BROTHERHOOD OF DOLPHINS

by

Ricardo Means Ybarra

Arte Público Press
Houston, Texas
1997

This volume is made possible through grants from the National Endowment for the Arts (a federal agency), Andrew W. Mellon Foundation, the Lila Wallace-Reader's Digest Fund and the City of Houston through The Cultural Arts Council of Houston, Harris County.

Recovering the past, creating the future

Arte Público Press
University of Houston
Houston, Texas 77204-2090

Cover illustration and design by Vega Design Group

Ybarra, Ricardo Means.
   Brotherhood of dolphins /
   Ricardo Means Ybarra.
      p.   cm.
   ISBN 1-55885-215-8 (pbk. : alk. paper)
   I. Title.
PS3575.B37B76   1997
813'.54—dc21   97-22188
                                        CIP

BROTHERHOOD
OF DOLPHINS

DEDICATION

for my father

ACKNOWLEDGMENTS

I wish to thank all those who fought to save, as well as those who labored to rebuild the Central Library.

And, to the following, my sincere appreciation for your help in making this novel possible: Tim Trujillo; Jack López Estevillo; Julie Popkin; Linda Feyder; Ben and Helen Saltman; B.J.; Rick and Pam Morgano; Bill and Cheri Pajares; Patty and the Deanman; Michael Manion; Battalion Chief Claude R. Creasy; Fire Station #10; Tom Brady, Engineer, and L.A. County Fire Station #107; Sparky Holloway; the librarians of the Central Library; Tom Trujillo; Angel Bautista; and Cynthia, *mi vida*, without whose constant love and support I might have turned to ash.

PREFACE

On April 29, 1986, the Central Library of Los Angeles burned in one of the most devastating fires in the history of Southern California. Seven hours, sixty companies and 350 firefighters were required to extinguish this arson.

Built in 1926, the Central Library was a valuable resource, a historical building as well as a place of study. In rebuilding, the original structure has been faithfully preserved and enlarged.

During my research, I wasn't surprised by the emotion of those involved: besides an estimated 200,000 books, the largest collection of patents and most of the magazine collection that were destroyed, another one and a half million volumes were damaged by smoke and water. But those numbers don't adequately represent the terrible loss expressed by everyone. It was Our Library that burned. The arsonist or arsonists were never found.

In using the Library as a subject, a source of cultural pride, I hope to have captured a reflection of the demanding, boisterous and conflicting beauty of our community in Los Angeles.

CHAPTER ONE

Sylvia Cruz wasn't using Engine Company 12's new Sears' power buffer. She was waxing the right front fender of the Fire Station's pumper, the massive La France relic that could still lavish fifteen hundred gallons a minute through eight two-and-a-half-inch hoses with T-shirts, T-shirts without holes, T-shirts that had been misplaced, T-shirts that were now carefully stacked on the chromed La France running board.

"Hey, Cruz, get your butt on the court; we're short a man."

Sylvia ignored the voice, but not the sound of the basketball, the lazy tempo increasing as if a drive down a lane was imminent, the only opponent, an opened bottle of Turtle Wax.

"Get that thing away from here, Bennett," Sylvia said sharply without looking up.

"Come on, now. We ain't going to be playing rough. Just a little exercise. Got to stay in shape, Cruz," Cornelius Bennett answered, dribbling away and then closer, alternating the dribble between hands, between legs, crouching as if to size up this new defender.

Sylvia stared into his face and snapped at the ball with a T-shirt. It connected, but Bennett didn't let the ball get away.

Cornelius smiled, winked, and continued dribbling. "Give that a try on the court. I know you're tough." He eyed the purple T-shirt, emblazoned with the gold Laker symbol, and then the stack on the fender. "Hey, where'd you pick up this rag pile? That's my Laker's tee in your hand," he said, his jaw dropping past a face elongated with concern. "I been missing that for a week now. I only wore it two, three times, and now look at it! How you going to get that polish out of it?"

"How you going to wear it without a collar?" Sylvia asked, grinning.

"You cut the collar off? What's the matter with you, Cruz?" Cornelius asked, his voice high enough to stuff a ball with two hands. "Serious infraction here, cutting up a man's Laker shirt. Won't look good on the report." Their eyes met as the ball hung in the air waiting for the feel of Cornelius's hands.

"The only infraction here is that thing on your upper lip. What is it? A smudge of grease?" Sylvia asked, mockingly.

Cornelius laughed. "I won't say a thing if you grow one." He continued chuckling.

Waxing the pumper was one thing but the "stash" was meant for the wall, a wall in the dining room where the portraits of Engine Company 12's finest hung, a wall glorified with the droopy upper lip, *bigotes* so thick they seemed to collect dust and force the glass away from the regulation 8 by 10 frames. Sylvia flicked the Laker T-shirt at Bennett's face.

"So I'll be the first smooth face on the wall, Corny. And I thought you'd never give in, never cop to that b.s."

"Oooh, Cruz, you one mean girl, aren't you? I thought I tol' you, never, never call me Corny. It don't fit my style," he crooned, smiling.

Sylvia Cruz started to touch her hair, and then let her hand fall away. Her hair was thick and black, and it shined in a straight line to the shoulders, in that style popular with modern East L.A. women. There was nothing left for her to rat-up over her forehead, nothing down her back, a cut like the Chicanas who were out busting down the door, getting theirs.

"You grow that thing, and your style will be seriously lacking," she said, stopping the impulse to pull her hair long, to feel for hair down the middle of her back.

"What, Cruz, you don't like a little fuzz to tickle your nose? Why don't you relax? Get out of that ol' outfit, tan your stilts, and sweat a bit."

Sylvia didn't respond; she knew why she was dressed in her "blues," why she worked the front of the station on downtown Spring Street as often as she could, always dressed crisp, in pants, never shorts. She was waiting for another considerate passerby to ask if she were out on work furlough from Sybil Brand, the Sheriff's Central Prison for Women. A nosy little old woman with a face like an uncooked dinner roll. Sylvia touched an ear, feeling the pierce. She didn't wear earrings, jewelry or make-up on the shift. It wasn't regulation. If she had had her hair, her make-up, and her look, she might have thought the prison question was funny, something to bring to a family dinner and frustrate Papa with. She wondered what it must feel like to be a "typical" firefighter now that Cornelius, the other boot, had started growing his "stash." But what was typical anymore? They weren't called firemen now.

"So when you gonna finish restoring La Frenchy here and get out on the court with us?" Cornelius asked, breaking into her thoughts and passing the basketball from hand to hand.

"When I finish," Sylvia said, dropping her hand to the fender.

"No need to worry 'bout it. You got all the shirts." Cornelius laughed loudly.

"I'm doing a job, Homer, so why don't you take your ball, your greasy face and get out of here."

"That is serious, Sylvia. Job fever. But my, you people doooo lay a fine shine down," Cornelius sang. "Can I fetch the Chief's boots for you?" he added, letting his eyes go sleepy, and smiling wide.

"Kiss my ass, Bennett."

"Don't tempt me now, Miz Croooze," Cornelius answered, smiling bigger.

Sylvia smiled back angelically, and then snatched the ball out of his hands. She faked a toss at a UPS truck passing by on the street. He jumped to the defense on the brick driveway, his arms extended, hands broad and flexing, head snaking back and forth in the fine smog of a morning in downtown Los Angeles.

Bennett faced the historic station house, its two under-sized garage bays stoically avenging themselves of the 'scrapers leaning in like neighbors at the fence by bathing in unhindered sun. Dull and square, Sylvia had thought on her first tour as a firefighter, like something from the Midwest, except that someone had curved the garage bays, outlining the arches in Moorish red brick. And the squat old building held other surprises, a brass pole, a Dalmatian, and that wall of photos. She faked another throw, and then, from inside the station house a bell rang like a phone gone crazy in a one-room apartment.

"Christ," she muttered, as the red light began to flash in its white cage between the spreading curves of the two arches.

"There goes the G-spot," Cornelius said, snatching the basketball out of her hands. "Grab that polish, girl; let's get on it," he shouted over his shoulder as he sprinted into the station.

Sylvia froze under the flashing red light, the bell still ringing, as she stared at half a fender gone white under drying polish. She forced herself to move, turning enough to catch her reflection in the section of the fender that she had finished polishing. "*Madre*," she swore, as she snatched up the pile of T-shirts. The woman who had stared at her from the fender looked too young and sweet to ever make it to the wall.

The alarm stopped, and the voice of the Chief, Battalion Chief Thomas Harrison, came over the Engine Company 12 loudspeaker. "All units are rolling. Let's get on it."

Sylvia turned away from the fender. Better not to look, she told herself, picking up the bottle of Turtle Wax and running to the lockers, thinking all the time about that fender turning white with polish, and her brother Ray, who'd be uptight about it.

It was the fourth call this shift. What was it this time? Another damn mattress fire? "Fucking lowlifes." She didn't want Ray to find out about that fender, that it hadn't been done right. She dumped the shirts and the Turtle Wax into a cabinet next to the equipment bay. Why'd she always have to think about her family during an alarm? Shovel heads are what they were. All they could talk about was brick and stone, except for Ray, the family *vato*, who had opened an auto body shop.

But it wasn't only the family, she thought, remembering her reflection in the fender. The woman staring out at her was too sweet-faced to take it easy. The type the nationals went nuts for, following her, whistling, clicking their tongues, banging on the sides of their cars, calling out, "*Oye mamacita*," or just, "*mami*." Eventually, one of them getting up the *huevos*— a nervous *mojado* in a polyester shirt with sweat stains under the arms, and baseball cap, coming on, speaking that polite wetback Spanish that must work so well among their women, talking low enough that the friends who were always bunched up eyeballing the move, couldn't hear the bullshit he was working. She'd let him follow her, about one step back, before she'd turn on him, throw her ample body and five-foot-seven-inch frame so that the Romeo would have to back up a step or two. Then she'd slice him in her best Echo Park *calo*, in language that let him know she wasn't interested in any rat-faced *piojo*, a head lice maggot. She might be a big, sweet-faced Chicana, but she wasn't that kind of Mexican, no way. Mama and Papa'd kill her, the *niñita*, the older three already married, Los Angeles City College education. They were already crazy because she'd joined the fire department, doing a man's work at twenty-one, with no babies, no husband, and no *novio* that they knew about. No, she'd better not bring home any nationals. There was a distinction to be made; Mama and Papa said so. She started laughing to herself as she opened her locker, thinking, what was the big deal about how long they'd been here anyway? Whose back wasn't wet in the U.S.A.? They could stop worrying about the nationals. Imagine, if I brought Cornelius home for dinner?

She pulled out her firefighter's jacket, tensing with the weight of the heavy yellow. Worrying like this was all Ray's fault, him and that damn fender. El Ray, the *vato*. She never could figure what he'd say or do. But he had backed her up about joining the Department, and had remained supportive even when Mama had started to cry. Maybe he'd just wanted to get her out of the body shop, Ray's Auto Body, so she wouldn't be hanging out, calling him Ramón in front of all his customers. "Ray. Call me Ray," he'd always say to her. But sometimes she slipped, and why shouldn't she call him Ramón? It was a beautiful name. It was their grandfather's name. So, what? Had he changed his name just because he didn't work with mortar and brick, or because the homies liked their American names better?

"Come on, Cruz, what's taking you?"

She looked into the face of Cornelius Bennett: smooth, tight, black and clean, and the sweet pink of his lips. Why was she worrying about that fender? Would Ray even care who she was draping? She wondered if he knew about Cornelius. *Orale*, what's a girl to do with a brother like that?

"Cruz, you best stop staring at my beautiful face and rig out, or I'll be worried about you. I'm lead man on the hose."

"Bennett, you're already nervous. It'll be the first real hose you ever held between your legs," Sylvia answered quickly, as she began to get into her turn-outs. She felt something against her feet inside the boots. She reached inside both boots and touched tubes wrapped in paper. She started to pull the objects out, but stopped. The men were too attentive. Cornelius was quiet. "Hoser *pendejos*," she shouted, pulling a tampon out of each boot, making sure to throw one in Bennett's laughingly innocent face. But the laughter ended abruptly as the Chief turned the corner. Cornelius quickly shoved Sylvia's arms through her jacket while she started snapping the clasps. She started past the Chief, standing at the doorway of operations, and didn't slow up as he yelled after her, "Commercial building, Cruz. You check your oxygen?"

"It's loaded," she shouted back over her shoulder. Harrison didn't offend her. He was straight with her, decent for an old hard-liner. She'd been around her brothers, father and grandfather enough to know about the sacredness of the workplace. She knew, too, that even though she had graduated top of her firefighting class in everything except physical strength, in the Chief's eyes she was a woman in the station, more than just an Affirmative Action nightmare.

She would be patient and ride with it as she did with the jokes and pranks. She wasn't shocked. She'd seen humiliation in the L.A. City schools and she'd grown up in a large family. In fact, she had expected worse than when they had partitioned off a toilet and shower for her, painted it pink, and put a catcher's mitt in the leftover urinal. But what she hadn't expected was the hostility from the wives, or her own stunned reaction. "Goddamn paddy bitches," she had told her brother Ray after the second picnic.

"Well, what did you expect," he had asked. "You're sleeping with their husbands. It doesn't matter that you're in another room."

She climbed into the pumper. "Very funny, Red," she shouted at Mike O'Neill, the driver, as she buckled into her seat.

"It wasn't me. Those guys are juveniles. I can't wait for them to grow up," O'Neill answered, spreading his teeth behind a huge red moustache.

"And what about you, Bro'? You wouldn't have been a part of that, would you?" Sylvia bored in on Cornelius.

Cornelius shrugged his shoulders and began to say something, but Red shouted over him as he put the pumper into first and started to wheel away from the Moorish red brick of the garage bay. "Cornel can't even find his own turn-outs, let alone yours. Right, Cornel? Didn't you tie them together with yellow thread like I told you?"

Sylvia laughed noiselessly and pointed a finger at him as Cornelius nodded his head up and down.

"I did just like you said, Red. You think it's okay to untie them now?"

O'Neill tried to shout something back, but it was lost as the pumper left the station with a roar and they entered Spring Street, sirens blaring and red light swinging, blinking red off the chrome pipes in front of her.

Sylvia watched the shadows turn into bright morning light. She felt her breathing slow as soon as they left. She could relax. The vibration of the motor, the chin strap rubbing under her jaw, the wind, the noise, and the yawing heads of the drivers stopping to let them pass, calmed her.

"Know where we're going?" Cornelius shouted at her.

She yelled back, cupping her mouth, "Office fire, downtown."

"We are downtown," he yelled back.

She shrugged her shoulders and watched the Times-Mirror building slide by. From her position she couldn't see the second-story deck, heavy with landscaping and two palm trees. She had always wanted to go up there. If there was a cafeteria, she would buy a Coke. It would be enough just to sit there for an hour in a garden above the streets. She looked at Cornelius, but he didn't look back. Perhaps she wasn't the only one to lose herself on the way to a fire. The heavy jacket, the boots, the helmet with its shield, the pumper's vibration up her spine. Buildings, cars, and people were outside, where no one could touch her, and since she was facing backwards, she couldn't see the fender. She'd stop worrying about it. Ray didn't have to know. She made a mental note to not look at the fender when they arrived. She just wouldn't go around that side of the truck.

They passed an office building under construction, the bottom half billowing with the wind, each level covered with cloth-like drapes at an open window. She saw ironworkers on an upper story opened to the sky. She wished that she could see what they were doing, moving steel into place, riveting, but they were so far away. She thought she saw movement, a yellow hard hat disappearing behind a post. She wondered if it felt as if the steel were moving, or whether he just felt the wind rushing between his legs? The building was almost out of view before she caught the legend spray-painted on the I-beam in red paint: "Sylvia, I love you. Will you marry me?" She smiled but she didn't laugh. Two pigeons flew over the pumper, one following the wings of the other. There was a cracked window on the sixth floor of the Union Bank high-rise. Blue sky slipped between buildings, but it wasn't the same sky framed in steel and yellow hard hats. A sign in a window at her left advertised the appearance of legendary singer, Ernie Andrews, at the Grand Avenue Bar. She liked Ernie Andrews, the way his deep voice opened her in a packed room. She realized that they were close to the Biltmore Hotel and the entrance to the Grand Avenue Bar. She had been here often, not just because it was close to the station, but because they had music in the afternoon. Jazz or salsa; it wasn't important which, because she came for *canciones en la tarde*, afternoon music in memory of her grandfather.

Her brother could call himself Ray all he wanted, but he couldn't forget who he was named after, could he? Ramón Santiago de la Rosa, the greatest mason Los Angeles would ever know. She envisioned her grandfather in his long-sleeved khaki shirt, the faded work pants, and his flat-soled boots worn and bleached from cement. The style never changed, except for Sunday when he wore black to mass for his wife. She saw his large face, filled with the authority of a foreman, a face traced with years of working in trenches and climbing scaffolding. She had liked his moustache, a grey, but elegantly trimmed *bigote* under the shadow of a huge nose, but what she had loved most were his ears. Papi said they were the ears of an *Indio*. That was why they were so large and why the ear-lobes were "*pura carne*." He said they would never stop growing, that someday he would have to buy an enormous *sombrero* to keep the sun off them. She had always wished that she could pierce them with a pirate's gold hoops, but this was a secret wish made only when she was at his shoulder and she would play with his ears, squeezing and rubbing the fleshy lobes he had called "pure beef."

He would always be waiting in the rocker at the living
room window when she arrived home from school. She would
put her books on the kitchen table, drink a half glass of water,
and then he would follow her out to the porch, asking her
about school and her walk home. Sometimes he would inquire
about any new admirers, and then he would roar with delight
when she would tell him that she wasn't interested in boys,
not those *mocosos tontos*.

"The boys are still snot-nosed brats," he would repeat as
he put on his hat, the stiff, reed-woven *sombrero Norteño*
favored by working men. By this time, she would be waiting
impatiently at the bottom of the wooden steps off the porch as
he cinched up the braided leather strap to the back of his
neck. She felt that he must be hurried along, but her Papi
wasn't one to be hurried when it came to his hat. It wasn't
that he was particular about his looks or his clothes, but,
when it came to the hat, he placed it with a degree of vanity,
so it wasn't until the sweat stains of the *sombrero* had found
their proper place that they would walk slowly to the *El
Mercado Flor de Valle* and into the back room where the other
jubilados had gathered around the fold-up *Tres Equis* table to
play cards.

Looking around her now, at Cornelius, the other firefighters, metal and axes, she had a sudden shortness of breath.
She felt the jacket, yellow and stiff, catching on callouses that
were part of her skin now. But still, in spite of the diesel
fumes, she could smell hanging clusters of chiles, warm *masa*,
the lime and salt filling the lids of *cerveza de bote* in the back
room of canned goods, sacks of beans and rice, and retired
men clasping hands in greeting. Chile, lime and salt. Chicken
bones cracking on the butcher's block. Heat that remained in
her *abuelito's* hat after the walk in the sun. The siren, the

pounding of the brakes and the motor, the slap of cards on the unsure legs of a metal beer table.

She was the loved *nieta*, the baby girl whose *quinceañera* was years away. There was no rush then for her to become a woman, to cook, clean, and have babies. How could she have been loved, admired, a member of this group of men, soaking it up, hanging at her Papi's shoulder, if she were a woman? And what would he have said about Cornelius?

Those were the best years: watching the cards and waiting for her grandfather to sing a *corrido*. Music in the afternoon. She would dream of it all day in school, and sometimes now, during her entire shift at the station. Waiting for the back room, her place outside the lights, the comfortable sack of beans, a singer, Ernie Andrews singing for her, her grandfather.

At school she'd been neither an outstanding student nor a failure. At home her quiet father had usually eaten alone while her mother worked in the kitchen. One older brother and three older sisters. Sylvia's afternoons had never been a secret or a worry. Her mother and older sisters had rarely walked the two doors down to bring her home or check on her homework. No one complained that she spent too much time with the *abuelo*, or wondered why she was rarely hungry for dinner. Why shouldn't she dream all day, as she did in the pumper now, of when her *abuelito* would lean back and sing with a voice of love, *traición* and happiness, of bricks and stones?

She had never cried in the back room of the Flor de Valle, although she had wanted to. Music in the afternoon. If she hadn't held them in then, would there be so many tears now? She could feel the goosebumps rise on her flesh, as they had in the room of cards, where she would prance unseen behind the Indian ears of her *abuelito*, like Bambi, the deer she had loved. And then she would feel the terror and wish that she could stop crying in the afternoon at linen-covered tables that didn't wobble. Was it for the better, she asked herself, that when his voice stopped, she would become a woman?

"Wake up and smell the coffee burning," Cornelius shouted.

She jerked her head at him, felt brakes grinding. She put her hand on the seat belt release. The street was filled with people pointing and staring. "This is it," she shouted.

"I believe so," Cornelius answered.

Sylvia thought for a moment that the alarm might be a mattress fire in the Biltmore. Lowlifes at the Biltmore? She watched Engine Company 10 pull in behind them, figuring they came as back-up. She peered into the windows of the Grand Avenue Bar, relieved when she could see that it wasn't music in the afternoon burning.

She saw a Division Chief squeeze his red car through the barricades as she unbuckled her seat belt. "*Hijo*," she said quietly.

"Must be a bad mutha," she heard Cornelius say.

She wondered where the fire was. There was no smoke, only people everywhere, coming from every building and storefront. She quickly turned to look at the Central Library as she heard a voice yell, "It's the library," and then Chief Harrison was shouting, and she was jumping down to run to the back of the pumper.

"We will take the West entrance, though I haven't yet received a positive location on the point of inception." Harrison stopped for a moment as he consulted a diagram he had on a clipboard. "The stairs are fifty feet in. The alarm was pulled on the second floor, but," he paused, "it may be in the stacks."

The stacks. She knew all about the stacks, a vertical workplace made up of seven tiers, where library workers stored books and collections not available to the public. They had been well versed on the Central Library. It was the most infamous fire hazard in the City, had always been, since it was built with book stacks like a chimney, two chimneys, one stack per side. Sylvia looked over her shoulder. Where was the smoke? There was still no smoke.

"We've been over this before. Douse it before it reaches the stacks. Goddamn, no smoke yet. I don't want to be hauling firefighters out of that oven, a goddamn kiln. Hit it before the chimney gets out of control. We'll worry about the books later." Chief Harrison hesitated a moment, looking into their eyes, and then asked, "Are there any questions?" When no one spoke, he continued, "Apparatus on. We're the first in. Watch your ass and your buddy. You know what this can do; don't go over your head." He held them for a moment with his eyes, "Good luck."

Cornelius and Sylvia followed two of Engine Company 12's most experienced "A shift" firefighters. Red, at the point, carried an axe and a crowbar. Jeff Howard, the crew captain, was wired to Harrison with a microphone. Cornelius and Sylvia were the third and fourth firefighters through the Fifth Street entrance. Cornelius had the nozzle, the inch and one-half hose draped over his shoulder. Sylvia knew there was six-foot-five with muscular legs under all that equipment. Maybe he had played football, she thought, pulling hose over her shoulder and running to keep up with him. As they made the entrance and followed the lead through a door, Sylvia wondered what it must have looked like when her grandfather worked here. Would it have been empty like it was now? Did footsteps echo with the same sound in these tall corridors? She saw the goddess in the foyer before they turned the corner. Had he placed the limestone blocks that framed her? She looked Asian or Indian, a Native-American, Latina? The almond shape of the eyes, the high forehead, erect, strong breasts free under the loose and clinging garment cinched at the waist, elaborate beadwork and headdress. The goddess held a tablet and a staff, the veins in her fingers showing clearly. Sylvia felt the goddess staring into her as if she wanted to speak, her nostrils widening as if she were trying to communicate something. Sylvia strained to listen, but could hear only boots, the breathing apparatus gurgling, and then Cornelius was charging up the stairs. Sylvia lunged after him, pulling hard on the hose, but she had to take one more look over her shoulder. Those eyes, they seemed to be following her.

They made the second floor, the history section, but there was still no smoke. The fire had to be in the tiers of the book stacks. She pulled in the hose, following Cornelius onto a catwalk in the tiers. The bookshelves were continuous from the first floor to the rotunda. The space was narrow. She felt a momentary fear of being trapped, the helmet restricting her vision, until she looked up. Above her there was open space between the ascending shelves and books, bindings rising beyond her headgear. They were at another corner, a tight right. She struggled, and Cornelius pulled her around. Another short flight of narrow stairs, along an identical row of books. She saw a pile of music, stacks of newspaper and bindings, everywhere bindings in purple, green, black and red. They continued on. She thought they must be at the fifth tier, but still no smoke, nothing but books. She didn't stop. The hose came easier now. There must be help below. She didn't want to think of her legs. They were heavy with exertion, but excitement drove them on. She tried to conserve her air, the regulator noisy as a steam kettle.

At the door to the fifth tier they finally found it. When Red hauled open the door, he was thrown back. Sylvia felt the surge as the back draft roared down the stairs, heat rolling out like music and, finally, a blur of smoke.

"Fifth tier. Out of control. I repeat, out of control," Sylvia heard Jeff scream into his mouthpiece. "Steam. Be ready for it," he shouted as Cornelius opened his nozzle. The water disappeared into smoke and returned as fog. Sylvia felt the piercing heat of water turned to vapor. Her scalp itched and crawled under the helmet. She wondered how long they could withstand it, her turn-outs filling with sweat, her eyes enlarging, dry and hard like eggs left too long in the pan. They couldn't. They had to make a retreat down the stairs.

Three times they went back at it, directing a full stream at the doorway and into the entrance they couldn't obtain. The walls of thick masonry, walls her grandfather had built, had absorbed the fire, just as the sandstone walls of a deep canyon hold the heat of the sun. The walls hissed. Through the open door stacks of books in their metal shelves glowed, racks fell as the metal turned molten, but the center of the fire wasn't here anymore. It had risen. This fire was moving. It was a chimney.

Sylvia noticed a sign over the door. The paint had blistered away so that only lines remained. "Art Section," she read. She heard Jeff yelling into the radio: "We can't enter the stacks from this floor. We have a chimney, I repeat, chimney. We're going to try the sixth tier." Jeff leaned over as he listened to the Chief's voice in his helmet. Then he straightened up, waved at them, and yelled, "We'll try to head it off at the sixth."

They retreated into a library room and advanced up stairs to the sixth tier landing. The heat pounded through the masonry. Sylvia could hear the flames, the crackling sound of an inferno clawing its way upward. She thought it would be a scene similar to that on the fifth. She was so intent on moving forward that she bumped into Cornelius who had stopped suddenly on the stairs. When she looked over his shoulder, she saw that it wasn't at all like the floor below. The fire was buckling the metal fire door. Here was the enemy at last.

Red used the crowbar again. Sylvia watched as the hard edge slid into the flames at the juncture of the door and the frame. She watched as it popped the door open and water from a full nozzle bounced back. A wall of heat. She was angered by the lack of power they had over the fire. Smoke and steam covered her. She pressed a gloved hand against Cornelius's back to find her bearings. There was too much steam here. The fire was rising up the stacks like the chimney that it was, but the wind it caused could create a back draft which would push the steam and smoke down through the fifth floor door and up the stairwell, attacking them from their back as well as from the door before them. She remembered this theory from a class at the academy. The water, now turned to vapor, would drop. The sudden change of temperature would cause a back draft. She remembered with sudden clarity that she hadn't been able to close the stairwell door behind them because of the hoses. She yelled. No one could hear her. She pounded on Cornelius's back. He moved forward another step, continuing to pour water into the stacks. "No more water," she screamed as a black fog exploded out the door, knocking Red and Jeff over. She turned and saw the back draft coming up the stairs like a truck on the freeway that suddenly fills your mirror.

Sylvia was lowest on the stairs and the first to drop into a protective crouch. It was enough to save her. The vapor and smoke from below was terrible, but it was nothing like the blast of super heated steam that seemed to wait a moment and then blow out suddenly through the sixth floor door to fell the firefighters. Sylvia didn't move for a moment. She wanted to stay huddled up like this, sweating, listening to the gurgling of her oxygen, trying to remember what the manual told her to do. What now? a voice inside her screamed. She couldn't think, yet she knew these were her friends, her lover, and suddenly she wasn't afraid. She crawled over Cornelius. She kept as low as she could. She was fighting to reach the nozzle which, still opened, was compounding the problem, causing more steam. She wrenched it from his hands, then, crawling blindly over the bodies, she took the nozzle and directed the spray over the silent men and down the stairs. She turned off the nozzle and slid Cornelius down the stairs past the smokestack at the fifth floor door. The room she left him in was filling with smoke, but it was clearer than the stairwell and there was visibility on the floor. It seemed to take forever. She became angry, arguing with herself to take her jacket and oxygen pack off so she could move faster. She went back twice more, keeping low. She felt as if her mind were detached, a moving energy, the goddess within her. Her arms and legs wanted to stop, they screamed at her to give up, but still she crawled up the stairs, feeling her way, trying to look through the visor into the eyes of the men lying beneath her. She fought back the urge to laugh, because this reminded her of sex; after-sex, she was still there, but the men were out cold. She felt like kissing each one after she had pulled him down the stairs, kissing joy and happiness into them, urging them on for another go.

After they were all off the stairs and away from the rising steam and smoke, Sylvia greedily sucked on the last of her air. She ignored the warning signs of overexertion combined with bottled oxygen. She had never been so sure of herself, never felt so clear and lucid, so fearless. She hefted the hose and the nozzle. She called to the goddess at the entry. "*La India*, it's just you and me now." She had known it at the entrance— those eyes were her eyes. Her grandfather had made them strong. She wouldn't need the helmet or the coat, just a loose slip that didn't cover her beauty. She would tackle the fire with the goddess, two women together, *mano a mano*. She heard the radio crackle. It was the Chief, that ass, what did he want? She was in control now; she knew what she was doing. She had the nozzle, the hose pulsing. Sylvia grabbed the microphone in Jeff's helmet, her voice snapping into it as if Harrison were a Romeo on the street, but she only heard the continuing crackle of Harrison's voice and she never felt the arms lifting her as everything went black before her visor.

CHAPTER 2

"Ray. Ray," he heard her shout. He turned to look at her in the driveway beyond the wide, thick, wooden rolling doors of the Quonset hut open to Glendale Boulevard, knowing that she couldn't see inside. Cecilia was hanging out the window of the Chevy Impala, his '58, as it rolled to a stop in the full sun of 12:30, glaring off the white Detroit hood that covered a tri-power, V-eight. She honked furiously, causing him to flinch, but still Ray didn't answer. Instead he took the dust cover from his face and let it hang under his chin.

He stared at her, seeing straight red hair hanging past the bottom frame of the window, one tiny ear with a pearl, the eyes of her Filipina mother that contrasted with her angular face. Dark red hair from her Irish father. Ray had tried to mix the colors once for a car he was spraying, but he had given up. Dark, but still red. He noticed her soft arm hanging out. Pudgy. After the baby she had put on a few, but he didn't mind. Why should he mind? He was big too, and she was his wife.

"Raaaay." The horn again.

He knew that the interior of the auto body shop—the chicken-wire in glass skylights, sunlight passing through the whirling rooftop fan onto the carefully laid out workbench of tools—reminded her of St. Teresa of Avila, the church a mile over the hill. Stained glass, candles flickering in alcoves at the feet of saints, and the altar. Was it possible to fall in love in a church or a body shop?

But it was just a shop. Vinny, his helper, looking up from a front fender, the concrete floor clean but spotted, a lav in a far corner under a dispenser of pink grainy soap, and his office in the back with the narrow bed, a closet of cleaned and pressed work clothes, and a shower. One item had been changed by Cecilia. She had surprised him.

In his office over the desk hung a calendar from St. Teresa's that he updated yearly. Everyone he knew had a calendar, even his Tía Sofía, so it never came as a surprise when he found an old one in a back room, a garage, or a drawer. He could remember the years from the pictures. San Martín de Porres was '81, the year Chato was killed in La Pantera Rosa bar. La Virgen de Guadalupe was '58, the year of his car. El Fray Junípero Serra was '68. He had shipped out of Camp Pendelton in time for the Tet offensive. The sermon on the Mount was '85, the year his daughter was born.

He remembered the pictures, the colors running together on the badly printed calendars, the holes in the corners where the tacks had severed the borders. San Martín holding his broom and crucifix in the hospital, light glowing behind his head, the dog and cat at his feet, a dove resting on the broom handle. The years hadn't affected San Martín, they would never touch him. The horn pounded again.

This year the picture over the calendar tear-offs was of the Sacred Heart of Jesus. There had been many Sacred Hearts over the years. Ray didn't have to go into his office to see it, that face loaded with some kind of problems, sad, yes, but strong. One finger touched the sword-pierced heart, blood dripping onto his white shirt, while the other hand stretched out for help, or was it understanding? Or was it love? Always blood. His church celebrated blood and pain. Ray knew. He wasn't a good Catholic; he only went to church when he was required to attend. Why did he go? Women made him go, especially one woman, a virgin—*La Madre*. If there was one thing you could hang with, he thought, it was the *Virgen*.

She hung in the middle of the wall, above and to the right of the calendar, a framed *Nuestra Virgen de Guadalupe* his mother had given him when he had opened the body shop. Lifted by an angel, surrounded by rays of light, that face and the light blue shawl covered with stars, the image exactly like the one he fingered around his neck. A *vato* could live with the *Virgen*, no problem, but there on the same wall was the calendar of the Snap-On Tool girl in the ripped wet T-shirt and the black thigh-high bikini bottoms where Cecilia had tacked it to the wall. Cecilia had wanted this, the only change she had made to his shop. It was just a picture, tacked on the wall with *La Virgen,* so why did he have such a hard time when the old *vatos* came in and, looking over their dark glasses, told him what they would do to that fine-looking *chavala* in the wet T-shirt.

The horn again. He wiped at his face, touching the narrow lines of his goatee, and heard the familiar car door open and slam.

"Ceci, what's goin' on, baby?" Ray asked, walking towards her with the paint sprayer in his right hand.

"Ramón, why don't you answer the goddamn phone? I called three times."

Ray pulled at his dust mask, turned to look at the car he was pin-striping, saw Vinny, who was staring at him, and then finally laid down the sprayer.

"What's the matter?" he asked suddenly. She only called him Ramón when she needed to catch his attention, not like his wild sister Sylvia who loved the name because it reminded her of their grandfather. Cecilia had first called him Ramón here in the shop before she had ever thought of marrying him. She had thought this was a garage, that he worked on engines. She had looked for grease under his fingernails. He looked past her at the Chevy, brilliant as holy light under the sun. He wondered if he was the one who was confused, the head of his wife tilted, chin almost touching shoulder, the impact wrench tight between breasts, taut nipples dripping water next to the blood-stained white shirt of the Sacred Heart of Jesus.

"Is it María Elena?" he asked, putting both hands on her arms.

Cecilia had insisted on naming their baby girl "María Elena" because she had seen the name on a stained glass window at St. Teresa's. She had made a connection with that young girl that he would never understand. He looked at her from arms length, saw the long neck and red hair. Was it chestnut? Her ears like tiny shells.

"We've got to go, Ray. Sylvia's in the hospital. She's gonna be alright. It was heat and smoke inhalation."

He reached out to her arms again, squeezed them for a moment, then released her. Turning to his helper, he said, "Vinny, lock up the shop when you've finished buffing out this *carrucho*." He walked into the office, Cecilia following him.

"How did it happen?" he asked as he stripped out of his overalls, put on a clean shirt and changed his socks and shoes.

"That big library downtown caught fire. You know, the old one. Her company was the first one in," she said, watching him tuck in his shirt.

"What about *mamá* and *papá*?"

"They're coming with us. They're waiting at home. Lupe will watch the baby," she said calmly before picking up the phone at the desk.

"Who're you calling?" Ray asked. He looked at her as she waited on the phone. He turned away as he heard her telling his mother they were on the way. He touched the *Virgen* around his neck as his eyes settled on nipples, sprayed water, and Snap-On tools.

Cecilia held out the keys as they left the shop. He took them, waited for her to slide across the seat under the steering wheel, and then he was in the car and shutting out everything.

"When did she go in?" he asked, as he turned right onto Glendale Boulevard.

"I'm not sure, but the fire started about ten this morning," she said, looking at him. "You know, Ray, I wish you'd get a message phone. It's times like this I need to get through to you."

He didn't answer. He didn't like answering the phone. If someone needed to talk to him, they could always come by, which they usually did, anyway.

"You don't have to answer every call," she said, sliding into his thoughts. "If you hear a message from someone you want to talk to, like your *vieja*," she said sarcastically, "then you stop the machine and answer the phone. It's not that big of a deal, Ray."

She didn't understand that if his clients and friends found out he had the machine, they would be calling and expecting him to return their calls. He didn't want to hurt anyone's feelings. The way it worked now, he didn't have to upset anyone, except for Cecilia. It was common knowledge that he didn't pick up the phone. They knew they had to come by. He weighed the situation, came to the conclusion that emergencies were rare, but constantly returning messages would be a hassle. Now all he had to do was convince Cecilia. He decided to blame it on Vicente.

"Baby, Vinny would be telling all his *chavalas* to call. Couldn't you see him listening to the phone all day, and then rushing over to write down names and numbers," he said without turning to look at her. He shifted his steering hand to his left and put his right on the back of the seat so that he could touch the back of her neck. "The boy's only twenty-two; you know what I mean?" He didn't wait for an answer. "How's *mamá*?" he asked.

"*Mamá's* real upset. She went for the palm fronds immediately and lit the candles. Of course, it's all your fault because you gave the go ahead to Sylvia. That's all she would talk about." Cecilia moved. It was just slight enough to put her neck out of reach. Ray noticed, but left his hand where it was as he wheeled the Chevy left across Glendale Boulevard and onto one of the small cross streets that lead into the hills of Elysian Heights and feed the crowds to Chavez Ravine, Dodger Stadium.

His family had been pushed out of the Ravine, named after the so-and-so Chavez. Whoever this person was, he wasn't a Chicano, because no homey called Chavez Ravine anything but Palo Verde or Loma. His parents had been starting out, living with his grandparents, Ramón and Carmen, but they hadn't lived in Loma because they were hard up. Palo Verde, centerfield of El Chavez Ravine, was a fine place to live, down and cool if you were a kid who liked to play in the hills and the dust of the one road that dropped into their barrio. In fact, everyone who lived in Loma had parked their cars at the top of the hill when it rained, because Loma was a dirt road where only families had lived until O'Malley and the Dodgers had come to town.

"They won't go with anyone else, you know. I offered to drive them, and Uncle Pete was home, but no, they insisted that you be the one," Cecilia said, turning to look at him, breaking into his reverie. Small, bungalow-style houses passed by. Ray saw twisted iron grillwork over windows and doors under the large porches, crabgrass lawns behind three foot high chain-link fences, and pots, always pots, geraniums and bougainvillaea; toys, bicycles and cars in the driveways, and people, kids everywhere, young men, *chavos* with the cars, mothers, grandparents on porches, and young girls, *las chavalas* in packs. He made a left on Echo Park Avenue, passed the Cuban *carnicería* across the street from the market he knew every inch of, the El Flor de Valle: blue linoleum floor worn away past the swing of the screen door, candy counter behind the cash register next to the cigarettes and liquor, *carnicería* along one side, the butcher's apron always bloodstained. There had once been a tortilla press in the back room where the old men would play cards, but now the tortillas came packaged. He flicked his head at the group of men standing near the doorway.

"We need a place of our own, Ray. I love your parents. *Mamá* and the girls help out with the baby, I know. It can be close by, honey. It's just that I want our own life. Ray?" she asked.

He had turned off Echo Park Avenue, backtracked up another hill, and down into the steep-sided valley commonly known as El Gallo. It wasn't a name that would show up in any street atlases, too small, too much a slip of the tongue, uttered as much in memory of his former barrio and the rooster that came to signify their desire to stay together as a community. How near was close by on a narrow street that didn't curve, filled with working class bungalows? It was quiet and humid with overshadowing trees, plants and gardens, hidden even from the sound of L.A. Ray knew every loquat tree, the way through all yards, every sleeping cat and the dogs that barked. He slowed as he passed his grandfather's. Half of

Loma was here. He knew everyone. At the house next door there hung a once popular swing under the covered porch. Rita had grown up there, and so had the boys. He turned back to look at his grandfather's house. The porch and straight cement walkway was painted red and bordered with roses, the house high off the ground with plenty of room to crawl to find newborn kittens. It hadn't changed. He and Cecilia could've moved in there. His *abuelo* Ramón had left the house to him. Ray had been the oldest grandson; that was the way it was supposed to be. But he had turned it over to Sylvia without thinking too hard over it. Some things were best done right, and if his grandfather's ghost was to be happy, it would be with Sylvia.

He pulled into the driveway two houses farther down from his grandfather's. He was careful and slow as he eased the Impala off the street, over the steep hump of a curve, and onto the two concrete paths on either side of grass that tried to grow in the driveway. His parents' home resembled the others. The growth, the short fences good for hiding nothing, a detached garage, useless for anything but storage because of its size. What had they left behind in Loma besides dust and blood spurting from an old rooster's neck? He thought of what Cecilia had said, but how could they move away? It was good here. He honked the horn twice, watched the screen door open and his mother appear; then he turned to Cecilia.

"We'll stop on the way back and look at a machine, baby, for the shop." He wouldn't say they would get one. He looked at her to see how she would take this. He knew better. Her expression told him that this wasn't what she wanted to hear, that ten minutes ago if he had agreed about the machine, he could have stalled her wish to move. He had missed an opportunity and now Cecilia would wait until they were alone. She had stored it, put it away until another time. He could tell by the way she slid out of the seat and held the door open for his mother and father. It struck him that they seemed smaller and older than usual, but he didn't want to notice it.

"Ramón, now is the time to talk to her," his mother told him in Spanish in the hospital elevator. He knew she meant Sylvia, and he knew she meant it was time to tell her to leave the fire department.

"Your *papá* worries all day and every night. It was bad enough that you gave her my father's house. How will she ever marry? It isn't right, *m'ijo*."

He took her hands in his, patted them and said, "She's gonna be all right, *mamá*," then the elevator stopped and Ray waited with the others for the doors to open. He stole a glance at his father, saw the somber face, the stoic line of his moustache. Ray held his hand over the elevator doors until they had all exited, and then they waited in a line against a wall painted light green as Cecilia went to the nurses' station and asked for Sylvia's room.

He waited again, holding open another door as they filed past him into a room that became more silent as the door closed behind him. His parents had stopped before crossing to the bed. He saw his mother's eyes flicker twice from her daughter's face with an oxygen tube inserted into her nose to the other bed in the corner. He recognized the face of Cornelius Bennett, and gestured with a nod of his head at the black hand that waved at him off the tight sheets.

Sylvia couldn't talk much, but she could smile. Her eyes lit up as Ray touched her knee. Cecilia rubbed her forehead; his mother spoke softly and kissed her face. He wanted to spend some time alone with her, but after a moment he knew he was just filling space, his mother and Cecilia talking non-stop. He left her bed and went over to the other side of the curtain.

"Anything I can get for you, homeboy?" he asked.

He was alarmed when Cornelius reached up and pulled the tubes out of his nose, speaking hoarsely, "It's good to see you, brutha."

"You better put that thing back in," Ray said, unsure about the worry he felt for this man, wondering suddenly if he was doing his sister. Ray was sure that they were an item, but why didn't it work him? Why didn't he worry? Was it because he liked Cornelius, that he trusted Sylvia's judgment? But what if he wasn't a proper older brother?

"No problem, we're gonna be fine. Overnight stay with pay and room service. Nothing to worry about," Cornelius said, placing the tubes back into his nose, and breathing deeply before speaking again. "Ray, Sylvia pulled us out. Me, Red and Jeff. She's one fine firefighter," Cornelius said, measuring his words. "Syl's all heart. You gotta be proud, Ray. I am." He smiled as he held on to Ray's hand.

Ray didn't smile, but he shook his head slightly as Cornelius squeezed his hand, holding on. Ray looked at their hands for a moment. His was smaller and meatier, and his fingernails weren't as pink. There wasn't any hair on either hand. He didn't say anything.

"What do ya'll hear about that fire?" Cornelius asked him finally, letting his hand go.

"They're calling it a disaster," he answered.

"Real bad," Cornelius said.

Ray waited again, rubbing his chin and looking at the face on the pillow.

"Thanks for stopping by, Ray."

"You take care, Cornelius," he said.

"I'll do my best," Cornelius answered.

Ray left him to stand at the foot of Sylvia's bed next to his father. His father acknowledged Ray with a sigh that showed the struggle of his reserve. Ray searched for words to comfort him, but all that came forth was the whiteness of his knuckles as he twisted the bed frame. Respectfully, he stood with his father hoping that it was enough. There would be time later. For now his wife and mother filled the space.

He didn't much listen, watched Sylvia, concerned with her labored breathing, the exhausted look of her eyes. He wanted a smoke, thought of inviting his father outside, but knew it wasn't right to leave. When the phone rang it startled everyone, Cecilia moving first to silence it.

"It's your Chief. Harrison," she said to Sylvia as she passed the phone. Sylvia attempted to be her animated self, but when she began to cough, she allowed Ceci to take back the phone to everyone's relief.

The door opened, it was their cousin Joe, his wife and their sister María. He talked briefly with his cousin and then caught Sylvia's eye amongst all the hugging and noise. Ray winked and she returned a thumbs up. Satisfied, he slipped out the door.

Alone on a veranda, where he could look out over Echo Park, the lights of Dodger Stadium struck him. There had been a crisis then, too. Loma, Palo Verde, Chavez Ravine. Maybe it hadn't been the greatest barrio; everyone always wanted out, to get a nice place on a real street with a toilet in the house. But for all the griping, no one had left until the Guzmáns made a big deal about it, the first to move out before the bulldozers came, to some suburb called Whittier. Was it Whittier or the Dodgers that had made them all leave? Old lady Trujillo would still be there, as sweet and friendly as was possible for a *viejita*, unlike the time she was interviewed on TV, calling the Dodgers, O'Malley, and Mayor Yorty *pinche desmadre cabrones, hijos de la chingada*, and a few other choice words until someone who understood Spanish had

called the station and told them that she wasn't exactly prais-
ing the city fathers or the Dodgers.

Ray would never go to the stadium or ever see the
Dodgers play because of the eviction, and he would never
move to Whittier. No way. How could anyone forget the barrio? Even if they wanted to forget how the mud stuck to their
shoes in the winter, there was no way to avoid remembering
those last days, the *viejita* Trujillo, that *panzón* O'Malley with
a body like an egg, his goddamn Brooklyn baseball team, and
the old *señor*, the Guzmán grandfather. That old man had
been one helluva *cabrón* to the fullest degree. Mean, but he
had loved his chickens and that rooster, that *pinche gallo* that
never left because they didn't allow no chickens in the sub-
urbs.

It had been dry the week before they left. Ray remembered it because the old man had been raising dust, stumbling
from house to house in the Loma, knocking on doors, getting
down with serious respect, as if he were asking on behalf of
his son for another's daughter, "If you would only take my
sweet *gallinas* that lay eggs like a goat shitting. And the
gallo."

Who could have taken them even if they had wanted such
wonderful hens? They all had their eviction notices and were
ready to fight until the last, except for the Guzmáns. And that
rooster he was trying to pass off. Anyone would've taken that
damn rooster and wrung its neck before the eviction notices
came. That shitbird was so *chingón* even the dogs stayed away
from its yard. The kids would toss rocks from more than twenty yards away until the old man came out with his machete.
Sometimes Ray would sneak over there just to see that
scrawny rooster perched on the old *señor*'s shoulder, picking
at the straw in the *sombrero* on the old man's head.

"*Maldita sea*," his father would say every night when some hen would start wailing and the rooster would crow for a good five minutes. No one would take that *gallo cabrón* from the old *señor*, even if only to throw him in the *mole*.

The day came when the Guzmáns had packed it all on Tony Guerrero's pick-up, all the men in the barrio hungover from the night before, complaining about their *crudas*, but working on the last of the barbecued chickens and Eastside beers left over and floating in a tub of warm water on the porch. The women had packed the last items and were cleaning up, and the kids were playing in the street as usual.

When it had been time for the Guzmáns to leave, there had been a lot of hugging and some crying. The Guzmán kids were the first ones in the old green Dodge and Ray had wondered how they could breathe in the back seat, lying on top of packages with their heads pressed to the felt headliner that was ripped in a hundred places. Mister Guzmán's fat head was twisted round farther than Ray had thought possible, and all he could see of the Guzmán kids were their hands waving against glass. He'd thought they'd back out, Mister Guzmán would grind the gears getting into first, there'd be a lot of dust mixed with exhaust, and that would be it. But they didn't make it out of the driveway. Tony Guerrero, who had just started his truck, waiting to follow them in his pick-up sagging from the load to the nice two bedroom house in Whittier with the bathroom that worked, switched his truck off suddenly, and Ray could still feel how the hair had climbed up his arms to the back of his skull so that he couldn't move a muscle.

"*Ay Dios, Papá!*" screamed Mrs. Guzmán. Ray could never remember whether he had fallen trying to get away, or if he had been knocked over. The old *señor's* howling had frozen him. Then that scrawny rooster had come running down the driveway, zeroing in on him with just a stump for a neck, and blood spurting so hot and hard that even after his *madre* had washed him and made him lay down, Ray thought that he would wake up like that Roy Campanella and have to go to Dodger games in a wheelchair. Ray had lain in his parents' bed all that afternoon, afraid to close his eyes, and had actually prayed that the scrawny old *gallo* would be alive to mount another hen. But there would never be the same noise again. It had taken the men fifteen minutes to get the machete out of the old *señor*'s hands, and in the evening, during the finest time to play, even the kids had been quiet.

The barrio never mentioned that rooster while they fought those bulldozers. Until the old lady Trujillo had to be pulled out of her house by the police, they wouldn't leave. Loma was their barrio, their home, their children, their old people, their mud, but when the porches went with a shove from the 'dozer blades it was time to get the hell out. None of them ever went to Whittier to visit the Guzmáns, but on warm evenings as their children played in the street and they sat on their porches in the new ravine many had moved to, who didn't proudly remember that tough, scrappy bird, a *chingón* until the end?

Christ, what had brought back memory lane, Ray wondered as his parents and wife left Sylvia's room and he went in to quickly say good-bye.

An hour and a half later, after they had dropped his parents back at home and were waiting in line for the Radio Shack cashier, Ray impatiently held a message phone box under his arm. Cecilia was reading the instructions she had dug out.

"Did the Chief ask you anything, baby?" Ray asked.

"You mean Tom?"

"Yeah, the brass."

"He seems like a decent guy. Sylvia likes him."

"Don't act too friendly with them. He's an administrator. I know his type from 'Nam." He looked knowingly at her. She was still reading.

"Are you listening to me? We got to watch these guys, let 'em know we're not going to settle for any bullshit. I saw you talking to him with one of your big smiles, and my mother ready to get on her knees and ask his blessing."

"He called to talk to Sylvia, and he's always very nice to your mother," Cecilia answered absentmindedly without taking her eyes off the instruction sheet.

He watched her face, set earnestly, her eyes darting quickly. She reached out and caressed his arm. His eyes widened and they moved up a step in line.

In the car, after the purchase of the answering machine, he waited through two signals before he spoke into the windshield. "You think Sylvia will be alright?"

"She's fine. She's there with Cornelius."

"What's that mean?" he asked quickly, throwing her a look.

"What do you think it means, Ray? They work together," she answered smoothly.

"Yeah?"

"Yeah, what?"

"They work together; that's right." He drove loosely, one hand on the lower part of the wheel, head eased back, butt slid forward, but he wasn't really loose, it was just a game he played with the Chevy.

"You know they're more than friends," she stated, slouching against the door.

"I don't want to talk about it," he answered low.

But Cecilia wouldn't let it pass. "So what if they are, Ray? At the hospital you couldn't get over there fast enough to make sure he was okay. And how many times have you invited him over with Sylvia? Three, four times. You guys play ping-pong, watch the Lakers. I didn't know you had a problem with it."

"Why didn't you just tell the fucking Chief that the brother is hammering my sister?"

"That's why you're so tight," Ceci said, laughing.

"I'm not tight. What's the big deal here?"

"You're the big deal, *viejo*," Cecilia said, sighing loudly and smiling at him. "The Chief said to call him anytime you want to talk about Sylvia's recovery."

"The fool can call the shop if he wants to talk to me."

Not more than a second passed before they both began to laugh and Ceci began to punch his arm until he swung it around her neck and hauled her face into his lap while he rubbed her chest and humped against her.

"You pig. *Cochino*," she screamed, laughing, grabbing his crotch and squeezing.

"I'll bet you told him I have an answering machine," Ray shouted, squeezing a breast and pinching the nipple.

"Ouch," she laughed, twisting his balls. "I didn't know we were buying one."

"Bullshit. You knew. Whooa, watch it with the jewels," Ray bellowed, rubbing her as she unzipped his pants. "Hey, what're you doing? We're in the neighborhood, hon."

"Can you believe the Chief calls you Ramón?"

"We're almost home, baby."

"Lupe's there."

"I know just the place, then. But hold off," Ray said, using both hands on the wheel to make a hard right. "Did he say my name sweet?" he asked, laughing.

"You want to get laid or you wanna know how some guy said your name?"

"Where'd you learn to talk dirty like that, wife," he groaned.

"He has a strong voice," she answered, grinning, but he didn't notice.

"Called me Ramón?" Ray asked, thinking of Sylvia, how he secretly enjoyed it that she called him that.

"Yeah, Ramón," she answered soft and low, stretching back to her side of the car, licking her lips as she waved him to her.

"*Oye mami*," Ray exhaled, so charged with relief and wanting her he worried that he couldn't hold back and quickly swung the Chevy over onto a vacant lot under a eucalyptus. There was a view of Silver Lake, but neither was interested in the blue water of a reservoir. She held him tight because that was what they both wanted. He felt her kisses, not like sweet blue water, lapping over his eyes, her warm, now salty lips.

"Sylvia's gonna be alright, Ramón."

"I love you, baby."

CHAPTER 3

"Chief Harrison, the Commander would like to see you when you have a minute," the aide said, shouting to be heard over the mechanical roar that accompanied a large fire. Harrison didn't bother to look up as he waved off the aide with the phone in his right hand. The Commander could wait a few minutes while he checked on Sylvia's condition. Leaning into the company pumper, the vibration a steady jangle against his back, he checked his watch and called the Queen of Angels Hospital.

As he waited to be connected, Harrison reviewed the current conditions before him. They had knocked down the fire in the northeast stack, the stack his Company 12 firefighters had been the first to enter, but then the library fire had slid across the seventh tier corridor and connected with the northwest stack. Smoke had been pouring from that side, out of the patent room, for the last hour. He saw two hook and ladders directing heavy streams through a smashed window. Steam and smoke poured out. They needed more access than an open window; in fact, they were busting through and making ventilation holes on the roof to relieve the heat from that corridor. Goddamn masonry. If it smashed down into the rotunda, the fire would continue in the center of the library.

It would take seven hours, twenty-two fire companies, four of his men hauled off in ambulances before they had the beast cornered. He cupped his free hand over his open ear to cut down the racket, and when the hospital patched him through to Sylvia's bed, he dropped it to slap the pumper. She wasn't in the ER! He told her to rest, commanded her to take it easy, that they had it under control and he'd be down later. When she handed the phone over to Cecilia, a family member, he talked longer than he wanted to.

He read his watch again, knew that it was time to meet with the old man, rubbed his face, and left his post at the pumper. Crossing the street, he stepped over lines of bulging four-inch hose and water in pools, water on asphalt.

The Commander had set up his headquarters on the sidewalk in front of the Grand Avenue Bar. The Commander always knew where to set up. Harrison watched a white-jacketed waiter bring out a tray loaded with thin china cups and two pitchers, one steaming, and lay it down on the table the old man was using.

"Here Tom, have a fresh cup of java," the Commander said, holding out the dainty white cup.

"I'll take it, Mack," Harrison answered. He sipped at the coffee, not caring how hot it was.

"We've got that roof broken open, Tom. Those hammer boys love to break and enter."

"Damn building was really built, wasn't it?" Harrison said as an answer.

"Don't build 'em like that anymore, thank God. Friggen hazard from day one," the Commander said, sipping his coffee. "Your men did a helluva job. I heard about Cruz."

"It was a pressure cooker in there, Mack. Backdrafts, the whole nine yards. I want a commendation for all of them, a special for Cruz."

"Over two thousand degrees in places," the Commander answered without slowing down. "I got the readings right here. How're they doing?"

"I just spoke with the hospital. Cruz was the big worry, tossed her oxygen before we got to her, sucked her bottle dry and still pulled those guys out."

"Uh-huh. She hooked up?"

"Didn't need life support. She's the real deal."

"Someone looking out for us. Goddamn, helluva fire, but there will not be any goddamn fatalities on our watch."

Harrison wiped his face but didn't comment. He didn't believe himself to be a superstitious man, didn't trust lady luck, but still he didn't want to push it.

"I'm gonna need one more big push. We gotta get at that seventh tier corridor before it ruptures, and you got the commendations," the Commander continued on with a nod at the library.

"I'm down to eight men," Harrison said, draining the cup and setting it down on the tray.

"New crew's coming in any minute," the commander said. "You go ahead and break off. You know the score. Get your men outta there, cool 'em off." The Commander reached out with his hand, shaking hands firmly; Harrison found himself re-crossing the street.

Harrison took the headset and leaned against the side of the pumper, clearing his throat before speaking. "Sam. Sam, do you read me?" He listened to the response. "Bring 'em out," he said, leaning harder into the pumper. He looked up to the roof a moment before he heard the jackhammers suddenly stop. They had finally broken through the roof. They'd knock it down soon.

A crowd inside a specially barricaded area anxiously cheered when they heard the hammers stop. He knew they were the librarians, library workers, because they wouldn't go home. How could they? He understood.

The "B" shift pulled in fresh and eager as the remaining eight firefighters from his "A" shift gathered around him at the side of the pumper, weary and soot-covered, even their eyes seeming to have a fine layer of smoke over them. They were a team, in it together. What did it have to do with fire? A chemical reaction, the reflection on cave walls?

Harrison cleared his throat, though it was already quiet, and then spoke. "You knocked down the northeast stack," he said, stopping to look at them. They had done it, and he wanted to give them the recognition; that was all the praise he needed to give. He continued with details, "The jackhammers have broken through on the northwest stack. Distributor nozzles have been placed in two of the access holes." He paused. "Water is boiling where it sits on the roof. Hook and ladders are hitting the patent room and teams are working their way up the tiers, but we're not going back in; it's almost dead and our shift is over." There were nods, but not an audible sound of relief or movement.

"What's the word, Chief?" a voice asked for all of them.

"They're at Queen of Angels. And the word is better than satisfactory. You can relax. They're on easy time, sipping milk shakes and watching you on the news." Only then did the team begin to unbuckle, helmets came off, knuckles cracked and water bottles passed around.

A few minutes later, he got a call from the Commander. "This one's going off, Tom. Your guys did a helluva job." Harrison held the headset about six inches from his ear. He could hear the old man perfectly. "Send them home. B shift can continue to check for hot spots." There was a slight pause. "Listen, Tom, I know you've been on your feet this whole time and Junior's coming in to replace you, but can you do me a favor?"

Harrison looked at the bronzed doors, thinking he wouldn't get much rest anyway. They knew he'd drop by the hospital and swing back over here. "What is it, Mack?" he asked.

"I have a Mrs. Delaney here. She's the head librarian." There was a short pause. "Can you imagine, Tom? These people haven't left." The Commander grunted, but he didn't have to explain. They both knew how the library workers felt. They'd seen it before. "I've been told to escort them in. Small groups, not for salvage. You understand, don't you?" he bellowed.

"Yeah, sure. I understand," Harrison answered back.

"I need someone like you to handle this, Tom."

Harrison knew what he wanted: a good image, visible concern, patience and consideration.

"I hate like hell to ask you, but we need it done."

"Sure Mack. I'll lead them in, but first I'm going to the hospital to check on my men," Harrison answered.

"Right and thanks, Tom."

Junior, the B shift captain, would be in charge of mop-up, which meant that Harrison's team could ride back to the station in the van, clean up, and head home. It would be late tonight before he could allow the librarians in, and they would have to be closely supervised. He'd have at least an hour to an hour and a half to buzz over to Queen of Angels Hospital and check in on the guys who were laid up. He realized that while he was making a check list he was staring at the valves on the pumper. There were six of them, yeah, that sounds right, he told himself, knowing it was time to leave.

In the hospital parking lot, he looked at his watch before getting out of the squad car. It read six-thirty. He decided to take the elevator up instead of the stairs, even though it was against his training and, if he would admit it, his superstitions, but he was tired and his crew members were on the fourth floor.

Later, after he'd checked in on all four of them and felt more than satisfied with their condition, he stopped in the cafeteria. He was seated, finishing a piece of pie, when he saw a head nurse rushing through the doors waving frantically at him. He waved back, thinking nothing of it until she called out his name sharply.

She continued her rush through the cafeteria to his table without the usual clipboard in her hands. He jumped up to meet her and felt sweat building on his forehead.

"What is it, Dolores?" he asked, almost shouting.

"It's Cruz, Tom. She's not responding. We've run her into intensive care," the head nurse said, touching his arm.

He didn't say anything. The lack of sleep in the last thirty hours, the smell of smoke on his jacket hit him solidly. He wanted to take his cap off and scratch his head. He thought of the elevator and cursed himself.

She let go of his arm. "It looks like cardiac arrest. Why don't you go on up. Third floor ER."

"Yeah, thanks Dolores. I know where it is," he heard himself mumble. Then he turned and headed for the stairs this time, taking them two at a time, up to the third floor where another nurse was waiting for him at the end of the hall.

"Chief Harrison," she called out, waving her arms.

The nurse led him through the intensive care unit to a bed in the corner. There were sheets drawn around some of the other beds, but not around this one. They had to have room. The nurse stopped and he saw the familiar dark machine with the two plunger-like ends like black curls of smoke, but the rest he saw in white. A white sheet on runners, Sylvia's bare chest, the doctors and nurses in caps and gowns. He twitched violently with Sylvia, once, twice, and then a third time. He wouldn't look away at the other machine, the one with the green screen that monitored her heartbeat, he didn't want to see if the line had straightened, level as the grout in a tile wall. A doctor passed him, rushing, a monstrous syringe in his hands, and he watched as it plunged into the bare chest of his firefighter with such force, it hurt the fillings in his teeth. But Sylvia jerked, kicked her legs, hacked into the oxygen mask and Harrison felt his own legs, couldn't stop their shaking, his hands fisted, fingernails tearing into his palms. The nurse, Dolores, shouted and hugged Sylvia, a doctor squeezed her hand, and Harrison had to lean against the bed to keep his feet firmly under him. Sylvia blinked. Harrison forced himself to turn away and check the other machine. It showed hills and valleys, the doctor already working at his gloves, as they covered the bare chest of Sylvia Cruz with the white sheet.

"My God," he whispered, rubbing the back of his neck furiously, working his clenched jaw until he felt the presence of the doctor.

"What happened?"

"Cardiac arrest. It must have been stress induced," the doctor answered, taking his glasses off to clean them. "From what I heard," the doctor continued, holding his glasses, "she fought a real battle. She's in great condition but she held the shock back until her body said it's time. And then she shut down big time."

"She's going to make it?"

"Don't see why not. You saw her, she was on the edge but she didn't give up."

Harrison stared hard into the doctor's face. Finally, he heard his voice come from a deep well, "Thanks, Doc." Not knowing what else to say, or if he could, he walked to the gurney and took Sylvia's hand in both of his.

She stared back at him, returning his hold on her with a weak squeeze.

"Damn you, I won't take anymore of your b.s. You got me this time. I'll have to report you in the future."

Sylvia smiled, squeezed once more and then closed her eyes. He jerked up to look at her machine, saw she was fine, maybe already asleep. He dropped her hand, placing it carefully at her side and turned wearily to leave the intensive care unit. He stopped outside in the corridor. He rubbed at the back of his neck again and tried to think of Sylvia. The more he tried to bring her into focus, the more she faded, and he found himself bringing up names and faces of all the firefighters he had known who had died. Darkened faces, the white circle around their eyes. He tried to bring himself back to Sylvia, but couldn't take his eyes off the walls. They were painted in two shades of green. A darker green on the bottom half where it was met by a lighter shade of green. They made a line where they met and he couldn't take his eyes off that green line as he remembered what Sylvia had told him about her grandfather. Her grandfather had been the greatest mason in Los Angeles. She had said he was the supervisor who had built the Central Library. She had told him that she wanted to be a firefighter in memory of her grandfather, to be useful, and to do something important. She had also said that he was a great singer of *corridos*. What's a *corrido*? Harrison asked himself as he finally took his eyes off the wall in the corridor and headed for the bright light at the foot of the stairs.

CHAPTER 4

Pete Escobedo was called in two days after the library fire, by Captain Jim Tucker at Evergreen. *El Chingón* was in one of his moods.

"Escahbeado, the fire department is conducting an investigation into the library fire. They haven't confirmed that it was arson. Now, that's not our jurisdiction until we get their say so, as you should well know, but in the time being, a fireman, a woman, for chris'sakes, was seriously injured in the line of duty. Name's Cruz, Sylvia Cruz. Affirmative action recruit," he spit out the words. Pete stood. He didn't plan to take a seat. He hadn't been invited in to sit down anyway, not for an affirmative action recruit.

"I heard about it," Pete said, conscious of staring at the pink skin that rolled out of Tucker's tightly buttoned collar.

"You did? Well, that's fine, because I'm putting you on it," Tucker said, looking down at his paperwork.

"Is this an investigation then, Sir?" Pete asked with a shade too much deference.

The Captain snapped his head up at him, squinting. "No," he growled, pointing one thick finger at Pete's chest. "Goddamn, this is not a goddamn investigation yet. Didn't I just say that, Escahbeado?" He didn't wait for an answer. "Here's the frigging sheet. You'll contact the family, not that I know what it'll help, but since you grew up in that area over there, and since the goddamn fire department wants to tell us how to run this police station, you're picked to engage in community relations," the Captain said, nearly strangling on the word "community." He threw the report on his desk and leaned back in his chair.

Pete picked up the report, three loose sheets, stared at it for a moment, and then returned his gaze to the Captain's neck. Tucker wasn't staring back; he was pulling at the skin under that very same chin as if a sudden thought had made itself clear. He let go of his neck and asked abruptly, "Are there any questions, Escahbeado?" He didn't wait for an answer. "Community relations, Escahbeado, you understand me. Then, get on it, but I don't want this interfering with the gang section, understand?"

Pete didn't answer. He understood. The Captain was telling him to add some of his own time and pass his card to the family to satisfy the community. To the Captain, Cruz was just another recruit to deal with. Pete was positive that Tucker didn't know that Sylvia Cruz was Ray's sister, that she had grown up in his neighborhood, his barrio, on his corner. The Captain had been working the last fifteen years in Evergreen and still treated East L.A. as if it were a foreign occupation: Beirut, Berlin, Beantown. Waiting for his retirement in Altadena. Pete understood. *El Chingón* wanted this one to slide on by with a minimum of time if it wasn't arson.

Pete had left the Captain's office as soon as those little round eyes had dropped to the desk again. He made his way through the squad room. Nine months a detective and he still had to share a desk with his partner, Tony Martínez, who wasn't in, so he had the mess to himself. He sat down, pulled a cigarette from a soft pack in the top drawer, and started reading the report. He hadn't gotten half way down the page before he was interrupted.

"Hey there, Angel," the detective said, rolling his name in Spanish. "Ahnhel." He had said it slowly, drawing it out. Pete didn't look up. He knew who was talking because nobody called him Angel in the squad room except for this redneck paddy. White boy in his late thirties going bare on top, stuck here at Evergreen as if it were a sentence. Pete had this detective down, the kind of lowbrow *chota* that never got out of his car, kept it rolling, called for a back-up if he had to take a leak.

No one else called him Angel except for his parents and the old folks. His homeys in Stairways had never called him "Ahnhel." If anything, he had always been "Sleepy," the name Coachy had used. Coachy had always called them the names they had wanted, the names they had dug up from comic books, the Saturday morning cartoons, one of the Seven Dwarfs, or their imaginations. They had all liked their Coachy, a blonde clean-cut P.E. major from UCLA. It was Coachy who had set up the games, when every park and school had summer leagues and recreation. It was Coachy who had taught him to wrestle and box.

He used "Pete" for the department, liked the way it sounded, his middle name once you translated it to English. It was the same with all the Chicanos in the department. No one used Juan, Jose or Pedro, and some of them, as soon as they made a little money, moved to Glendale, Burbank, Northridge, or way the hell out to Diamond Bar. Clean little suburb as far away from the barrio as possible.

So this dumb paddy was at it again, but did he really know what he was implying? Did he know the put down, a *gabacho* using the Spanish of their *madres*, using his name with that tongue? Pete looked around the squad room and felt the tenseness in the others. These *paisanos*, they knew, the paddy wasn't that stupid or naive, and they didn't like it either. Although the paddy detective weighed more than him and was about six inches taller, Pete didn't care; this kind of shit couldn't go on. He didn't look up. Pete wanted the tenseness to sweat, to chill his backbone, to tighten his wiry body.

"You got a toaster, huh?"

Pete ignored him. He put aside the hospital report on Sylvia Cruz, then started on the disaster report by a Chief Harrison of the fire department. The detective started to leave. Pete continued to read, thinking that he really didn't want this trouble in the squad room, that he'd get this guy sometime on the outside, but the paddy stopped and turned, smiling as if he were a good buddy.

"You gonna start your investigation at Olvera Street, Ahnhel?"

That was when Pete came out of the chair slowly, adjusting his pants. The detective tensed up when Pete stopped in front of him but the stupid grin remained on his face as he made a sly effort to back down, saying, "Just keeping it light, *primo*."

There it was again. "*Primo*," cousin, but Pete didn't need to think about it this time and hit him in the face twice with rapid short strikes. When the detective got his hands up, Pete went after his ribs, wailing, as he had on the heavy bag in the playground under Coachy's supervision. He liked the way the grunts became smaller as the big man tried to get some air. He liked the way he himself was breathing, the way his body worked: smooth, quick and accurate inside, like the famous "homeboy" boxer, Danny Red López. "Your mother must have picked up some shit off a corncob to breed someone as stupid as you," Pete said into the detective's ear, but loud enough for the others to hear as he stopped and watched the big guy slide off the desk onto the floor. He looked up then to see that the squad room, all of them, including the other paddy rollers, had made a wall in front of Tucker's glass office so the *chingón* couldn't see what was going on. Pete looked down, thought about giving him another pop in the face, but knew he was finished; he felt good. Then there was the roar of Lieutenant Jesse Vasconcelos, "What the hell's goin' on here?"

Pete sat down at his desk, picked up the report again, and looked at the lieutenant with a "what gives" expression. Tony Martínez, who must have come in during the fight, was talking to the lieutenant. "*Compa*, this poor guy has been working too hard. Look how he slipped and fell on that desk. You okay, Joe?" Tony asked, turning to the detective, who was now sitting against the edge of the desk, breathing hard, trying not to moan and hold his guts all at the same time.

"Shut your fat mouth, Martínez," the lieutenant yelled, "or I'll kick you back on beat in Terrace."

Pete read on.

"Right, *jefe*. I was just shoving outta here. Working on a squeal right now, *ahorita*," Martínez answered quickly, nodding his head at Pete before turning on his heels.

"If the rest of you aren't busy, I can find something for you to do. Clear out—now!" the Lieutenant bellowed, approaching the front of Pete's desk. "I want to see you in my office in five minutes, Escobedo."

Pete placed the report in a file folder and laid it on a stack that was already tumbling. He reached into the top drawer for the cigarettes and pulled one out, but he didn't light it. His eyes fell on his business cards. "Detective, Evergreen Division," it read in small print under his name, Pete Escobedo. No Ahnhel. His *padres* hadn't known any better, proud of the culture, their culture, *La Raza*. What had they known about naming their children, the fights he'd had in school? Angel Pete, they'd called him, anglicized, and even some of the Chicano and Mexican kids had joined in. His par-

ents didn't understand what it was like out of their neighborhood, that he could only be *Angelito* at the *panadería* or the
barber shop, that his name didn't sit right with the others,
that it never would, not in a high school or a department of
cops. That's why he used his middle name, Pete. Pete had a
good ring to it. "Pete," he whispered to himself, never Pedro.
"Pete," he said again, and then like he couldn't help it,
"Angel," drawing it out, "Ahnhel."

He got up and went into the bathroom. Staring in the
mirror, he brushed back the thick straight black hair that lay
close to his scalp with his fingers, touched the neat black
moustache and looked into his dark eyes. "Ahnhel," he repeated, turning sideways to survey his face. His nose was like a
beak, but his face still looked thin without the round cheeks of
his father and mother. At five foot six he was much taller than
his parents. Thin, but strong. He'd had to learn to be strong.
Ahnhel. He went into the lieutenant's office and stood there
with a serious expression while Vasconcelos went dark around
the eyes about division relations. "You'd better keep the snot
off your nose, Escobedo, if you want a permanent place here,"
were the lieutenant's final words, except that he used *"mocos"*
instead of snot, a word that irritated Pete because its meaning
was like a slap to the back of a child's head. That was the
thing about their *madre's* language; words had other mean-
ings.

"I don't want no trouble, 'tenant," Pete said, shrugging as
he left the office.

He returned to his desk and sat down as if nothing had
happened. Then he made an appointment with the Fire Chief,
Tom Harrison, for that afternoon. *El Chingón* had said there
wasn't to be an investigation yet, community relations only.
But there was a double meaning in the message, just as Sylvia
Cruz is community, family, neighborhood, his people.

With an hour and a half to kill before his appointment, he left Evergreen, drove west and crossed the L.A. river, a concrete-lined geographical boundary that separated east Los Angeles from downtown, from everywhere for that matter. He always knew he was crossing over at the halfway point on the bridge, as if it were a causeway, the border that distinct. Perhaps it was the barren walls of the concrete river that made him reflect on the quality of Los Angeles. And as he drove west he crossed other bridges, imaginary, but he clearly saw a city of barrios, neighborhoods like his own in Echo Park, sharing borders with Silver Lake although one was mainly Latino and the other upwardly mobile.

In Silver Lake, he stopped at Annette's, a condo with a view of the Silver Lake reservoir. She wasn't at home and suddenly he felt awkward, the street quiet and reserved, the lake fenced in and no children or families. He should have called first, they'd only been dating for a couple of weeks, but he was light-headed after the fight at the station. What had he wanted from her? Clearly, he should have called, her type expected a call, he admonished himself, as he drove back to Echo Park.

Sunset Boulevard in Echo Park was congested, the sidewalks busy. He checked the barber shop hoping for a trim, but it was filled up and he couldn't wait.

Finally, he knew where he had to go. He'd been to Engine Company 12 at least five times through grammar and junior high. It had seemed like every new *gringa* teacher with high ideals had hauled them off to the fire station. He parked behind a red and white Dodge, checked his hair in the mirror, got out of the car and put on his jacket.

He had to wait five minutes for Chief Harrison in the station office.

"You read the prelim, Detective Escobedo?" Harrison asked.

"Yes, I did."

"Good. What else can I do for you?"

"Background, Chief," Pete answered. He waited a moment. "What was unusual about that fire?"

"That's difficult to answer, detective," Harrison answered, rubbing his hands thoughtfully. "It was a very busy fire. Can you be more specific?"

"Yeah, I could be more specific, Chief Harrison, but the only thing I know about fires is that when they're too hot they burn my steaks," Pete paused. "I want to find this arsonist." He looked at Harrison but he was thinking about Sylvia. Should he let Harrison know how close he was to her? He watched Harrison take hold of a coffee cup and pull a measured sip.

"We haven't identified it as an arson yet."

"No, you haven't," Pete answered too quickly. He knew he should hold back. He toned down his next question. "But, you must have a feeling one way or the other?"

"The Fire Inspector's report won't come in for several days," Harrison answered, locking onto Pete's eyes before looking at his notes.

"I see." Pete paused, hoping that a moment would give him more. Pass and return, he told himself. "So you were at the hospital with Sylvia Cruz?"

"I visited her at around six-thirty, stopped in to see the others. I was having a cup of coffee when she went under."

"Was she that close?" Pete asked calmly, checking the chief's expression.

"It was hell. I was there."

"You didn't expect it?"

"It can happen. Sylvia is strong, capable. She seemed fine when I first saw her. It would've been a loss, a loss to everyone," he repeated, speaking into the rubbing of his hands.

The man took it hard, Pete thought, then asked, "She's going to be okay?"

"It's looking good. I was with her this morning. She doesn't much remember it. Bounced back like a kid."

"Will Cruz have a place here? After she recovers, of course."

"If she passes the medical, Sylvia's on my team," Harrison stated, shaking his head.

"Was Sylvia Cruz accepted in your Company?"

"Still is," the Chief answered quickly. "She was a recruit, but she's good. She's going to receive a commendation for heroism. She pulled three men out of the fire."

"No problems with the men?" Pete asked, brushing at his coat.

Harrison moved forward in his chair. "She got along fine with everyone. She experienced the usual hazing, nothing serious. Why so many questions, Detective? What does this have to do with the fire?" Harrison asked tautly.

Harrison's eyes weren't cool now; they were angry and set hard. Pete held them. "Just wondering how it works here, Chief. I have no idea."

"We're professionals. I'm sure you understand that," Harrison answered.

Pete nodded his head. The man was wound tight, but he was straight. He was all right for a *jefe*. A boss who was ready to fight for his people, had gone right to the hospital to check up on them. Pete glanced at his watch, a half hour had passed. He hadn't learned anything new, but it hadn't been a waste of time.

"And if it was arson that almost killed one of your team?" Pete asked.

"You're getting my full cooperation, Detective. We're already plenty upset around here."

"You'll give me a call when the report comes in?"

"I'm not holding a thing back from you. I want to nail the bastard," Harrison answered, spreading his palms out.

"Chief Harrison," Pete said respectfully, rising as he extended his hand, "thank you for all your help. I've taken up too much of your time, but I would like to talk to some of your men."

"Anyone in particular?" Harrison answered with a question.

Pete looked up and around the room. He listened to the sounds of the firehouse, heard a ball game going on. "Who was she closest to?"

"Cornelius Bennett," Harrison answered. "You'll probably find him in the back, working out, Detective."

"Thanks again," Pete said as he left the office. Harrison was a pro, but he wasn't able to hide his feelings, the sharp sense, tuned up high. Pete knew it was arson, the Chief had as much as told him so.

He went directly to the back, following the sound of the bouncing ball to a small cement court against the wall of the firehouse. There was a wooden backboard for handball, a hoop near the top of the backboard, and a hose drying rack off to the side. He watched the eight men. Four who were shirtless had control of the game. One of the players swooped in between two defenders for a easy lay-up. He was checked hard, but still made the basket effortlessly. "You gave me an open lane," he shouted, grinning. The two shirts who had been beat, had their hands on their knees, breathing hard.

Pete saw his opening and shouted, "Where can I find Cornelius Bennett?"

"Polishing the pumper," a shirt answered back.

"The pumper," Pete said, and then turned back into the station house. He wandered over to the pumper and looked at all the chrome and dials, saw the firefighter working on a fender. Pete noticed that it hadn't been polished properly, that it was being rubbed out. He also noticed that the firefighter was black.

"Cornelius Bennett?" he asked.

"The same. What can I do for you?" Cornelius answered without turning around.

"Detective Escobedo, LAPD. I want to ask you a few questions regarding the Central Library fire."

Bennett turned, looked Pete over, capped the can of rubbing compound, dropped the T-shirt he was using as a rag, and stood up. "Sure thing."

"It'll only take a few minutes, Mr. Bennett," Pete said, touching his shirt and tie while stepping back. The guy was at least a foot taller.

"Call me Cornelius."

"Why don't you tell me what you know about the fire, Mr. Bennett," Pete said, not offering his first name.

He heard about the fire, heard what he already knew about Sylvia's heroism. Then he asked about her situation in the Company.

Bennett told him that Cruz was a fine firefighter; they all liked her. They had been close. There was a glimmer in his eyes. Cruz and Bennett, recruits, adjoining lockers, same pumper. They'd been close, real close. Pete didn't have to work hard to bring up Sylvia's proper and strict family. This relationship wouldn't be something that Sylvia would announce at supper time. The report had some *real* blood in it now, Pete thought, no doubt about it. If he was right, and he was sure that he was, how would Ray feel if he knew? Well, it was Sylvia's ride, and she's a fine *chavala*, smart too. Better let this one slide.

"You were in the same hospital room with Sylvia Cruz?" Pete asked pointedly.

"Yes, they had to put us in a room together. It's a crowded hospital," Cornelius pointed out. "Her family came by, early afternoon, the whole family. I talked to Ray. Ray is Syl's brother," Cornelius said.

Pete paused before answering. "Yeah, I know him."

"Good people."

"They are. So you were in the room when she lapsed into... "

"Cardiac arrest! Right after the Chief left. Her monitor went off and all hell broke loose."

"What exactly happened?" Pete asked, feeling in his pocket for a cigarette.

"Full emergency procedure. They wheeled Sylvia out on the gurney. I thought... Man, I thought it was the last time I'd see her," Cornelius said, looking down at the fender.

Pete let the quiet seep in before he struck a match. "How did the fire start?"

"Could've been many causes. Electrical. A smoker, Detective," he said, raising his eyebrows at Pete.

"Was it arson?"

"That's not my department."

"But you know what they use."

"Usually a high flammable. Starts with lighter fluid on up to the exotic. A fire's not too difficult to start. It's the finishing that's tough."

"Thanks for your time, Cornelius," Pete said finally.

"Any time. Let me know if there's anything I can do," Cornelius answered.

"Here's my card. Get back to me if anything comes up. I'll let you get back to work," Pete said.

Later, on the ride back to his station house, Pete was thinking about that fender, how much sweat it would take to get off that dried polish when he remembered where he was, saw the sign, and had to cross three lanes of traffic to make the First Avenue exit. He made a left at the bottom of the off-ramp and went back under the freeway, gunning it through a yellow light. He looked in his rearview mirror and watched two cars follow him. "Goddamn L.A. drivers," he said aloud reaching down to punch the radio to another station. Lousy music. He tried a Mexican station. Commercials as usual, a lawyer talking so fast he couldn't begin to understand him. Mexican stations. They must be raking it in with all the commercials. He reached into the map pocket on the driver's door and pulled out three tapes. Music came on as he was fumbling. It was *Norteño*, but he wasn't interested and slid in *Los Lobos*. Better, much better, he muttered as he turned up the volume.

He passed a Russian graveyard loaded with trees, and then a Jewish cemetery surrounded by a high fence covered with ivy. He had to swerve and brake hard to miss a car that had drifted into his lane. "*Chinga su...*," he grumbled as he pulled up close, hoping that it was some young *vatos* he could hassle, but it was only an ancient couple, Korean or Chinese, the old man's eyeglass frames rigid over his clenched jaws, the old lady bowing slightly as she gave him a nervous smile.

"*Buenas tardes*," he yelled to them and returned their wave. Two blocks later, as he turned left into the Evergreen parking lot, barely beating a hearse followed by its parade, he wondered what it was about Boyle Heights that made people want to be buried here.

CHAPTER 5

The morning began with fog. That was how he remembered it. Fleshy fog in the buds of the creeping morning glory that had been blooming since early April. Interior fog in the backdrop of Encinitas streets, flickering images of cars, and the click-clack of wiper blades.

Billy Johnson stopped before crossing the railroad tracks to shoot a long hostile look at the sixty watt lamp of sun. Below the sun, the traffic signal at the road to Beacon's beach had turned red, but it didn't glow. It was dull and dark. It was as black as a pot of dried-out beans. Fog. Why fog? June was the month for fog in this strip of a beach town, and it was only the end of April. Now he had to find another place to live— again. He studied the wet rust of the railroad tracks, knowing that he couldn't stay in Peter's backyard because his girl- friend, Debbie, was too uptight. What did she know? She was L.A. She smoked, drank too much coffee and ate veal. Didn't she see he was only there to help them? Hadn't he shown them how to grow and press wheat grass? Hadn't he explained the powers of pyramids, and blessed them with smoking sage? His knowledge alone should be enough. But it was Debbie's fault he had to move. Bitch!

He picked up a eucalyptus nut from among the sharp stones between the tracks and licked its spiky haircut, the del- icate green hairs with fuzzy yellow tops that spread out from the crown of the nut. Now this was sweet and good. This was why he collected seeds, because seeds are perfect microcosms, the centers of the universe. He collected a handful of the nuts, pocketed them in his flannel shirt and stepped down the embankment. But as he crossed the street to the donut shop, the anger returned. Debbie's diet was retro; that was why she was so hostile. He had read it while massaging her feet. The toxins were in her liver; he could feel it when he pressed between her toes. I will be the new revolution but Debbie will never be a part of it, Billy told himself as he opened the wooden screen door and entered the donut shop.

"Heya, Wheelyam. You want to work today? Cook leave for two days. Come on, you fry donuts tonight, eh?"

She was alone inside the donut shop, a woman who looked too small and thin to speak so aggressively. He pulled at the hair he had tied back in a ponytail, tight, thin, honey-blond hair that grew long from the sides of his crown. She kept her eyes on him as she quickly wiped her delicate hands on a white towel. She could be fourteen or forty. He thought she was thirty-six because she was Vietnamese. Under the fluorescent lights, his skin was the same bleached color as the fog on the windows. He touched his glasses as if to make sure his eyes were still blue as he ignored her, staring instead at the pink icing on a tray of cake donuts. He liked the way she called him William.

"Did'ya try that tea I gave you the other day?" he asked slowly, the corners of his mouth turning down so that his lips looked even thinner and bluer than usual. "That is a local herb. It grows here specially because this place is sacred. One of the Mount Palomar triangulation points. So is Disneyland, which explains its popularity. That plant's been perfecting itself here for over ten thousand years. It was meant to grow," he said, stretching his pink nose over the counter and crooking his head sideways. He exaggerated the word "meant," as if it were a seed stuck on his tongue. "Do you realize the healing effect that tea would have on your customers instead of coffee." He played with this word too, pausing to look her over before fighting with the dispenser for a napkin to wipe his glasses.

"Do ya know what I mean, Mrs. Nguyen?" He waited a moment, cocking his head. "You have the power to change all of your customers into smiling happy people. Instead of leaving here with bad breath and their hearts getting angry over work, they'll arrive in a blissed-out state. They won't even notice that their intestines will be completely plugged up for six hours from one of your grease balls."

"Wheelyam! These are Americans come in here. They don't want tea. We make good donut and coffee. Hills Brothers. Where you get this crazy ideas?" she asked with a laugh. But the laugh wasn't real; it was just part of her voice.

"I know what I'm talking about, Mrs. Nguyen." He pressed in on her, head jerking, hands behind his back. He rarely used his hands to make a point. "You see, the reason why Americans aren't as skinny as you, or as healthy, is because they haven't learned to deal with ten thousand years of oppression. They just love Ronnie and Nancy."

She laughed again, but stopped short to flip up both hands. Her voice had the musical quality of a video arcade as she spoke to him. "You like to tell me crazy ideas, don't you, Wheelyam? You think I buy the tea from you? Sure, if I know it sells, but Thao don't think so. This the land of opportunity, Wheelyam. You very smart. You should have big house and wife, huh?" She gave him a big smile before she turned to change a filter in the coffee machine.

He finished wiping his glasses, staring through them into the exposed array of fluorescent tubes before putting them on and looking at her. "You think it's so great, you should try Oklahoma."

"We already lived in Texas. We were settled there," she shot back at him.

Billy paid no attention to what she said. "You see what we're about to go through here is the expulsion of cultural idiocy. Rejuvenate the planet, Mrs. Nguyen. We will align once again with Nature," he said, touching the bridge of his glasses. "The whole world will follow because we'll be pollution free, happy, and rich. Our kids will cavort with the dolphins. California is the place. Look, even the Italians are wild about California. They know, Mrs. Nguyen. They know."

"The Italians?" she responded. "They make good shoes, but too expensive."

"You're stuck on leather," he clucked. "It's the beef mentality, but we're going to break out of it. That's why the Italians need us. They're searching, Mrs. Nguyen, searching for a way to rid themselves of the Vatican."

"The Vatican?" she asked, perplexed.

He bent over the counter. "The Vatican is a corporate culture vacuum. We need to open up the institutions, give away all their art, Mrs. Nguyen," he answered, his eyebrows arching over the top of his glasses. "I'm working on it right now with the Milanese. First thing I'd do is send the *Pietá* to Belize. Ship all the Vatican art to Third World countries in boxes, not even tell the countries they were coming. Let them decide what to do with it." He paused, but he wasn't waiting for a response. She gave him one, anyway.

"What you talking about, Wheelyam? Those countries already have art."

He smiled the thin smile. "That's right, they have art which reveres Nature, but we're so bent over by the *idea* of Raphael and Michelangelo that we've lost it. Let me explain it to you this way," he said, leaning over the counter. "The Trinity is a pyramid, Nature." He brought out his hands and made a triangle, staring through his fingers at her. "It's not the hocus pocus they sell you, it has always been the new art. Nature. Get it? The pyramid." Billy shifted his gaze from her to his fingers, opening and closing the triangle.

"I know what the Holy Trinity is. Father, Son and Holy Ghost. I understand; I'm good Catholic," she answered, waving her hands up at his face to emphasize her position or to clear the air between them.

Billy frowned and leaned back. "We'll see. Just think of the dolphins, that's who we are, a brotherhood, and the Italians will go crazy over my new ideas because they know. They know."

Mrs. Nguyen brushed away a few strands of hair that had fallen over her forehead, but she continued to look him straight in the face, aware suddenly that he had stopped talking, that his voice had been as low and modulated as the fluorescent hum from above. She hadn't noticed the lights before, the power surges apparent now. Maybe, she thought, it wasn't only the sound of his voice, but also the movement of his head and eyes that amused her so much. She turned away, as if to get something from the back of the shop, because she didn't want him to see her smiling.

She picked up a tray of cinnamon rolls as she spoke over her shoulder. "What about Vietnam? You send art to Vietnam?"

"No," he answered, pouring himself a cup of coffee. "Vietnam doesn't need Vatican art. That would be like shipping over pneumonia. That art is nothing more than heavy water in the lungs." He added a huge slug of milk to his coffee and watched as the milk blossomed from the center. He focused on several large droplets of milk which had clung to the lip of the styrofoam cup before he licked them away. "Vietnam is already spiritually advanced. What they need is tea from Encinitas. That tea I gave you will heal your whole country."

She laughed and flung up her hands as the screen door squeaked. Billy watched as two surfers came in, poured coffee, and ordered maple bars and cinnamon rolls. They slouched against the counter in neon shorts, flip-flops, and all-cotton sweat shirts. They were basic beach blond, reflecting color, neither talking. Billy returned to his own coffee, opened up two packets of sugar, and let them slide slowly into the blossom he had created.

"You know what propels your board on a wave?" Billy asked, as he stirred his coffee.

"Huh?" one said, his mouth full of maple bar.

"Air bubbles, trapped air bubbles. You should study the dolphins. They're covered with tiny hairs that trap air bubbles. That's why they can swim so fast. Water flows around them. They just slip right through," he said with his eyes as well as his mouth. "You could do it with synthetics, but it has to be micro. Right now you're only standing in one place. You think you're moving, but it's just the wave." He was staring at them with the half-smile that he had perfected. A smile that made his already thin lips thinner, as if someone had drawn a line there with a pink marks-a-lot. He continued to stir his coffee with a red and white plastic stirrer, and waited. The surfers paid their bill and left without responding. The screen door banged shut and Billy smiled big for the first time that morning.

"I could revolutionize surfing, but no one could handle it. They want to abuse the wave," he told Mrs. Nguyen.

She smiled at him. "So you come in tonight?"

"I don't know," he answered heavily. "I'd have to do coffee enemas for a week to get rid of the grease in my liver."

"Ten o'clock, tonight."

"All right. I got a telephone bill I have to pay, anyway. How about a couple of cinnamon rolls?"

"Aiie, Wheelyam, I think you don't like these grease balls." But she picked up two rolls, placed them on wax paper, and slid them across the counter top.

"One's because I need to feel blocked up. It's good for my creative energy. The other one's to look at and remember what it's like to work here."

"Yeah, yeah. Okay. Tonight," she said hurriedly as the screen door opened and two customers walked in. "George, Howard, how you this morning?" she sang out.

"Later, Mrs. Nguyen," Billy said as he walked out on the wet wooden porch. The fog was still thick, would remain thick until nine or nine-thirty, but the sun was high enough now so that the glow overhead was steady, and the flickering had stopped. He looked at the white above him. It was beginning to happen, a new start. Then he bit into a cinnamon roll and crossed the highway back to the railroad tracks.

Billy walked in the Amtrak roadbed, rolling at the hip like a sailor. It was his torso that caused it—short powerful legs on a long waist, combined with his six-foot-two-inch height, and the cotton surgical pants, low on his hips, that he had salvaged from a friend who drove ambulances. He had tied the pants below the roll of fat over his hip bones, the only area of fat on his body. He walked slowly, not because he was almost thirty-six, but because he wasn't in a hurry. He was never in a hurry, and he didn't believe in exercise, anyway. The joggers and the bike riders had too much Catholic guilt; why else would they do something so unpleasant? He didn't listen for the train or pace himself to step on the wooden crossmembers, though he remembered that as a kid he would have seen how many he could leap over, balancing to avoid falling off the oil-soaked wood. He didn't care that the sharp stones between the rails dug through his flip-flops and into his feet; he was wishing for pockets. Had there been pockets in his cotton drawstring pants, he could have walked and had some place to put his hands.

He stopped when he came to the trestle that crossed over a highway underpass. Watching the cars, he remembered with distaste the cinnamon roll he had eaten. He leaned over the edge of the trestle, absorbing the stroke of air as the cars passed underneath him. He planned a lunch of cooked beets. Beets. Would they ever understand that cars were killing the planet or that beets were an aphrodisiac? He squatted in the middle of the rails and made an elaborate gesture of spreading his hands over one rail. There was a famous cowboy painting he had seen of an Indian with his ear to the rail, but in the painting there had been a prairie.

Cars. Too much energy. He would take a pot of beets over to Jesús. Eat some beans and beets with Jesús and talk culture. Jesús was culturally aware; he just didn't know it because he had everything going for him: a family, a wife, and a place to live. Jesús knew how to live, which was why it was so good to talk to him. Happy with less. The only thing that Jesús really didn't understand was dolphins. He didn't see dolphins. If there was one thing he would do, it would be to educate Jesús, show him dolphins. The dolphins would teach Jesús as they had taught him.

Billy looked up and down the rails until, confident that the Amtrak wouldn't catch him in the middle of the trestle, he started to cross. He didn't look for a place to put his hands now; he was moving too fast to worry about his hands. When he reached the other side of the trestle he looked north and south. He felt disappointed. He had never been caught on the trestle. He trudged slowly off the embankment, sliding down the side so that his flip-flops filled with sharp stones. When he reached level dirt he balanced on one foot and then the other. Once the stones were cleared, he continued walking past the edge of the business section of Encinitas, one of a string of small beach towns eighty miles to the south of Los Angeles, and headed up the hill to Maggie's.

Maggie's house was more than halfway up a hill overlooking the ocean. It was set against the hillside on the upper part of the street. The house wandered across the luxury of two skinny beach lots. Even to his untrained eye, it was obvious where sections had been added on. Unsupervised local construction, an Encinitas original. Squatty walls of chunky used concrete, stones, bricks, and even tires meandered step-like up from the street. The front door was open, a *corazón de trigo* hanging where the knocker should be. He yelled inside, "Maggie, Maggie," then entered. Maggie was living alone these days. It wasn't a big house, but she had plenty of room. He should have brought her something, he thought, and then looked at the second cinnamon roll wrapped in wax paper.

He heard her faint reply. "Who is it? Come on through; I'm in the side yard. Who is it?"

"It's Billy," he shouted back as he walked through the room, not looking at the books and art work that were scattered everywhere. Paintings leaned against the wall waiting for space. Pots to be glazed, sculpture, a loom with a half-finished rug. He had seen it all before. He placed the cinnamon roll on a bookshelf, passed through the kitchen and out onto a sloping cement patio surrounded by sandstone rocks and a low, cracked concrete wall. In the center was a fountain which she used as a barbecue pit. Maggie had her skinny, bent back turned to him. A long grey braid of hair hung down the center.

Her bare ankles and feet, thin as they were, collided incessantly under the frayed edge of the pink cotton housecoat she wore. She was watering the oleanders, jimsonweed, wandering jew and iceplant that grew alongside the sandstone wall, the water only a dribble out of a hose the width of a thick pencil. She didn't let the water fall in any one place, but waved the hose like a wand as she fidgeted along the wall.

"Maggie, you don't need to water those plants. They're drought resistant, except for the wandering jew. They belong here," Billy said to her back.

"What," she squawked, turning and giving him a puzzled look. "What's that?"

He didn't move closer, and as he spoke, he couldn't take his eyes off the thin stream of water now splashing on the cement patio and her feet. "Those plants you're watering are drought resistant. They don't need to be watered," he repeated loudly, feeling himself grow angry at her lack of attention and waste of water.

"Billy, I don't have the time to put in any plants, and if I did, it wouldn't be roses, but I like to water, and plants can always use water," she snapped at him. "What're you doing anyway? Why aren't you working? With the sun coming out like this, and you loving plants so much, you should get out there and bend your back. Do something productive. God, I hate waste," she said from her curved spine as she continued to sprinkle water over sandstone, patio, and plants.

"I'm working on something big right now and I can't," he paused, "waste time on mind-numbing work. The planet's suffering enough as it is."

She turned back again, giving Billy such a look that it seemed to him the water dribbling out of the hose in her right hand might be connected in some way to her face and begin gurgling out of her open mouth. Her face was a mass of wrinkles, lips twitching, her eyes so wide open that her eyebrows seemed to disappear into her forehead, the hair pulled back straight from it.

"I don't have a room for you, Billy, if that's what you're looking for."

"Maggie, that's not what I came here for," Billy lied with a tired voice and a sideways tilt of his head. "I have a very crucial matter to talk to you about," he pleaded.

"Pick walnuts for a week and you'll know what sleep's good for," she answered, turning back to the sandstone wall with the hose.

"There won't be any walnuts to pick if the Saguaro cactus cannot survive. Why do you think the Aztecs looked for the site of a flowering cactus to establish their empire? They knew the true meaning of growth."

"They were also looking for an eagle with a snake in its talons," Maggie shot back.

"Times were hostile, more so now," he said, continuing fast. "I am putting together a consortium of the most liberated, sensitive minds in Southern California. Their backgrounds are in plant growth, construction, electronics, and oceanography. We're all linked by our desire for a natural order and the polarity of mathematics. We're going to create Califia, Maggie, the new and revived Arcadia. It's going to start here in the trine of the Mount Palomar triangle." He paused, noticing that the hose had remained in one spot for more than three breaths. "We need you as an artist," he continued, "because there must be a recording of this new order." He paused, but began quickly again as the hose started to wiggle. "You understand nature, and you will be called upon to express it like you never have before."

"What is this bullshit?" Maggie asked impatiently. She dropped the hose onto the patio and sat in a metal patio rocker that badly needed paint. When she had set it in motion she spoke. "Why, can I ask you, would you want me as the artist? What I produce is dabbling. Crap, if you don't know."

Billy sat on a unbroken section of the concrete wall, and looked at the dribbling hose before he spoke. "That's not true," he said seriously. "You are centered; that's why your work hasn't been accepted. But it soon will be honored."

"Oh, Billy," she exhaled. "I haven't received such a goosing in a long time. Who are these great minds?" she asked with only a hint of the former sarcasm in her voice.

His friends flashed before his eyes, but he knew that they, like Jesús, didn't understand him. What he needed was a woman to mother his many children and a true brother at his side. A clear mind not like all this mess and this fog. "It's coming together," he stated profoundly. "I have a presentation scheduled at the Unitarian Church. A local shaman will cover us with a sagebrush blessing so that the spirit will enter us all, and then I'll start the dialogue. It will seem as if a circle has been drawn around everyone present. We will be the Brotherhood of Dolphins. And sisters," he added quickly. "Everyone in that circle will understand."

Billy moved closer, letting his eyes settle on the bunched wrinkles of her forehead before he squatted on the cement patio and reached for one of her feet. "Here, I can see you need a foot massage." Maggie let him raise her right foot. It was bony, the toenails cracked and yellow. Billy eyed the approaching circle of water from the hose, angry about the waste, chiding himself for not turning it off before he started on her foot.

"It sounds like your usual bunch of nonsense to me," Maggie said, relaxing into the back of the rocker, but watching him carefully over the tip of her large nose.

"That's just it, Maggie. I've been working up to this all my life. Think of how many people you know who have said that I was capable of great things. It takes time, time."

"I've seen and heard it all, believe me," she said through closed eyes.

"Yes, you have," he said. "You are a great resource. This is not a youth movement. Women and elders are to be revered." He hesitated a moment, as if he felt something in her foot. "You need to drink mate tea, Maggie; I can feel it in your kidneys. Feel it?" He pressed hard into the soft meat next to her big toe, just as he had with Debbie before she had thrown him out of Peter's backyard. Maggie gasped. Billy continued. "I'm working out the toxins now, but I'd recommend a one day fast and lots of mate tea. I'll get it for you."

"I think you're right. I've had a lot of stress lately. I need to clean out my system," she said as she gasped again.

"Creativity in the modern world doesn't relieve stress, but it will when we return to Nature." He put down her right foot and lifted up her left. He placed it on his knee, felt the circle of water lap over his flip-flops, and started to rub for a moment. He stopped. The name flashed as if sunlight had burst through onto the patio. Billy hadn't seen him in years, but they had once been best friends in high school. He went back to her feet, hardly able to control his excitement.

"What I need, Maggie, is to reunite with the spiritual center of Califia, the original Dolphin Brother. His roots are deep; he is the true Californio."

"Calls himself a Spaniard, probably?" she growled.

"Calasan." The name spouted off his tongue and Billy had to stop the massage. "He is an old soul, and what is really fantastic is that he is so completely one that he doesn't have any realization of it. I have to contact him and bring him here." He began to rub forcefully again, feeling the section of her foot that gave her the greatest pleasure, hoping that it would dull her brain, that she would relax enough so he could get something from her, if not a room.

"Maggie, can I use your phone? I need your help; my phone was disconnected."

"So this is what you wanted. Now we're getting to it. My phone," she said, her eyes opening wide. He could feel the tension in her foot.

"It's important," he said, trying to maintain the soothing rub and keep the tension out of his voice.

"Well, I admire what you've cooked up for the entertainment value of it, but using my phone is out of the question. You don't seem to remember that my phone is tapped, and I don't want to get into any more trouble with those FBI assholes."

"That was twenty years ago when Angela Davis lived here," Billy said, looking from the water on the patio to the faucet, and thinking again that he should turn it off.

"It's never stopped. I've been organizing for a long time, you know. Angela was just a student then," Maggie answered, closing her eyes. "They were looking to trump up some charges. They busted down my doors after Angela engineered that prison escape at Soledad. They broke in here more than once, and now they're looking for Sandinistas or illegals because I work with the mission. I can't even let the patriots come near my house." She sat up, pulling her foot out of his grasp.

"But Angela was a long time ago. They don't even care about her anymore."

"What?" she snapped. The water had now covered the patio. He rubbed his thighs nervously before pulling her foot back to his knees. "That's what you think, Billy. I've been around." She sat up straight, pulling her left foot from his grasp.

"It's just a simple call, Maggie," Billy sputtered, trying to calm the constricted feeling in his chest, the short breaths, his hands knotting.

"I don't think so. What about Jane? Jane has a good job and her own place, and I know you've been seeing a lot of her lately."

"I don't really want to go into it, but Jane has a long way to go. She's into the money mode. I've brought a lot of peace and love into her life, but she doesn't understand it yet. What she wants is a house and a good car. She's frightened by her heart," Billy said angrily.

"Well, she seems alright to me, woman working her butt off to make it, and with a child too. Men freeloading off women; times haven't changed a bit."

"What I give her can't be bought, Maggie. That's the main problem with this culture. I provide love, reassurance, good food. You love my massages, don't you? I do them with love. What should I charge? Love and understanding are taken for granted," Billy snapped, exhaling with the anger that had built up in him from this morning. A day that had begun in fog and Debbie throwing him out.

"Love is fine, but food on the table is another thing altogether. I don't know what makes it swing, and why you can't make it stick. Seems like a woman would never leave if the loving was as good as you say it is."

"Women in this society have been too conditioned to receive. They could lead us back to the center, but they've become hooked by plastic. And I can't find the right one who knows it," he spat out at the flood on the patio.

"The right one, you say. That's your problem right there. They're individuals; they don't have any God-given gifts to save men, believe me," she said angrily.

He looked up at her, squinting because she was a blur to him. His head hurt and he was having trouble focusing. The water around his feet felt cool, but the gurgling of the hose was now as annoying as her voice. He spoke slowly because it was difficult to breathe.

"This should be a place where young women can gather and, just by your presence, retrieve the gifts that will save mankind." His voice wavered and lost its calmness as he thought of Debbie again. He imagined shoving the dribbling hose down Debbie's throat to clean out her insides for good.

Maggie was quiet for a long moment. When she spoke, she added a whimsical smile. "Well, I can see that reality has escaped us once again. I have to get back to work. I can't spend my day talking nonsense."

Billy couldn't think of anything to say. He was still envisioning Debbie with his left hand behind her head, forcing it down as he shoved the hose deeper. Maggie stared at him with an intense far-off smile. He knew she didn't believe in the importance of this call. Maybe he should have brought her beets.

"Well," she said, putting both hands on the arms of the rocker and raising herself. "What do you say? I got work to do," she said, turning her back on him.

He stared at the back of her head. Maggie wouldn't help him out. She was shutting him out like Debbie had, like his ex-wife had. She wasn't a real woman. Billy jumped up, the hose in his hand. He could see the sun. He didn't need Maggie or Debbie, or Mrs. Nguyen; his life was beginning like the fog disappearing. "What about the water, Maggie?" he whispered into her ear.

"What?" Maggie croaked, clawing at the lime-green plastic hose that now circled her neck and snapped her head back.

"Don't you know? I'm a Dolphin Brother," he whispered as he tightened his grip, shoved his knee into her back, forcing her to the wet patio. Water hissed from the end of the hose like the dry bubbling he heard in her throat as he twisted the hose hard against the back of her neck. Maggie's bare feet, the hard yellow nails scratching at the cement, left trails of blood to float in the puddled water, her thin hands clawed at the hose tearing a line into her throat, her eyes rolled back, white and wide. Billy waited until her toes curled back, her hands falling limp before releasing the pressure on the hose. Maggie sucked in rattling air as Billy licked her ear and tore through the flimsy material to reach her breasts. "Have you ever been this close to a man, Maggie?"

A croak bubbled from her mouth.

"What was that? Not hard enough? I'll give you hard." He pulled her up tighter, twisting the thin green hose until the dribble from its end stopped again. She made one last tired slap at her throat and when he could feel the fight leave, he threw her down, lying on her, ear to chest, his hand clamped over her nose and mouth. Fascinated by the faint gurgling and the last shudder, he spread his fingers over her lips as one last thin bubble of mucous popped from her open mouth, staining a finger.

He remained on her, softly stroking her forehead, and didn't stand up until several minutes had passed. He brushed at his front side to remove the strand of her saliva on his finger and realized that he was growing erect. He thought of relieving himself but it didn't seem appropriate. Billy stared at her. Maggie had always been too busy to know a good thing. She had always needed to fill her space with activity. She could have helped me. Look at where she lived, all the space and wasted water. She should have known better. He went to shut off the water.

In the house, he went into the living room, picked up the cinnamon roll, bit into it and chewed while thoughtfully reading the front page report of the Los Angeles library fire in the morning newspaper. The report called it the destruction of a cultural institution. Billy was pleased and read all the articles, absorbed with the details. When he finished he decided on three paintings, returning with them to the garden. They made a nice fire in the old fountain. Billy wouldn't look at Maggie until he had lit the bundle of sage he always carried with him, the stems tied together with a red thread. Blowing on the dried herb until it began to smoke, he made elaborate circles around Maggie and finally the barbecue pit, holding the smoking sage aloft until, tiring of the ritual, he tossed it, into the flames. He stood at the pit for a moment longer, pleased with the way the smoke had mingled with the last of the fog, then he walked slowly down through the dirt gardens to the basement room that Angela Davis had lived in when she was a student. He stood with his hand on the door, a full sheet of plywood warped with the moisture and sun. Inside, a black and red mural still filled the back wall. On the wall to his left, in darkness, a pencil drawing was tacked up. He pulled on the cord to the overhead bulb and crossed over to the drawing. It was a crude portrait of Maggie. It was signed, "Angela Davis." He studied it for a moment, though he remembered it well. He crossed over to the metal sink and cupboard built against the wall near the door and, reaching under the sink, felt around among the pipes, then higher until he felt the Sir Walter Raleigh tin. He grinned after he had shaken it, pried open the lid, and had seen the makings of one good joint in the bottom. He couldn't remember having left any weed here. My lucky day, he told himself. He looked around the room for a piece of paper or a plastic baggy, but the room was clean. He looked outside at the jumble of a yard. He thought of using the Sir Walter Raleigh tin, but decided against it. Instead, he carefully untacked the Angela Davis drawing, creased it in the middle, emptied the marijuana into the crease, and folded the drawing up like an envelope. He started out of the room, remembered the light, went back to turn it off, and looked at the empty white patch that had once been an Angela Davis. "Now, that's art," he said aloud.

CHAPTER 6

Pete moved one shuffling step forward with the line winding through the Cruz's backyard. Nothing's changed, he thought. There was the lime tree, two orange and a loquat so tight together in a corner of the yard that grass would never grow there. Mud was splattered along the cement foundation of the house where *Señora* Cruz watered her plants with too much pressure from the hose. The house, like all the old clapboard houses in El Gallo, this ravine between two hills, sat high on its foundation. Under the porch was still the small door with the wooden latch that had taken them into the dark of whelping cats and dogs. The small door hadn't changed, but there was something different about the house. The round wringer washing machine was gone from the back porch; in its place were a washer and dryer, square, white and gleaming. He remembered clothes disappearing into the hungry yellow lips of the wringer, the round *panzón* of a washer, water spilling over the sides, the back porch vibrating and then the clothesline pulley screeching like a crow. It relieved him to see that the rusted wire wrapped around the pulley was still stretched to the cottage built alongside the garage.

The food line shifted, and he was carried forward with it. He looked carefully around the shoulder of the huge red and black dress in front of him. He knew it belonged to Marta, a checker at the Pioneer Market, but he didn't want Marta to know he was behind her. He wondered if she'd left her skinny man at home. Her husband would be uncomfortable here since everyone knew Marta had cinched his *huevos*, and besides, he'd get tight and want to start a fight. She'd probably made him stay at home with her kids. He searched faces, knew most of them. There by the back porch were his mother and father. His *mamá* was unusually quiet, while his *papá* graciously nodded as Paco the electrician chewed on his ear. His gaze drifted to a group of good-looking *chavalas*, young women in tight black dresses. Someone was occupying their time. Nothing's changed here, he thought again.

An hour ago he had left his parents' house, but instead of taking the car, he had walked through their backyard, opened the wooden gate and stepped onto the cement stairway that started on Allesandro, went up over the hill under the trees and bushes of other backyards, and down into the ravine. Before he started up the steps he had turned and stared, momentarily shocked by the quality of light, the garden, the worn smallness of the house with its half curtains at every window. He felt reluctant to take a step up, feeling a caution he had never known in this place. How long had it been, and why had he decided to walk here? With every step he felt more familiar, but still not hidden. "Stairways." Hadn't they hung out here because it had made them feel invisible? These same steps, the old group. Since he'd stopped coming, had the trees and bushes parted, or was it just the angle of the sun today? He noticed the litters of leaf and sowbugs exposed in the corners of cement steps. He had started to hurry, taking two at a time, aware that he was climbing in fine clothes, that the sound of these shoes was out of place. He hurried to get there, to the widened platform, to the landing that was most hidden, that had sheltered them like a cave, that needed tightness to enter. He had to see his *placa*, even faded, the squares they had all tagged, to remember his first smoke, the *chavalas* he had kissed.

The line moved forward and he was carried with its traffic, lost on the highway with his own thoughts. And then he bumped into her.

"Hey, watch it, *pendejo*," Marta said, turning. "Oh, Pete, hey, how you doing, honey? Haven't seen you for a long time," sweetening her big face with a smile.

"I'm hanging on to you. Don't stop so sudden," he answered back. He knew she laughed, but he didn't hear what she said next as he retreated back into memory.

At the landing he had been angry at first, their place a mess of broken beer bottles and butts. He remembered kicking them out of the way, scuffing at the cement with his good shoes, knowing that if his *placa* was still there, he wouldn't be able to read it under all the new spray-painted shit. But then he had felt it, the chiseled letters, "Sleepy," and that strange relaxation had come to his throat, and he was invisible again... until Marta punched him in the shoulder.

"Hey, dream boy, I'm talking to you."

At the top of the stairways, he had forced himself to stop. He wouldn't need to hurry now, he had told himself. As he looked back down into the tunnel of trees, he realized that he would never forget, that he was still alive here, and that he could return anytime.

He mumbled at Marta, but she wasn't paying attention anymore. They'd finally reached the table, and Marta was taking her sweet time loading up. Pete decided he wasn't hungry and left the line. He bumped into *Tiá* Sofía. They hugged, and he kissed her on both cheeks. He, Ray and Sylvia had spent lots of time growing up at Sofía's house down the street. She had the house that was always full with Uncle Pete's wild musician friends and labor radicals. Sometimes, they'd play music and Sofía would sing, but mostly she would make them laugh. He looked past her for Sylvia and found Ray.

"*¿Qué pasa, vato?*" he asked.

"Think she'll want to be a firefighter after tonight?" Ray asked.

"Where is she?"

Cecilia joined them. "In that bunch," she said, pointing at a group laughing and shouting.

It was Cecilia who brought it up. "Was it arson?" she asked.

"They haven't made it official," Pete answered, looking at them both.

"And you're in on it?" Ray asked.

"So far. I talked with Chief Harrison and he's kicking butt to get the final report in."

Cecilia scrunched her face. She was about to say something when they heard Sofía call out, "Carmen, over here, *m'ija*." Pete turned to see a young woman walk gracefully to Sofía. He thought that he had just glanced at her, but a gentle push from Cecilia told him that he was holding the glance for too long.

"Is that Sofía's gawky little kid? The *traviesa* we teased 'til she ran to *mamá* crying," Pete asked over his shoulder. He backed up slowly, bumping into Ray.

"That's the one. Go get something to eat and we'll talk later. In the house," Ray said.

"Don't forget it's a celebration, Pete," Cecilia added with a knowing grin.

"Yeah," Pete answered, "I'll catch you inside."

Pete watched them walk away, thinking that yes, they'd get together and talk, but first he should say hello to the wild one who had caused this party and then to the brat who had grown up, but when he turned back, Sylvia and Carmen were gone and he had to mingle with the crowd, working his way slowly in order to find them.

He checked out Uncle Pete, Carmen's *papá*, who had made good playing the *marimbas* with Eddie Cano. Uncle Pete carried on while cooking *carne asada* at the barbecue. He heard the group of *chavalas* again, and wondered who was entertaining them. When he caught the low bass of Bobby Ramón, who had been an outfielder in the minor leagues, he knew. He spotted Bobby's wife, a tiny, well-built woman from Pomona who had bleached her hair so vigorously, it had taken on the look and shine of a football helmet. Bobby knew how to entertain. Pete would make sure to stop by and say hello. He wondered how many of the good-lookers were married. One, her back to him on the other side of Bobby's wife, had a sweet figure, thin, but with great legs. He thought of Annette for a moment, in the condo with a view of Silver Lake, and then was glad he hadn't brought her when the woman turned, showing him a face of full lips, large moist eyes, and small gold rings in her ears visible before fine swept-back hair. It was Carmen. Again he decided to wait and struck up a conversation with a group of *viejos*.

The old men were pleased to know that he had become a detective before he was forty, an early age, they said, over and over, as if they couldn't get over it. He was thirty-two; he hadn't accomplished much, but they were happy for him. Such a stubborn kid, who would have thought?

"You could have still been on the other side," someone remarked. Another said it wasn't like Mexico, where connections got you places. They thought that it was hard work, his hard work, and luck, always luck. He didn't tell them the truth; why should he? Yes, he supposed that he had worked hard at it, but there were still rumors that the department had been forced to go over others to pick him. Fuck the department; he was pedaling as fast as he could.

He knew he had stayed with the *viejos* for too long when he started to miss questions, had to repeat himself, working hard at it. Why hadn't he learned his mother's language better? Thankfully, music from the speakers started up. Ray had wanted it this way for Sylvia, Pete thought; after her recovery there should be a good time. Anyway, Sylvia loved to party. After a few songs, a couple in their fifties came out onto the concrete patio. He watched as they got into the *cumbia* without hesitation, their faces serious. Pete smiled, knowing the positive effects of the *cumbia*, and where it led. They had all the steps, moving as only a couple who had spent that much time together could. Pete turned in order to take leave of the old men diplomatically, but saw that he could slip away unnoticed as they concentrated on the churn of hips, those gorgeous polka-dotted *nalgas*.

He bumped into Vinny, who worked at Ray's shop, and a friend of Vinny's he didn't know, who was introduced to him as Louie. They were standing at the edge of the tables, but they weren't eating. Pete could see they were high, and when they asked him if he wanted to go smoke a *pito*, he wasn't surprised or annoyed. What could he do, bust them? After a minute, he left to chat with several of the good-lookers. They were excitedly waiting for the old-timer music to finish so they could get down. He knew he would be wanted; he was available and he could dance, but he wasn't looking to dance until he'd talked to Carmen.

Ray came over to him and they both looked up. The night carried a rumble of Dodger Stadium noise from the *pinche* Chavez Ravine over the hill.

"You ready to go inside?" Ray asked stoically.

"I haven't even said hello to Sylvia," Pete answered as he picked out Carmen walking to a table and sitting down. "Where is she?"

"I'm right here, *loco*." The happy voice of Sylvia Cruz punctured his stare. She grabbed him by the arm. "Boy, you got it bad, staring the dog face at my *prima*. What about me?"

"You still here? I thought we got rid of you. Dammit, give me an *abrazo*." He hugged her tight. "Welcome back," he said, kissing her on the cheek.

"Is that all I get? A kiss on the cheek?"

"Shhh. Your brother's here, but I'll take care of you later."

"Dream on, Romeo. I'll introduce you to Julieta later."

"Would you?"

"Don't look at me that way. Carmen can handle herself. She's not a baby anymore."

"I noticed."

"She'll eat you alive."

"I don't want to break this love triangle up, but my wife's waiting inside," Ray said.

"Take him away, he's not interested in me. He's *loco* for my best friend."

"This homeboy's investigating your fire."

"I know. He's already interrogated everyone at the station. That's why I couldn't invite them over."

"What do you think, Sylvia?" Pete asked quietly.

She turned to him, the happiness cleared, replaced by a somber tone. "Get this bastard before he does it again."

Ray's eyebrows raised up. "What?"

"He burned our library, our books, the building our *abuelo* built. I could feel every one of the stones and bricks *papi* touched, and the goddess in the entry. I'm glad you're on it, Pete. I'm so pleased I might even speak highly of you to Carmen."

Pete smiled at Ray.

"You ready for that *fría?*" Ray asked finally.

"I could use one now," Pete answered.

"You better dance with me, dude," Sylvia said, her exuberance returning.

"You got it."

"Catch you two later." She hugged her brother and went over to Carmen.

"You sure you want to go in the house?" Ray asked, following Pete's stare. "Carmen turned out fine, didn't she?"

"Very fine," he answered, catching her eye for the first time and smiling before she returned her attention to Sylvia.

"Let's do it, she's waiting and I can see you can't take care of yourself, old man," Ray teased him.

"Not now," Pete said, knowing that Ray was enjoying this too much. Pete shouldn't have let on. Ray could be like a kid, needling an exposed soft spot and never letting up. No, he didn't want Ray around.

"In the house," Pete said, nudging Ray, who was grinning wickedly, up the stairs and through the kitchen. In the dining room on the table was the bar, and an open cooler of beer in ice on two chairs. He took a glass and filled it with ice, then poured in whiskey until the ice floated. *Señora* Cruz came in and asked him in Spanish if he had eaten. Pete hadn't, but assured her that he would, that the food smelled *muy rica*. Ray took him by the arm and led him to his parents' bedroom. They drifted through the living room and the soft tongue of his parents' culture. He felt the love of family, the texture so beautiful he wanted to forget that he had to do business, that English was what he must use to be a man in his world. English led him away from this world. Listening, he wanted to stop, his ear sprouting lilies, his tongue curling around purple grapes. He heard the voice of his childhood; a swing on a rope, loquats by the handful among the bees, a cat under the lime tree, and then he followed Ray.

Ray closed the door. There were lacy curtains on one window, a chair in the corner, an overhead light, Cecilia sitting on the bed. A neat and simple room. Ray went over to her and sat down. He gestured at the chair, but Pete waved it off, preferring to stand with his back to the dresser loaded down with statues, pictures of the kids, and candles burning under the large framed Virgin of Guadalupe.

"So when does the investigation begin?" Ray asked.

"I already started it on the sly, before the final report arrives," Pete answered. "There will be a special squad set up to track down the arsonist," Pete answered, looking at the two of them, catching their eyes, "but even if they take me off it, I'll be watching out, and I'll be there when the time comes."

"We know you will, Pete." It was Cecilia who spoke up. "Is there anything we can do to help?"

Pete leaned against the dresser. "Not yet. What about Sylvia, she's taking it hard."

"She's real angry, Pete. We'll do what we can. We just don't want it to affect her work. She's got a good future," Cecilia spoke up, swivelling on the bed, and then patting Ray's leg.

"I don't want her to get too involved, Pete," Ray spoke up.

"I'll keep it low key as much as possible with her."

"Thanks, Pete," Ceci said.

"Hey."

"We're just so happy she wasn't..."

"Isn't this a party?" Ray asked, hugging Ceci. "Let's get out of here. I'm thirsty."

"Go on, honey, I need to check on the baby." She started to cry.

"It's okay, *Mamá*. Sylvia's okay," Ray said, holding her, rubbing her face.

"Is she, Ray? What about the next fire?" Ceci asked, staring up into his eyes. Ray didn't answer her. Like stains on a bedspread, her questions were impossible to ignore. Always there as much as you wanted to take your mind off them.

Pete knew there weren't any words to cover up their fears. Sylvia wouldn't back down; she had made it clear she was returning to the station, something about making it to the wall.

Cecilia pushed away, patted Ray on the rear and said, "She's as hard-headed as you, husband. Now, I've gotta go find that baby of ours." They watched as Cecilia left.

Ray took Pete's glass. They walked out through the living room and into the kitchen. Pete didn't say a word as he filled the glass with ice cubes.

"Harrison is a stand-up dude and so is Bennett. Sylvia's sure of it," Ray announced, as much to himself as to Pete, before he went to the cooler for another Budweiser.

Pete waited a moment for Ray to continue, but Ray was quiet. That would be all he would say for right now; it was hard for him to put his trust in the men Sylvia worked with. Pete downed his second whiskey and Ray filled it again.

"Let's go outside, detective. There's someone I know you want to meet."

CHAPTER 7

Billy Johnson couldn't decide where to smoke the pot. He had stopped at the end of Maggie's road where it crossed the busy street that went either up the hill to the freeway or down to the beach. He felt for the Angela Davis sketch in his shirt pocket to make sure that it was still folded, but what he needed was rolling papers. There were papers in the tepee at David's, but that was four miles away in Leucadia. Linda, the wheat grass lady, had her greenhouse only a mile away, but he didn't want to get high and listen to the freeway. Jesús was working, but he didn't like smoking *mota* anyway. If he walked to David's, he could get high in the tepee. He could lay down and stare up at the sky and the clouds through the crossing poles and open flaps and meditate on the Brotherhood of Dolphins. He looked down Cardiff Avenue, his eyes following the straight line over the railroad tracks and into an ocean that had bloomed from the fog of morning into plentiful blue. He didn't wonder that the fog would leave; his mind was occupied with the smell of sage he had left burning in Maggie's barbecue pit like fog burnt away by the sun.

He walked down Cardiff Avenue, crossed Pacific Coast Highway where the road ended, and entered the State Park through a hole in the fence. He was surrounded by antennas, motor homes, surfers in vans, children, frisbees, dogs on chains, bicycles and barbecues. He floated from one rock song to another, wanting to recognize the songs and forget the smell of gasoline engines. This was good. These people were lost. Look at them, camping, crammed in between the Highway and the ocean in dippy dirt spaces. They wouldn't know what to do with themselves in real nature—Baja—listening to the waves, watching the moon and the dolphins.

He should have taken his ex-wife to Baja. She had believed in him at the beginning of their marriage before she had become negative and paranoid. But where was she now? If he could find her, he could show her that he was on the brink of unbelievable wealth and power. A new age where his ideas would flower. Perhaps it wouldn't have helped to take her to Baja, to commune with dolphins. Women weren't all that perceptive, like Debbie who had kicked him out of her backyard. His fists clenched and he pictured Maggie, Maggie struggling on the concrete patio underneath him. Well, she had been an exalted being; it was right that she would help him begin the Brotherhood of Dolphins.

Billy entered what was clearly a surfer's campsite. Three surfer girls lounged on foldout chairs drinking Corona. He didn't consider how he looked, slouching in his white cotton drawstrings, worn and faded red flannel shirt, and flip flops gone thin and wide as he entered their space, his shadow covering a girl's tight belly.

"You know the radiation factor is especially high this year," he announced. He was pleased when they all looked at him.

"Are you a walking umbrella or something?" the girl in his shade asked, turning to her friends and opening her mouth wide in a silent laugh.

"The ozone layer is so depleted over the poles that we are being flooded with radiation. It's a Doppler effect; it bounces across the ocean and off the stratosphere, arriving to penetrate your bare skin," Billy said with his mock smile.

"Oh my god, Lisa, get me the sunscreen," one shrieked, laughing.

"I'm melting," another said, and all three howled at each other.

"In fifteen years you'll be paying a plastic surgeon. He'll have to go in with a laser. It'll be a year of band-aids," Billy said dryly.

"Will I lose my tattoo?" one asked, flexing her stomach to draw his attention to the multi-colored butterfly that had landed so low under her navel, one wing was hidden under the edge of her Brazilian thong bikini.

"You'll be covered with tattoos," he answered. The three girls squealed and he wondered if she had shaved for her tattoo.

"So what are you? The sun guard?" the girl in his shade said, adjusting her sunglasses with the tips of her red nails.

"You wanta rub some lotion on me, mister sun guard?" another asked saucily. They leaned in again, laughing together inside the space they encircled. Billy smiled back and grinned. He pulled on the tail of his hair.

"You should be in Baja swimming with the dolphins," he said, grinning larger.

"I hate Mexico. Those men in T.J. are always trying to rub my buns," one said.

"I already have my dolphin," the tattooed girl in his shade said. "He's out surfing now, keeping his little porpy wet."

"Here's to Mexico," the third girl hooted, taking a long pull from her Corona.

Billy laughed with them this time, but after they had finished laughing he stood there quietly, not grinning anymore as they told each other Ensenada and Tijuana horror stories.

"You got any rolling papers?" he asked finally. "I just need a couple of papers."

"Whatta you got to smoke? Aren't you gonna share, mister sun man?" one asked.

"It's back at my campsite. I'll go get it," Billy lied.

"Bring me a popsicle; the radiation is burning my insides," the butterfly girl ordered.

He could hear them laughing as he walked away. He made sure to saunter smoothly even though he was pissed off. TJ, sure, they had probably never had a decent orgasm either. Now he'd really like to smoke that joint. He strolled faster, hustling to get out of this campsite and away from all these fools. He headed for the Coast Highway, away from the rocky beach, and onto a walkway on the edge of the cliffs and the state park. Billy trudged on, ignoring the speeding cars. He could have walked on the Amtrak rails across the highway, but instead he focused on the last patch of fog ahead of him in Encinitas. It was all he could do. Unsteady with anger, his vision blurred; head aching, he wanted to get out of this bright sun.

Finally entering Encinitas and the final wisps of fog, he touched the pot in his shirt pocket and felt a momentary relief. Was it the sun that had reminded him of Maggie, the sun clearing on her patio? Hadn't he blessed her with sage and the fire? The smoke had been strong, a cleansing. Suddenly tired and hungry, he didn't want to feel brightness or surfer girls or Maggie.

At the Dean Witter brokerage house, Billy stopped. Through the glass door was the sound of heavy phones. He remembered that he wanted to call Calasan and bring him into his fold. He needed a phone he could use for free. The urge was overpowering to enter the building, and with a nod from a secretary, pick up a phone. He stared at the door, seemingly closed of its own free will, stared at his reflection for a moment, then turned, crossed the street and entered Gene's.

The cafe was busy, the exhaust fan sucking, newspapers piled on the full counter, and Sal. He didn't like Gene's because of Sal, but he wanted to clear his head with coffee. He selected an *L.A. Times* business section from the stack next to the cash register, sat down at the counter and waited for coffee.

"*Buenas*, Sal," Billy said as a thick white mug was placed before him. The young Chicano with glistening, razor-sharp hair and no moustache grunted back, "Got deep-fried abalone with eggs, or you just jamming with mud this morning?"

"Hand me the honey, Sal," Billy answered.

"You're not going to put honey in coffee, man?"

"Oh yeah, it gives the beans a subtle aroma of orange," Billy said. He poured the honey directly into the center of the coffee, added cream and let it sit for a moment before he used a spoon. He read and half-listened as Sal made his rounds, the spoon still in the mug of coffee.

"Look at this, Sal." He turned the folded paper in Sal's direction. "The Japanese are buying the Brentwood Country Club. They've fished out the ocean and now they're buying into the leisure class of L.A."

"Who the fuck cares," Sal answered from the cash register. His T-shirt was tight as he worked the bills, showing the twenty-four-year-old muscles that Billy knew would turn to fat in six years. "Hey, Eugene, where's those hash browns, man," he yelled.

Billy took his first sip of coffee, pretending to read the paper, waiting again until Sal was in his area, in his own circle of noise.

"You should talk to Eugene. Tell him to boycott all seafood. It's just money to Sony and Toshiba. More war games on video. We can stop it here," Billy said, looking up from the paper with a furrowed forehead.

"You're paranoid, dude. Here, drink some more coffee," Sal said without slowing down, pouring coffee to the rim of the white mug.

A man with a crew-cut in a plumbing supply shirt that couldn't stretch enough to cover his belt spoke up next. "Yeah, I had to go out two hundred miles to hook tuna. Took two days to catch my limit. Nothing around here except for bottom garbage."

Billy looked at the big man and let his eyebrows move up enough to extend his wrinkle to the few hairs left on the top of his head. He took off his glasses, cleaned them with the edge of his T-shirt which he'd pulled out from under his sweater, and then cocked an ear at the butter on the griddle, at a group of men discussing golf, and at the elusive Sal. When Billy spoke again, he talked as he methodically cleaned his glasses. The man with the crew cut lowered his head as if to catch a reflection of sound off Billy's glasses. "If we don't stop the Japanese from fishing out the waters, the only boat you'll be going out on is the one in a Nintendo game."

"Yeah," the big man answered as he stuck his lips to a coffee mug. "We ran across two of their factory boats, nets spread out for miles."

"You see any dolphin in their nets?" Billy asked quickly, adjusting his glasses on his nose.

The man rubbed a hand across the flesh tightly packed under the plumbing logo. "No, we didn't come that close. We only saw the Japs because the Captain knew where they were, said the rice eaters always know where to find the tuna."

"It's just profits. That's all the fish are, is profits. They don't care about the dolphins," Billy answered smugly after a moment had passed.

"They're efficient bastards," Sal spoke, slowing before he placed an order at the griddle, "but that ain't gonna stop nobody from buying fish."

"That's what you think now, Sal, but I want to tell you that the time is coming for us to take back Nature, to develop Nature."

"Whattya talking about, stopping fishing to save a few dolphins?" the big man asked scornfully.

"I'm talking about cultural institutions. Art," Billy answered sarcastically.

Sal hissed and then laughed. "Art? What you want, a few T-shirts with 'Save the Dolphin' airbrushed on the front for twenty bucks?"

"No, it's time to discard our theories of enlightened art," he answered slowly, "and we're going to start it here in Encinitas," Billy said, looking at Sal.

"You're crazy, man," Sal said, slapping the counter.

"What is real is that this area holds antiquities and beauty greater than the Getty museum. Art must once again be created within Nature. Oil, electronic, fishing money creates pollution so terrible it's killing the seguaro in Arizona and the oaks on Palomar. We can just stop our busy lives and sit quietly, letting the rain fall in a mist so the plants can grow and the animals can live. Then we will see the return of the Condor and we will see the return of the real Californio, a true Dolphin brother." Billy took a drink of water and then peered over the glass, staring directly at Sal. Calasan and the Brotherhood of the Dolphins; that's why I'm here, Billy thought. To create.

Sal let out a low whistle before moving off with a full pot of coffee. "Jeezus, what you been smoking?" he yelled from the end of the counter nearest the front window.

A few heads turned. The plumbing supply T-shirt folded both hands around his cup of coffee and, measuring his words, asked, "Overthrow big business? Is that it? By tossing all the art?"

"Sheet no, he gonna keep it all for himself," Sal shouted as he moved away from the window. "Hey, Howie, you want a Picasso to add to your collection? Billy here let you have one if you keep it out in the garage." Howie and Sal both laughed.

Billy didn't wait for the laughter to subside as he spoke to the big man on his right loudly enough for Sal to hear. "It's time that the multinational corporations answered our desires. If we take away the hedonistic charity they call philanthropy, the blessing of art they have enslaved us with, then they will have to listen and realize that real art is Nature, has always been Nature. Then we can go about healing the planet and you will catch tuna off the Oceanside breakwater."

The door opened and a young woman entered. She paused nervously, startled by Sal's loud response and the ensuing laughter. "The only thing you'll ever catch at the Oceanside breakwater is scrawny cats or the clap."

The woman, for lack of space, had to sit at Billy's left.

Sal slapped a mug down and reached for another pot. He filled the mug rapidly and then pulled out his order book. "There is a special today," he said, then leaned in and whispered, letting his eyes flicker over at Billy, "but I wouldn't order it right now if you happen to be an art lover." He leaned back, snorted a laugh and winked.

Billy touched his ponytail, his gaze lingering over the woman in sweatpants. She was perfect, he concluded, touching his glasses. Very thin, some would say skinny, vegetarian thin, not runner's thin. She wore glasses and had mousy brown hair that she had tried to perm, but it hadn't had much effect. She stooped a bit and seemed shy, nervous. She had no tan and a very round face for such a thin neck. He watched her bury her head into the menu, and then returned to the man on his right.

The big man was twisting his mug in a counter-clockwise circle. He twisted it at least fourteen times, the mug scraping the counter top, before he spoke. "You know, I got three kids. I'd like to see them grow up and settle here, but I just don't know anymore. There's so many of these goddamn condos, and how they gonna afford a house? I grew up here and I don't hardly recognize it no more." He started twisting again, speaking into the mug. "What we got to do is get rid of the developers. I'd like to hitch them up to the back of my truck and drag them over to the other side of Pendleton, and then I'd build a goddamn wall there with a sign that says, 'If you're from L.A. then just turn the hell around;' that's what I'd do. Build a wall around North County. That way, we could keep them the hell out, and all the Mex's and other illegal immigrants." The big man's voice had steadily risen so that by the time he had drawled out "illegal" everyone in the cafe was looking at him and Billy.

"Hey, whatt'ya all saying about Mexicans?" Sal spoke up loudly from the cash register.

Billy ignored them by looking past Sal and out between the painted lettering on the front window. He checked his watch and searched the menu laying on the counter in front of the woman next to him.

"Sal, I don't mean you," the big man growled, waving his palms. "You're all right. It's all your goddamn compadrays crossing the border and them Orientals."

Sal walked over fast, put the coffee pot on the counter next to Billy and leaned in, his hands on the counter, until he was eye level with the top of the crew-cut. "They ain't my *com-*

padres, man, but that don't give you the right to talk that way. Understand?"

Billy shifted in his seat, glanced sideways, and then raised his hands off the counter top in an attempt to bring the conversation back to his subject, but he was ignored by Sal who continued.

"My family was here before yours left their cave. You want to start talking about cleaning up Encinitas? Then we can start with lazy, beer-sucking *pendejos* like you."

"You hold on, Sal. You're lucky we taught you to speak English or you'd just be another greaser selling oranges on the off-ramp," the big man bellowed, the plumbing supply logo swelling as his finger jabbed the air an inch from Sal's chest.

"Right now, *hijo de la chingada*," Sal shouted, untying his apron and throwing it to the floor.

The man got off his stool. Billy could see that he was bigger, much larger than Sal, but what really impressed him was the ability of his belly to hover an inch over the top of the counter. Billy's mouth opened. He wanted to say something clever, but it was Eugene who restored order, or possibly it was the meat cleaver slamming past home into the chopping block. The meat cleaver, still vibrating, might have been enough to insure silence; however, Eugene added, "Shut up the both of yous," and standing, one hand on his hip, the other holding the two-foot knife sharpener like a thick épée, he brought all eyes to focus on the steel. Eggs popped, bacon sizzled, the stuffed sailfish hanging on the back wall grinned deviously, and the ventilator seemed to amplify its chant; hummnn nahh, hummnn nahh, hummnn nahh.

Billy turned away from the sailfish to look at the woman next to him. His immediate thought was how to get her out of here, to give her a massage and rub her thighs. He peered past the woman to look for activity in Dean Witter's across the street, but couldn't see a thing. He thought about going to the teepee at Dave's to smoke his pot, but what he really wanted was to get into a hot tub with the thin woman next to him and make her dinner and then maybe she'd make love to him. Then again, maybe he should go to the race track at Del Mar to see about a job washing dishes, then stop in to see Jesús, eat beans, drink beer and see if he couldn't talk Jesús into going to Baja with him next week to build another pyramid. He realized that his eyes hurt, that he was straining them, his eyebrows pricked up so high. He pulled a napkin out of its dispenser and very deliberately started to clean his glasses again.

"You, Jack, can leave. Right now," Eugene said with the authority of a look caused by too much gin the night before and two feet of steel to back him up.

Jack, the T-shirted plumber of fish, went over to the cash register and said in a voice loud enough for the secretaries in Dean Witter to punch their hold buttons, "Eugene, this used to be a good establishment 'fore you let these dumbfucks in here. How much I owe you?"

"Fuck you," Sal shouted, pointing his finger at the plumbing logo.

"Fuck you, José," he answered.

"I'll kick your knuckle-dragging fat ass, *culero*," Sal said.

"Yeah, you and ten taco benders, wetback."

"Outaa here," Eugene muttered.

The big man tossed a ten at the cash register and stomped out, slamming the screen door behind him. Sal stood at the plate glass window and laid both hands against the glass, saluting the crew-cut with both middle fingers while mouthing the descriptive combination of words that begin with mother.

As soon as the plumber's truck had lit off into the sunrise, leaving the smell of burning rubber for the secretaries at Dean Witter, the cafe erupted into applause.

"Way to go, Sal."

"You showed him, Eugene."

"Get rid of that dumbfuck."

"What a helmet."

Eugene acknowledged the jubilation by turning back to the griddle and lighting an unfiltered Camel. Sal high-fived the patrons, flexed his muscles and promised to kick ass without his *primos*. Several minutes later, after he had whipped his apron back on, he leaned over the counter in front of Billy and said, "Hey, way to go. Coffee's on me bro'." He extended his right hand for a slap.

Billy reached for the honey, ignoring Sal's hand, but he wished he could bum a cigarette from Eugene—or at least an omelette. Sal must have read his thoughts, placing a leftover order of hashbrowns, a cold egg, and sausage in front of him.

Billy smiled weakly, peppered his egg and hash browns and went to work.

"I agree with you. What you said about big business," the woman at his side whispered. She was shy. She barely looked at him.

"It's the cultural institutions that have to make the statement," he answered her.

"We must protect our natural resources. I'm glad you spoke up."

Billy stared at her before placing his fork at the edge of his plate. He leaned over to whisper, "The revolution is beginning here, now."

"I don't know. L.A. is growing closer."

"You're so right." He gave her his biggest smile. "I've got an important appointment I can't miss, but could we meet later at the Universal Life meeting tonight? I know you'd like it."

"I was planning to go," she answered, surprised. "I'll see you there."

"Great. My name's Billy."

"Barbara."

He shook her skinny hand and got up. Standing, he realized that he hadn't finished the plate of greasy food. He could eat more, but he suddenly wasn't hungry. She was beautiful. She wasn't like Maggie.

"Take 'er easy, bro'," Sal shouted after Billy. Billy felt that the whole cafe was watching him.

"Ciao, Sal," he answered as he left. He looked at the sky, emptied of any fog, as he walked briskly into the bright sun.

CHAPTER 8

Pete woke to the sound of a trash truck. When he sat up to look out the window into the late morning of Silver Lake, the trash truck was gone. "What the hell?" he muttered. He focused on the room. It wasn't his room, but he had been here before, an orderly room filled with cute things. He heard the grinding of gears again, and waited for the clank when the jaws stopped and the box loaded with garbage banged forward and released its contents into the top of the truck. The grinding stopped, and then he smelled coffee, bitter and strong, french roast. He studied the nightstand to his right. A brass lamp with a glass shade, a white clam shell holding crystals, round black stones and a ceramic frog; a tiny round cactus in a small pot, the burned stick and trail of ash that remained of incense.

Pete worked himself out of bed. Why did he always feel so thin after a night of drinking? His stomach tightened and his legs twisted when meeting the floor. He didn't remember how he had gotten here, but he had an idea that if he got out of here now, he wouldn't have to remember last night. He picked his shirt off the floor, but hesitated because he was already remembering, and he didn't want to, not now, not here in this condo with this woman. His shirt was still in his hand when Annette entered. She carried a black-lacquered tray holding two thick white mugs, a creamer, and a sugar bowl. She was wearing a shorty kimono, but he knew instinctively that she was nude underneath it as he tried to focus on the tray in her hands. Then he remembered. He had been at a table in Ray's backyard with a plate of *carnitas, frijoles*, and salad. He had been reaching for a *tortilla* when Carmen came over and sat down next to him. Had he touched his food?

"What're you doing, lover?" Annette asked sweetly, placing the tray on the floor and taking the shirt from his hand. "You're in a big hurry this morning, not like last night. Uhmm," she said, leaning over and rubbing his pants. "The coffee can wait." She pulled the sash that held the kimono together and let it fall to the floor.

His eyes followed the kimono to the floor and then back up above her face onto the blond hair, pulled back and held in place with two white combs. She rubbed him harder. He took her hand and held it. When Carmen had smiled at him, his hand had frozen in the *tortilla* tray.

"Weren't you gonna come up and say hello to me, or do you still think I'm a brat?" Carmen had asked. He hoped he had smiled and even laughed. He remembered looking at her teeth, how white and perfect they had looked between lips that soft and red.

"Annette," he began stridently, before switching to a softer tone. "Baby, look, I'm sorry, but I gotta get going. There's this case I'm working on, and I have to jump on it." Maybe she didn't hear him. Her face and all that blond hair was in his chest, and she had taken his hand, placed it on her breast, and was teaching it how to rub.

His hand was flat, the fingers straight and stiff as she worked it over the left and then the right breast. His hand moved, but it could have been a door knob that he was turning, trying to let himself out.

Carmen had taken his hand and led him home, to Sofía and Uncle Pete's house. It had been like that the whole day, a reunion. Sofía had made them dance, and then when she had left the room, he remembered a slow dance; his hand had slid down to Carmen's rear as he held her close.

"You're not getting out of here, Petey." Annette worked at his buckle, and then started on his pants. He tried to stop her as his thoughts drifted back to Carmen.

He and Carmen had started a kiss that lasted through one song, and then another. The room was spinning, but not from the booze. He had wanted to suck her tongue down his throat. He couldn't touch her face enough; he tried to learn her face with his lips. He kissed her so hard their teeth met. They rubbed her tight skirt high as Carmen bit into his neck.

"Come to baby, Petey," Annette said, pushing against him while working his pants past his knees so that he fell awk-wardly back onto the bed.

Had it been him or had it been Carmen? Or had they slipped to the floor together? She had wrapped her hands around his neck, and he could feel her under him.

"Annette, sugar." But she was pulling on him hard, and then he was inside of her.

He pictured Carmen, her hair thrown back, the light sweat on her upper lip and forehead, kissing him, and holding him tighter. Her dress had pushed up higher and he had slid against nylon, her breath coming quickly between her lips. They had dry-humped slowly, melting into one continuous thrust and ride.

He didn't open his eyes. Annette fucked him hard, the way she liked it, her arms leaning over his shoulders, fingers clawing the sheets, blond hair sweeping his face.

It was Carmen who had slithered out of her nylons. He hadn't wanted to push it with her, but there she was, in black, silky panties. He had kept his hand there, cupping her, kissing her eyes, before snaking between her legs again, allowing himself to move only with her pressure. He didn't press heavily against her, just enough to move together, feel her through his own underwear, pants, and her panties, as if he were there, touching her, as if his cock were sliding between her lips but not penetrating, burrowing up and out and bursting through to their bellies.

"Ohh baby, ohh baby, fuck me harder, ohh, ohh." Annette came, but wanted more.

In his mind he was with Carmen; he hadn't wanted to stop her, but he had to unzip his pants. Then the door had opened and *Tía* Sofía had walked into the room. Heat rose to his cheeks. His mother culture had bored through him with guilt.

He waited five minutes, or what he thought was five minutes. Annette was still breathing heavily. He sat on the bed as he put on his clothes. She touched his back.

"When will you be back, lover," she asked, exhaling on the word "lover."

Pete picked up his coat and tie. "As soon as I finish this case. I'll call you tomorrow," he lied, leaving the room without ever touching his coffee.

He drove the long mile to Echo Park, weaving wildly in and out of lanes scattered with Sunday drivers. He pushed the car hard, not relaxing even as he drove the streets he knew so well. Why had he gone to see Annette after last night? He told himself he was unattached and young. But then why hadn't he taken Annette to the party, brought her to his town to meet his people? It made him uncomfortable to think in terms of barrios, borders, people. He would call Annette tomorrow.

At the El Patio Bar on Sunset, near the corner of Echo Park and Sunset, he retreated into the relief of the cool dark and the layers of bottles behind the bar.

"¿Qué onda, jóven?"

"Tap, Lalo."

"Chasin' the dog, eh? Christ, I dragged in like you a few times." Lalo placed the beer on a napkin filled with cartoons of a pot-bellied, lewd, middle-aged man chasing around a blonde starlet with torpedo breasts. The captions were in Spanish. Pete had never bothered to read them. He took a drink.

"Feel better?" Lalo asked.

Pete didn't answer. He was the only customer.

He lit a cigarette, stubbed it out and then finished the beer slowly.

"¿Otra?"

"Yeah, hit me with another." He looked at the bubbles rising in the glass for a long time before he took a sip. He lit another cigarette but left it in an ashtray as he went to the jukebox. He selected three songs, thinking, I'll just listen to these, finish my beer, and go on over to Sofía's. He reflected on last night. Carmen. Annette. Carmen. Had he made a fool of himself with her, too? Carmen, so sweet. It was time to put his house in order, but he listened to the songs and drank the beer. Lalo put up another, and a stack of quarters. Pete stacked and re-stacked the quarters, returned to the jukebox and selected the same three songs. It was still early, he told himself, he could run up a tab—he was good for it; Lalo had told him so—but then his father appeared in the seat next to him, his papá who rarely came into El Patio anymore, pleased to find Pete here alone. They had a drink together, and Pete played the same three songs, songs he hoped his father would twirl his glass to. Pete wasn't hungry, but he went home after the last song, his old man clapping him one on the back because *mamá* was waiting with a big Sunday dinner.

The family was waiting at the table when they walked in: his older sister Carla with her three kids, his brother, Sergio, his wife and two kids, Moni, his youngest sister, who had just finished high school; and German, the baby at sixteen. Pete asked Carla why her husband Danny was working on a Sunday night. The dinner table turned quiet. He left the table wishing he hadn't brought it up, Carla's glaring eyes following him to the sofa.

When he woke up, it was dark and the TV was loud. His mother was watching *Siempre en Domingo*. He wondered how he could have slept through this racket. He watched a young pop group—they couldn't have been older than sixteen—lip-synching a Michael Jackson song. The camera flashed into the audience from time to time to show the viewers how much fun the audience was having. The kids were moving around in their seats, but the grandmothers never smiled; *abuelitas* with earrings.

"*Mamá*," he said, rising from the sofa. "I'm going now. Thanks for the dinner."

She turned and looked at him for a moment. "*¿Dormiste bien, m'ijo? ¿Cuándo regresas?*"

"I'll stop by during the week," he answered, bending to kiss her on the forehead.

"Eh?" she asked.

"I'll come by during the week," he repeated in Spanish. "*Buenas noches, Mamá.*"

"*Que le vaya bien*," she answered, hugging him long and hard before turning back to the TV.

He left by the kitchen door, stopped, jangled the keys in his pocket, and then headed across the yard to the gate. He stopped again and looked back at the house in the dark, blue light from the TV passing through the curtains. It had been his home and, growing up, he had never thought he would leave the ravine, but now he had his own apartment, not far away, but still he didn't come to Sunday dinners often enough. Finally, he opened the gate and turned up the stairs. He didn't stop at the landing, but rushed to the top of the stairway. There he lit a *fravo* and looked out over the valley where the streetcar tracks were buried, the famous Red Cars hauled away the year he was born. He could see the darkened playground of St. Teresa's grammar school, lights in the rooms of apartments and houses. He watched cars descend at the end of the freeway onto Glendale Boulevard, and he wondered what the drivers were listening to, if they were talking to someone in the seats beside them, or if they were silent because of the turn. He listened to an owl. Why hadn't he driven his car instead of walking the steps? The owl left and Pete turned, heading down into the ravine toward Carmen's house.

The stairs went straight down the hill through the overgrowth. They didn't zig and zag like the stairways on other hills, though there was a landing after every twelfth stair. He had counted them many times.

There was a crowd and music in Carmen's house, but the streetlight at either end of the block wasn't enough to expose him. He didn't know how long he stood there. He admired the retaining wall, built of rock, that Sylvia's grandfather had built. Flowers and flowering vines grew at the top of the wall and hung over. Grass grew to the front porch. One elm tree draped the house. It was an old style bungalow with big beams on the wooden porch. For the first time, he noticed how thick the beams were in the construction of the porch. He guessed that it was an attempt at creative design. The door was open, and he could hear Uncle Pete playing the piano and someone with a saxophone. He saw Sofía moving back and

forth, and Carmen, leaning on one elbow at the fireplace man-
tle, talking to an earnest young man with a Cuban-style
beard.

He watched the house until a car cruised slowly by, the
driver giving him a long look in the splash of headlights. Then
he walked back up the stairways. He didn't slow at the top,
but continued down quickly, through his parents' yard, not
pausing once until he got into his car and headed down to
Glendale Boulevard. At the Lake, he turned left at the Aimee
McPherson Temple. He would have driven past the Lake as
usual, but he saw Ray's '58, so he stopped. He knew where he
would find Ray, but after he had gotten out of his car and
walked a few feet, he hesitated. It wasn't because the Lake
was so quiet and dark, a black expanse of water, larger and
deeper when the water shone in the night. No, he knew it
wasn't the lake that made him hesitate. It was this feeling
again, returning, like he had felt yesterday at the stairways
and at Sylvia's party. Why? He hadn't ever really left, had he?
Then, why was it so quiet and dark? He pushed himself forward, and then felt a feeling of relief when he heard the
ducks. How had he missed them before! There was squawking, the beating of wings. Now the sounds that he knew as
well as the cross tattooed in the soft meat between his thumb
and first finger came easily to him. Frogs. The rustle of the
wind over water lilies. Lilies with leaves as big as manhole
covers. He remembered the time, on a dare, when he had
stepped on one. He had been nine years old, and he had
thought he could walk across them to the other side. He had
fallen in up to his belly button, and his *mamá* had had to
wash his shoes because they were filled with black muck. Now
he heard the paddle boats, the ones the *viejos* used with their
grandkids in the afternoon and lovers rented at sundown, rubbing against the little pier. He also heard the Hollywood

Freeway, a radio in some apartment, a mother yelling at her kids, but these sounds didn't interfere with the sounds of the lake. He walked to the bridge that crossed to the island, hopped the barricade and, careful of where he stepped because of the burned holes in the wood, crossed the bridge. He couldn't see Ray on the island obscured by the pom-pom bushes that encircled it, but when he stepped onto the hard-packed dirt and whistled softly, he heard him.

"I'm over here, Angel," Ray said, using the hard "g" in Angel.

"Feeding your babies, *vato*?" Pete asked.

"Yeah, man, feeding them."

They didn't say anything more for a moment, instead looking out over the water through a break in the bushes at a spot where the fountain stood silent in the middle of the lake.

"The mama kitty still here, Ray?" Pete asked, not taking his eyes off the water.

"No, she's been gone about four or five years. There's new mamas now, and more babies," Ray said softly.

"They let you pet them yet?"

"No," Ray said after a long pause. "There's one who's a little braver than the others; sometimes she eats out of my hand, but you know I don't try to pet them. I think they like it that way. I'm here; they know me; I'm the man with the cans. That's fine enough for them."

"What about Beto? He still come around?"

"No, Beto always wanted to pet them."

"Yeah, that sounds like Beto." Pete waited a good five minutes. They were standing side by side staring out at the lake. "Ray, I caused a scene with Carmen at Sofía's," he said finally, easing it out, wondering if he had brought it up right, and thankful for the dark so that Ray couldn't see his face.

"I haven't heard nothing about it, homer, but you don't need to do any explaining with me."

Pete flicked a stone into the lake but it fell short of the glassy spot where the fountain rested. "I gotta run, bro'," he finally spoke to Ray's outline.

"You'll do right, Pete. Look around before you leave; this will always be your home," Ray said.

Pete walked back across the bridge and drove to his apartment over the hill from Echo Park Lake. He let himself in and sat on the balcony, ignoring the flashing light on his message machine. He sat for a long time, the apartment dark behind him, staring at a spot where a fountain stood silent in the lake.

CHAPTER 9

"**B**arbara, this is the start of the primo-design factor. Califia, the Brotherhood of Dolphins, healing Mother California. We're going to open a window into the Third World that will blow minds. And we are the thieves who have stolen the show." Billy stood in her kitchen, his head slightly bowed, his voice rising and falling. He picked an artichoke up off the counter and held it up. "Now, this is design," he stated.

Barbara turned from the living room window that she had just opened. She knew that he was excited. He had been this way at the Unitarian Fellowship meeting; in fact, he had been waiting for her in the parking lot. She still wasn't sure what it was all about, but she felt more alive than she had in years, perhaps ever. She wondered about this feeling, and about Billy. At the meeting before the lecture had begun, Billy had spoken with the Sandinistas who were there to ask for medical aid. Maggie, a woman Barbara had always admired, hadn't shown up yet. It had caused a slight panic, Maggie the tireless organizer, always so punctual. Billy had volunteered to translate, in Maggie's absence. It hadn't surprised her that he was fluent in Spanish; somehow it just seemed natural because he was so knowledgeable. He knew so much about their country and their art, so much that when pressed, one of the Sandinistas had given him the phone number, a card of the Nicaraguan artist whose work was on display. An artist and a woman, but hadn't Billy seemed too ecstatic? The card like a talisman, sacredly treasured. She made herself stop analyzing and looked at him; he was still gazing at the artichoke. When he put it down, he opened her refrigerator without hesitation and stood there, his hand on the door, inspecting what she had.

He wasn't like anyone she had ever known. She guessed he didn't work, or at least not much, and he didn't have a car. He thinks a lot, there's so much going on in his head all the time. She'd never been with a thinker like him before. She surprised herself by imagining him making love to her. She hadn't made love in six months; the last time had been a disaster. It shocked her that she was even thinking of it. She imagined pulling on his ponytail while he entered her. She hoped he wasn't too rough. That was how the last one had been. She had cried after he left. She felt her face, wondering if she was blotching. She'd have to excuse herself and go into the bathroom.

"I'll be right back," she said, walking towards the bathroom.

"You don't have any beer," he called out after her.

No, she didn't, she thought. I'll have to buy beer for the next time he comes. She remembered a bottle of red wine she had saved for a special occasion. She'd bring that out.

"I have to introduce you to Jesús," she heard him say as she shut the door. When she returned, he was on the phone. She looked at the clock over the stove. It was late, 11:30. Would he call his friend this late? She tried to listen, but he was talking too low. She opened a cupboard, found the bottle of wine, and set it on the counter. Her sister had given it to her for her thirty-fourth birthday. She was glad she wasn't a drinker. Cabernet Sauvignon, she read. She hoped it was good. The phone clicked as she poured the wine.

"I hope you like red wine," she said loudly, too loudly.

"Ah, Cabernet. What year is it?" he asked, his body close behind her in the kitchen now.

She grabbed clumsily for the bottle. "Oh, uhm, 1984," she answered nervously.

Billy took a whiff, held the glass in his fingers to look closely into the wine, and then took a sip.

"Oak," he sighed, "great flavor." He lifted his glass to hers and toasted, "To the Brotherhood of Dolphins." They clicked glasses and she took her first sip. She decided to take off her glasses; if she were going to drink wine late at night with this man, she didn't need to see clearly. She took them off and left them on the counter. Billy took his own glasses off and put hers on. "Your right eye is stronger than mine."

"Oh?" she asked uncertainly, wondering if she should put her glasses back on. She didn't want to appear silly.

"Barbara, I'm going to be incredibly wealthy." Billy looked at her, smiling as he waited for her response.

"It sounds great," she said finally, still not sure how he would do this.

"We'll be lunching with the Arabs and going to the opera in Berlin in three weeks."

"So quickly?"

"The time has come. They'll be sending jets to pick us up, and showering us with money just to consider them."

"Oh," was all Barbara could think of to say. She took another sip of wine. She felt hot in the kitchen under the light and wondered if he would suggest moving to the living room. Billy finished his glass and poured himself another. "To Califia," he announced, as he touched her glass and moved closer. He took a slow drink, staring at her over the edge of his glass. She tried to look back at him, but she couldn't see him very well this close up. He was closer now. She looked at his thin lips; she could smell his garlic breath. I hope he doesn't want to kiss me now, she thought; it's too bright in here. She took a step back. Caught off guard, Billy lost his balance and lurched forward. A big slop of wine hit the floor.

"Oh, I'm so sorry," she said, putting her glass down quickly and reaching out to touch his arms.

"It's okay," Billy murmured, pulling her to him.

Barbara tried to turn her face. She didn't like it in the kitchen, and now there was wine on the floor. But he mashed her face, her hands still on his arms.

"Uhh, Billy," she finally got out as he nibbled and slurped on her neck, "why don't we go into the living room?" She had trouble pushing him away; he had an idiotic grin on his face as he straightened his glasses. She worried; what if he was insatiable? There were those stories of intelligent men, how they couldn't get enough. And what if, like her, he hadn't made love to someone in six months? He was still grinning at her, and, although she couldn't focus properly, she had felt it: he was hard.

"Come on," Billy said, but he didn't pull her. Instead he took the glasses and the wine bottle, walked into the living room, and sat on the floor, leaning against the couch.

She watched in horror as he sat on the floor. What if he spilled his wine? She reached for her glasses, touched her hair, and cleaned the wine off the linoleum. She took a long time to wipe up the floor and rinse out the sponge. He was looking at one of her books; he was intent, studious. She felt better. "What did your friend say?" she called out. Billy ignored her. She eventually had to come out of the kitchen, but she left the bright lights on. She stood next to him. "Did you talk to your friend?" she asked again.

"This is an amazing book. I studied here, in Firenze, for a year of college," he said into the book.

She stared down. He was looking at the *David*, one of her favorites, but she had always wondered why Michelangelo had made his thing so tiny and pointy. But who could she ask?

"I saw the most incredible works of art on every corner, in walls, in houses, in bars, in the middle of streets. Art to them is like our McDonald's. They do their wash in a da Vinci fountain and cook under the gaze of Giotto. But the Italians are starving for new art. I sent a friend of mine in Milano an airbrushed wave, you know, surfer art, and he says they're crazy for it." Billy stopped talking and gazed at the *David* again before impatiently turning the pages.

"I'd love to go there," Barbara said, then added, "Did you talk to your friend?"

Billy shut the book, but he didn't replace it on the coffee table. He took another sip of wine, looked at Barbara, and pushed his glasses up. He reached for her right foot, slid off her shoe, and started to massage the arch. "You're very tense," he said.

Tense? She was rigid, she thought.

"Let it go," he said soothingly. He worked diligently on her foot, and Barbara felt herself start to relax. She took a sip of wine. He moved closer now, and started rubbing the other foot. She sighed as he worked the sole. "I talked with Calasan. He's bored with his life, but he'd never say so. We're going to meet in L.A., at his grandfather's house. He was glad to talk to me, but he seemed tired. He probably drinks too much now. It's been a few years since we were together, but Barbara, I'm going to bring him down and take him to my pyramids in Baja, to sing with the dolphins. He'll be blown away."

Barbara murmured an "uh-huh." He had talked before of the pyramids in Baja, California, and the dolphins, but she was feeling too good, so good that she didn't notice that he wasn't rubbing her feet anymore with his hands, that he had brought both of her feet together like a cup and was rubbing something hard and warm between them. She didn't mind that he was kissing her knees; he could work himself up higher, and it would be alright with her. When he jerked and moaned a little, she felt something warm and sticky on her legs and against the soles of her feet, but she figured it must just be wine because he went down and licked it off. She felt good, knew he would be a wonderful lover because he was so intelligent, forgetting for the moment, the worry, that maybe he couldn't be satisfied.

CHAPTER 10

Pete decided to take Earl Street. He was in Silver Lake after finishing his shift at Evergreen, when he had driven by Annette's condo with every intention of stopping. There would be no easy way to leave and when he saw her vacant parking spot he knew he would wind through the hills and shoot straight up a steep one. He had never liked this hill—walking up or down on its narrow sidewalk—but his nephew, Carla's boy, worked him over whenever they went for a drive, "Pete, please, Uncle Pete," and Pete would do it, sometimes driving down the hill which scared him more than going up, goosing it in the middle to hear his nephew and the other kids scream. There were more hills, one over by the Ravine, where you could go up and down twice, and then there was Fargo Street, which was supposedly the steepest street around, but Earl Street was long and dense with trees and houses; at least it gave the most thrill.

As he turned left up the street, crossing Glendale Boulevard in heavy traffic, he could see the line of sunset halfway up the hill. The top half of the hill was golden, honey-looking through the last layers of smog. He rarely noticed the smog at sunset. He immediately thought of Dodger Stadium after batting practice, when the crew dragged the infield before the start of the game, when he could look out over that icy green field into the fried hills of his old neighborhood. He accelerated up the hill, easing down in his seat so that all he could see was the top of the car hood and a splat of blue between the trees at the top of the hill. At the crest, he kept low, turned left on instinct, rose up in his seat at the last possible moment on a windy, narrow road with typical bungalows and cliff-hanging modern homes. Before turning down the other side of the hill, he stopped and looked at the L.A. sunset, pink and orange with no clouds, vapor trails leading to Burbank Airport, Silver Lake Reservoir, a deep placid blue, the air calm, carrying the growth of new weeds, the sunset of automobiles.

Pete dropped his arm out the window so it hung against the door and slid his shades into place. An old man came towards him, pulled at one end by a tiny white poodle and a fat black dog who stopped often to scratch at a hairless patch on his backside. When the poodle reached the door, he eyed Pete and yapped, continuing as the old man yanked the leash, and said, "Now shut your face, Angel, honey."

Pete smiled at the old man. The old man looked into the car, acknowledging Pete's smile and, winking at him, said, "She thinks she's the queen around here. Drives old Horace crazy."

Pete shook his head and watched as the old man and the black dog dragged off in his side mirror. Still smiling, Pete drove over the rise, but the smile disappeared once he hit the shade of the hill. Bringing the car to a stop, he bent over to look through the passenger window at a house on the upper slope. He saw the cages, at least a dozen of them, but no *monos*. When they were kids, there had always been ten or twelve monkeys and the baboon. Whenever they came the monkeys would go nuts, climbing over one another, running around in their cages, squawking and grabbing at their outstretched fingers. To bother the monkeys was why he and his friends would sneak up the hill alongside the cages. But there had also been a baboon, a baboon with a nose like a dog and no tail, that wouldn't entertain, that just sat and stared morosely at them. Pete stopped the car. He envisioned the sad eyes of the baboon.

They had tried to get the baboon going, but poking him with a stick only made him move to the far corner of the cage where he would circle once, sit, and then turn to stare at them again. They began to bring him carrots, loquats, bananas, an uncooked hotdog. He'd take their gifts, sniff once, lick at the object sometimes, and then let it just roll out of his thick-fingered hand and return to his stare, not blinking, but moving only his eyes from boy to boy.

It was Pete's friend, Chuy, who had grabbed the Butterfinger from his other friend Flaco, the orange paper pulled down like a banana peel, the chocolate readied for Flaco's first bite. Giggling like the maniac he was, Chuy had shoved it through the chicken wire and Flaco had jumped him quick. Pete and the others would have had to straighten them out, except that everyone stopped to watch the baboon. He had grabbed the Butterfinger, sniffed it, licked it, and then taken a small bite. Even Flaco had had to grow quiet. What Pete would never forget was watching that first taste, as if he were savoring it himself. The powerful baboon had chewed thoughtfully, glancing at them from time to time, giving them small looks, before taking another sweet little bite down to the paper. The baboon carefully tore back the wrapper so that enough of the candy bar was exposed to nibble again. Pete had pushed his face against the cage, his cheeks recording the twists and circles of wire.

After that, they had returned at least once a week with Mars bars, Baby Ruths, licorice, but nothing pleased the

baboon more than the Butterfingers which they always handed to him in the wrapper because they liked to watch him
patiently tear open the paper and chew graciously, elegantly,
with dignity.

Pete continued to look up at the cages until his foot fal-
tered against the brake pedal and the car began to creep slowly
forward. As the car slid down the hill, he had to turn backwards in the seat in order to see the last rusting corner of a
cage under an orange sky. He cruised slowly over the
Glendale Freeway and up Baxter Street past his parents'
house. He drove slowly because he was staring straight ahead,
but not seeing, and even the sky turning blue-black in front of
him and the beginning of night didn't pick him up. He turned
right at the ravine and parked across from Sofía's house, but
he sat in the car until lights appeared in all the houses on the
street.

Sofía answered the door, failing to recognize him for a
moment as he stood on the unlit porch. Then suddenly, she
was grabbing him by both arms and pulling him in. "Where
have you been, honey?" she asked, winking and smiling at
him. She hugged him affectionately. He said something to her,
but he wasn't sure what it was. He felt nervous from seeing
Sofía, unsure of how he would be accepted after that night
with Carmen.

Uncle Pete noticed him, raised his hand, and yelled,
"Come on in, close that damn door," and went back to his conversation with a young long hair.

Pete figured he was a musician by the way he was bop-
ping his head to everything Uncle Pete said. Sofía asked him
if he wanted a drink, and this time he heard himself speak.

"A beer?" she asked.

"Fine," he answered. He was still standing just inside the
door when she returned so that she had to yell at him to sit

down. She came over, sat down next to him, and handed him an ice cold Bohemia.

"Now, tell me, have you been so busy that you couldn't come by?"

Pete shrugged his shoulders and Sofía, as usual, read his thoughts.

"So," she said humorously, "a busy day, but Carmen has to return to Stanford in three days. I know she wants to see you again. Why didn't you call?"

"I was too busy, *Tía*. I couldn't call," he answered finally, the relief so heavy it was difficult to talk. He remembered the night he had stood outside watching them in the living room, too nervous to come in.

"Oh, bull roar," she shouted merrily. "So busy the cat got your tongue. *Hijo*, how long have I known you." She leaned back and laughed heartily. "Well, you blew it tonight, home-boy; Carmen is out." She winked and then burst out laughing again. "I'll tell her you were here, though, and that you'll be back tomorrow night. Am I right?" she asked, laughing some more.

"*Tiá*," was all he could say.

"I'm making *arroz con pollo* and you are coming for dinner. Now tell me, what's new with the fire?"

He waited a moment. What would he tell Sofía? He had the arson report in his car, faxed over late that afternoon by Chief Harrison. He had thumbed through it at the end of his shift, searching for details that might make sense to him. The fire had been set in a storeroom used for art and exhibits. The room hadn't been locked; however, the area was closed to the public. Pete knew that with so many library personnel and the loose enforcement of the library it would be a simple matter to slip into the storeroom. According to Harrison, whom he had called, the arsonist had picked a room adjacent to the infamous stacks. It was either luck or careful planning. The arsonist had used paper, easily attainable in a library; then it had just been a simple matter of closing the door and mingling with the library patrons. Two or three minutes at the most was all the time it would take, Harrison concluded.

"Why would someone set fire to a library?" he had asked.

"A sickness. What else?"

"It would be someone so... cruel, someone who wants to hurt as many as possible."

"This one doesn't care for others."

Pete said good-bye to Uncle Pete, told Sofía he'd be back tomorrow night for dinner, and was out the door into the dark night of the ravine. Planning to go to Evergreen and work on the arson files again, he started up the car and drove three blocks down the ravine, one block farther than he would normally have gone, when he realized that he was in the Salvadoran barrio. Out of force of habit, he would normally have turned at the block before. He grinned. Here he was a detective, and still he found himself feeling cautious, as if he had crossed into a foreign land at night.

A girl walked up the street towards him. She was hugging herself with her arms, striding quickly. Not wanting to stare, he shot her a quick look as he passed her. He stepped on the brakes when he realized that it was Carmen. "Carmen!" he shouted, backing up. She stopped cautiously, and when she recognized him, came around to the passenger door which he had opened, and got in. He could see that she was crying.

"What happened?" he asked, touching her head lightly.

"Nothing, Pete, nothing."

"Nothing? Why are you crying? Come on, you can tell me," he said, rubbing her shiny hair.

"Just a lousy date," she repeated, looking up at him. He could see where the tears had melted eyeliner onto her cheeks. He rubbed harder at her head, trying to relax himself.

"What, did he try something with you?" he tried to ask calmly.

"No, Pete, it wasn't that. I just didn't want to be with him."

"And that's why you had to walk home by yourself?" He heard his voice rise, so sharp it seemed to cut across the headlights on the street.

"Pete, I can walk home by myself. Calm down. He didn't do anything to me. I just didn't want to be with him."

"Where? Where is he, Carmen?" he said angrily.

"No, Pete. I don't want any trouble. We were at a club. I just didn't like it there." She reached out to him, but he held her hands away from him.

"Which club?" he asked calmly. "Tell me, I won't cause any problems, just tell me which club. Carmen?"

"I don't want you to go there," she said hugging herself.

"Just tell me which club. I won't do a thing."

"I don't want any problems. I have to see him at school," she blurted out.

"A college boy? Some college boy did this to you?" His voice was rising again. He tried to bring it down. "Where is he from? The Westside?"

"No, he's not a *gabacho*," Carmen answered angrily, reading his thoughts. "He's from around here. In fact, he lives in this neighborhood," she shot at him, and then touched her lips with her fingers as if to retrieve the words that had just slipped out.

"*Chinga...*, a *Salvatrucha*?" he almost screamed. He stared ahead for a moment, breathing deeply. "Okay, it's alright, Carmen; you're gonna be alright. I'm gonna take you home now," he said, putting the car into reverse and driving backwards the three blocks without swerving. He stopped hard in front of Sofía's, ran around to Carmen's door, opened it and waited for her to get out. Sofía was at the front door. "*M'ija*," she called out, "is that you?"

Carmen ignored her mother. "Pete, we're not kids anymore. Why are you acting this way, you of all people, a detective? Please, come into the house. I don't want you to leave. Pete!" she screamed.

He closed the passenger door, marched to his side of the car, and jumped in.

"*Mamá*," Carmen yelled. "Stop him!"

He heard Sofía yell, "Angel," but it didn't do any good, because he was already gone and he wasn't looking in the rear-view mirror. He didn't slow up until he parked near the El Guanaco night club. He felt under the seat for the *filero* tucked into the wires of the upholstery and stuck the switchblade in the sock of his right foot. His police pistol was in the glove compartment, which he locked before heading for the night club.

He stopped five feet from the door, as if he'd come up against a wall. It wasn't the darkness; there was light along the walls and, hanging over the middle of the dance floor, a mirrored ball flickered across the room and his face. What stopped him were the women. For a moment, he was alone in a room with women, women sitting at tables holding their arms, or touching their hair. He would have walked out then, because what could he do in a room full of women, when a slow *cumbia* came over the loudspeakers and men rushed from the bar to the tables of waiting women. Pete remembered that he'd stopped in here once when it was called Mi Casita and had been a Cuban hang-out. The Salvadoran barrio had been Cuban then, although he had stepped around it just as carefully. He had come in here with Paco, a Cuban detective. They had both been starting out in the department, and they had come here for a couple of beers. Neighborhoods changed. The *cubanos* had moved up or out, and the Salvadorans had taken their place, but what had changed really? They still stared at each other across the streets and made low comments. He wondered what Paco, the *cubano*, would think of this place now, and where was Paco? Out in the Valley, softening up in Northridge maybe?

Pete studied the women. They dressed differently, but it was their faces that caught him. Faces like the women of his barrio. And their style of speech, although different, had a texture he was very familiar with, words he barely understood over music that was slow, the kind of romantic stuff he only heard on the A.M. stations. It wasn't so bad here, although he could understand that Carmen might have felt out of place. Pete decided he was ready to leave it at that; he could see what had happened, and he was about to turn and leave when he saw him, the slim dude with the trimmed beard. It was the same guy he'd seen through the window at Sofía's, but now he was chatting up a girl as if he were having a great time. Pete talked to himself, being a detective came up, the department. He was not a gangster, his *cholo* days as buried as his tag on the stairways. He was a man in his barrio and he couldn't calm down, and the longer he stood there and watched the student, the more he thought of Carmen having to walk through *their* neighborhood alone at night, their barrio. They just didn't have any respect, not just this dude, but the whole 'hood was to blame, and then he couldn't stop himself as he moved into the crowd of men.

He didn't care that they could sense his presence, or that he heard someone swear "Chicano" as he elbowed his way up to the bar next to the stud. He stared at him with an intense, cold look that blocked out everything other than the object of the stare. The guy didn't look like a student; maybe twenty-seven or even thirty, he looked more like a professional, an attorney or a bank official, too old to be pulling shit, too care-free as he leaned into a cute *chavala* in black. Pete turned away and ordered a Cuba Libre. The bartender called it a "coobah," gave him a hostile look, and waited impatiently to be paid. Pete tossed a five on the counter, took one sip, and turned back to Carmen's former date. He asked slowly, in what he thought was a low voice, "What kind of *cabrón* would let a girl walk home alone at night?" The noise around them snapped shut as all stared. The student rubbed his beard, looked briefly at Pete, and then ignored him, leaning away to say something to the *chavala* he was working on.

Pete took a full gulp of the 'coobah,' almost gouging his eye out with the straw. He grabbed at the straw, tapping it angrily on the side of the glass. "Hey, asshole, didn't your mother teach you to be polite?" Pete asked louder, taking another sip, concentrating on his stare, getting properly irri-tated, the beard grating on him, until he could feel the knife against his leg when the guy touched his face again.

The man brushed the sides of his jacket and said in Spanish, "Since when does a ravine dog know his own mother?" There were whistles.

"*Tu abuela me la pela,*" Pete answered back, bringing it down from mothers to grandmothers. He felt his eyes turn black as he smiled and then flicked his straw into the stu-dent's face.

"What is this?" the Salvadoran shouted in English while wiping rum and Coke from his face. "Why would you come in here, in front of all of these people, my friends? You are alone," he said with sarcasm, gesturing to his right and left with his hands and eyes. "We can trade insults, or we can talk and clear up this problem between us."

Pete casually bent over, came up with his knife opened, pressing the point against the soft section of throat below the section where the student's beard had been shaven clean. The bar was silent. The ball continued twirling, and in the flashes of light Pete could see the indentation of flesh, the reflection of whiskers on the blade, and the adam's apple quivering. "Tell me," Pete said, thinking that in all his years of fighting he had never cut a man, never used it. What would Carmen think? And his parents, Sofía, Ray? "Why'd you let Carmen walk home alone?" he shouted, trying to block out his thoughts, the tightening of his eyes, the shortened breath.

"Carmen? You're here about Carmen?" the student grunted nervously, his eyes flickering on Pete's hand.

"Yes, Carmen," Pete answered, relaxing the point of the knife so that it rested on the knot of a tie. Blades weren't used much anymore. He thought of the gunshot wounds he had seen. They were ugly holes, not like the clean entry of thin metal. How hard would he have to push? It would come naturally, he guessed, but maybe he should go for the belly. A stick like this in the throat would do him in. He didn't even know this guy. He thought of kids dying from warfare in the streets.

"You're the cause of this then."

"Fuck you." What had kids done to deserve death? Like termites after a rain, flying into the sun to dry their wings.

The student leaned forward, the blade moving with him. "You must be Pete."

Pete felt a muscle twitch in his jaw, but he said nothing.

"Carmen wanted to talk about you. I didn't want to hear it; she's my date, you know what I mean? She became furious, said you were just a childhood friend and then she left. Can you understand? I felt it. She was alive when she spoke of you."

Pete squeezed the handle of the blade, touched the throat once more and pulled it away. He closed it carefully and slid it into his pocket. He continued to stare at the student, but he had lost his concentration. What would Paco think of this place now? It wasn't a dump. He should at least hit this fool, because he had come in here. He tried to bring up the hate again, but instead he remembered how he hated funerals in sunlight. He leaned against the bar and ordered another "coobah." It came quickly this time. He would have this drink, relax a moment, and then leave.

He had just lifted the drink to his lips when they flew through the door. He tried to wave them off as Ray hit somebody. A chair was hurtled, and the screaming and yelling began. Pete raised his drink as Vinny flew over a table, landing against him. He picked Vinny up, but held him back. "Let's go," he shouted in Vinny's ear. "The bulls are coming." He turned and looked at the student, but he didn't say a word. On the way out he pulled some guy off of Chuy, and the group hit the sidewalk, the whine of a siren at their backs.

They walked quickly up the street and into the El Patio bar. They took over a whole end of the bar, kidding each other as if it were a reunion after an afternoon softball game. Ray roared when he saw Chuy's shiner. When Ray's cousin, Shorty, came back inside to tell them that the cops had cleared out, Pete ordered another round.

Flaco punched Pete in the arm, taunting him, "Getting old and slow, Sleepy."

"And you're getting fat," Pete shouted back, pummeling Flaco's belly.

"Yeah, yeah, come on, but watchale, I ain't no *pinche menso* college student," Flaco answered back, getting into a crouch and sparring.

Pete thought of the empty cages and the baboon. He wanted to tell Flaco and Chuy he'd been up there that afternoon, but Flaco had turned to slip punches with Chuy. Just like old times. He turned back to the bar. "How'd you know where to find me?" Pete asked Ray.

"It wasn't too hard, *pendejo*. I could've heard Sofía screaming from my shop," Ray answered.

"Too much."

"Yeah, too much," Ray repeated.

"Uh-oh, here comes Sofía," Shorty announced, ducking his head under the darkness of the bar top.

No one turned, all heads drooping lower as if that would hide them, but it didn't help. Pete felt himself turned around.

"Oh, *hijo*," Sofía exclaimed. Pete looked over her shoulder and saw Carmen. "You bum," she added, before turning to swear at Ray.

"What got into you?" she demanded of the group.

"Fucking *Salvatruchas*," Chuy answered.

"Why is it *Salvatruchas*? You are the ones acting like kids, fighting like you did when you were on the stairways."

"They think they're better than us," someone said.

"That's the way it is, isn't it?" Sofía answered angrily. "When you're on the bottom of the heap, who do you fight with? Your brothers."

"Not *my* brothers," Flaco replied.

"You're Puerto Rican, Flaco. If you're not brothers, then why are you hanging with these *mexicanos*?" No one answered. "Why are we wasting our time fighting each other? Latinos fighting one another."

"You don't understand, *vieja*."

"No political shit," said another.

Sofía walked up to the face of the man who had just spoken. "I do understand, *joven*. I fought some battles: Delano, the Vietnam War, education for all of you. We did it for you, your *madres* and *padres*, for a better life, not so you could fight among yourselves. *¿Qué dices tú?* What do you know of pride? Eh?"

There was no answer.

"The barrio's our strength, united we can help each other, fight *racismo*, but this, this thing tonight is a waste of time, a waste of your lives."

"You don' understand, *Tía*."

"Hell, I don't," Sofía said, spitting out the words. "I've already buried one child."

"*Mamá*," Carmen said quietly, touching her arm. "Let's go now."

"Yeah, we heard enough," Flaco said over his shoulder, but he was immediately shouted down by the others.

"*Respeto*."

"Shut up."

"*Pendejo*."

"Chill out."

"No, *m'ija*. Relax. It's time to put this aside," Sofía said to Carmen.

"Cuba for *la Tiá*, and what are you having Carmen?" Ray asked, standing with Pete and opening a space for them.

"Stoli on the rocks," Carmen answered.

"Carmen, they don't stock that here," Ray said.

"Sure they do. There's a bottle I left with Sal six months ago. I knew you *mensos* wouldn't touch it."

Everyone laughed at this, talking all at once while Carmen and Sofía sat at the bar. The drinks came and they quieted when Sofía raised her glass, "*Hijos*, I love you, like the one son I buried. Don't ever forget how beautiful you are. *Viva y salud.*"

The toast was loud. The guys slapped one another and spoke earnestly to Sofía. Pete watched Sofía brush at eyes that still searched for the lost son. Wouldn't he have been here tonight? He would have fought for his sister's pride, Pete thought. Sofía had strong ideas; look at the way she had raised her daughter. But how could you change a way of life other than to leave the neighborhood? He looked around at the others. Who could leave this? They were his brothers; they had come to save his ass. He looked into his beer, the color of a Butterfinger, then down to the cartoons on the napkin. He tried to focus on the girl with the volcanoes on her chest, but he couldn't shake the afternoon at the cages. If he went back and knocked on the door, would they know what had happened to the baboon? He wanted to know if they had sent the baboon to a zoo or whether his last days on the hill under the orange sunsets had at least been as peaceful, decent, and sweet as the delicate nibbles he had taken from the candy bar. He felt his face for the twisted marks of the chicken wire, hoping that if he could just feel them, he would know things hadn't changed.

They hung out at the bar for another round, then left in a group. Carmen drove home with Pete, but they were silent in the car. He wanted to talk to her, but didn't know how to start. He drove slowly, inspecting the homes in the ravine as if their heavy-lidded porches could tell him something.

When he stopped in front of her house, Carmen turned to look at him. He waited for a long minute, hoping that she wouldn't say anything. He had a twist in his stomach like he hadn't felt since those long ago moments before a wrestling match. When the silence had gone on too long, it was he who spoke past her into the amber glow of the window and the reflection of his face.

"See you tomorrow night, huh?"

Carmen jerked the door open and slammed it hard behind her. She walked quickly around the back of the Trans-Am and was on the sidewalk before he finally stopped staring at the dash lights and put it into park to follow her.

"Carmen. Carmen, talk to me!" Pete was standing in the middle of the street. The engine hummed methodically, exhaust fumes swirling in the lights from Sofía's house.

"Now you want to talk about it? Two hours ago you wouldn't listen to me."

She had stopped at the driveway. Pete knew she wanted him to talk to her. He went over and touched the roof of his car. He wanted to pound it. "I didn't mean to cause any problems. I was gonna walk out of there, but then I saw him and it worked me up."

"*Machismo.* Showing off on my account. I'm not that way, Pete. I'm a woman now; I can take care of my own life."

"Hey, just because you're in a university doesn't mean you can't use some help when you're back at home," Pete shot back.

Carmen advanced three feet, facing him, one hand working the air and the other confidently on her hip. "I know that man. We go to school together and yes, he's a *salvadoreño*. Now I wonder if he thinks I'm a racist or that I need protection, worse, that I want it from you."

Pete watched Sofía cross the living room twice. A porch light went on across the street. He could lean in to shut off the engine and flick off his car lights, but he didn't want to move. "Is that right?" he asked finally. "This guy is more than a friend to you."

"You mean, was he my *novio*?" she asked, annoyed again. "Yeah, we got to know each other. We were more than friends, Pete."

He wasn't shocked, but then he hadn't expected her to be so open with him on the street. "Then what about the other night?" he growled, feeling the heat from his chest under his hands.

"I felt something for you the other night," she said angrily. Then she paused, searching for the answer in his face. "You see," she paused again, and continued more quietly, "I kept track of you, everything you were doing. I was proud of what you had accomplished and I wanted to see what you were all about, now that we're older. I guess it was a thing I had for you, and for some crazy reason I hoped you felt the same way about me, even though you hadn't seen me all these years. For all you knew, I was that kid with the scraped-up knees, but all I wanted was for you to see me, and to like me for what I have become... But I don't think you can do that," she said, breathing hard.

Pete rested his hand on the top of his car, thinking he should turn the engine off. She wasn't more than ten feet away from him, and she looked beautiful with her serious face. He reached in and turned the key, but immediately wished he hadn't when he heard the silence. "I haven't changed, Carmen. This is still my barrio. And it's yours too, and it always will be yours. We can't change that." He waited for her to say something, but when she didn't, he continued. "This school business has gone to your head; you've forgotten where you come from."

"That's it!" she shot back. "You can't feel good about my success even though I feel good about yours. And I'm not leaving the barrio. This is my home and always will be. Besides, who are you to talk? You've left too."

"Oh yeah, an apartment six blocks away," Pete answered angrily, bitten by her remark that he'd left the ravine. "Some kind of special type at Stanford," he said vehemently. "You have all the boys drooling. You don't even look like a *chavala* anymore. What did you do, come back to the old corner to see what it was like? A little research to see if a *vato* can pound as well?" They stared at one another. The street was quiet. Pete felt his strength leaving him; if he hadn't gone to Silver Lake earlier he wouldn't have been on such a downer all night. Those damn cages. Then he wished he could take back what he had just said.

"Research!" She laughed. "I make love because I want to, because I like the person I'm with. You ought to try it sometime. I can see it would be a new experience for you." She turned and walked up the driveway. He watched her open the front door, enter and close it without once turning around to look at him. He pounded the vinyl top of the car three, four times, turned back to look into the house, and saw only the back wall, a print of Siquieros over the fireplace. "Damn you, Pete," he muttered, then got into the car and drove to Evergreen station.

At the station there were only two duty officers. He went to his desk and read through the arson file again, making new notes. He underlined "storeroom" three times, but his list was short: art, library personnel recently fired, Chief Harrison, Sylvia and Bennett. He thought of Bennett—he was sure that he and Sylvia were draping. What was it with these women? What did they see in these other men? He was trying to work himself up again when he saw the message to call Annette. Annette, the blond. He stubbed out his cigarette. It was time to go home. He couldn't make sense of anything, not the world, not his neighborhood, not tonight. Maybe Carmen was right. Who was he to talk? Annette, a blond he wouldn't ever bring around. A *jaina* who'd never been east of the river. Who was he to talk?

CHAPTER 11

Billy woke up earlier than usual. He looked over at the clock on the other side of Barbara's head. It read six-fifteen. He hadn't slept much last night, the second night that he hadn't slept well. He'd stayed up late working on an art piece he wanted to bring with him today, but he hadn't finished it. He had thought that maybe if he smoked a little weed it would help, but then he had gotten so stoned that he hadn't felt like driving over to Harold's house to run it off on the computer printer. Instead, he had laid out the photos of seven women that he had taken and stared at them, planning which section of each photo he would magnify so highly that it became dots on a large sheet of paper. Then he would paint in the dots, using only one color so that the face would barely be identifiable against the white background. It would show the spirit of women, their inner beauty, the soul that men needed and desired. He wouldn't name the women—that wasn't what was important; he would give them each a number, a large number, which would appear in the lower right-hand corner. The idea was women, strong women, and there was no need for an explanation; he only had to show the seven pieces and it would hit deep inside; that was why he used dots. Dots are the way we see; the universe nothing more than points of light. Superimpose it on one's retina as dots, and it wouldn't ever disappear.

He had talked to Barbara about it until she had fallen asleep. She had been upset. One of the pictures was of

Maggie. The picture, so soon after Maggie's murder had made her cry. It upset him that he couldn't tell her why Maggie was his centerpiece, only that his art would glorify her memory. And then, when leaving for the bedroom, too weary to listen anymore, Barbara had said that the idea reminded her of Warhol. He had bristled at the comparison.

"Warhol doesn't know a thing about women. Just wait; you'll see. It's an important piece whose time has come," he had told her as she fell into bed.

But he had been so excited about the idea that he couldn't sleep, and when he had gotten into bed with Barbara later, she had barely awoken as he entered her.

She didn't understand, but at least she was lending him her car to drive up to L.A. She was supportive, but he wished now that he had finished the pictures so he could take them along to show the artist on the calling card he'd taken from the Sandinista. He would meet Lourdes María Monroy today in downtown L.A. Lourdes, the artist, would understand his ideas.

He got out of bed and put on the new grey shirt with turquoise stripes that Barbara had bought him. He added white pants and black shoes that she had also picked out and paid for. He didn't really care what he wore, but she had insisted. He made coffee and looked in the refrigerator for something to munch on. There were two slices of leftover pepperoni pizza. He chewed on one piece as he waited for the water to boil. It was alright; his body could handle this garbage since he usually led such a clean life. He'd take a coffee enema when he got back, to purify himself of the toxins he would absorb in Los Angeles.

He ate the other piece of pizza as he poured the hot water into the filter. He'd only have two cups. He pulled out the cream and sugar, and rolled almost half a cup of cream into his coffee cup. He saw the container of wheat grass juice that he'd made Barbara buy the night before. It was unopened. He should drink a glass for the pure energy it would give him. Barbara wouldn't miss it; she didn't like the way it tasted. He was trying to bring her around, but in one week of living with her he couldn't change much; she still craved flesh and grease.

He looked through Barbara's purse as he drank his second cup of coffee, found two twenty dollar bills, and stuck them in his pants. In the bathroom, Billy sat on the john while he brushed his teeth, satisfied that the coffee had gone right to work on his colon. He finished up and brushed his hair back, making sure that the ponytail was tight. Then, he went into the front room to stare at the photos laid out on the floor. They looked great. He should take a picture of Barbara to make it eight. Why not? He'd brought so much into her life in the last week. She had so much more now that he lived with her. He did that for people. A portrait. Barbara would be pleased.

He went into the bedroom to give her a kiss, but instead he pulled down the blankets and nuzzled her tiny breasts. He felt himself growing hard, and he would have slipped in, but he had to make that appointment. "I'll call you when I finish up in L.A.," he whispered.

"Drive carefully," she said sleepily, giving him a hug.

Billy left the apartment and got into the Honda Accord which was parked on the street. The car ran smoothly, and the gas tank was always full. Barbara was very concerned about material things. He didn't let the engine warm up, just threw it right into gear. He headed down Highway One in fog, crossed the train tracks and made a right. There was traffic on the highway, not heavy, commuters drinking coffee, breathing sadly in their cocoons as they hurried to some dead job. He wouldn't ever live that way, not for any kind of money, rushing every day. He turned left into the dirt parking lot of the donut shop. The fluorescent lights seemed brighter than usual; maybe they had added bulbs, or maybe it was the fog outside, the fog again.

"Wheelyam, good morning. I not see you for several days."

"I've been busy, real busy. I'm heading up to L.A. to sell one of my projects," he said tiredly, hoping that it sounded as if he couldn't care less.

"Oh, you have buyer?" Mrs. Nguyen asked. "You be a rich man soon."

"I'm already there, Mrs. Nguyen," he said, letting his eyebrows rise and his head slope to one side, his thin lips tightening into a tiny smile.

"Well, you look nice," she said in her friendly voice as she went back to carry a tray of fresh cinnamon rolls to the counter.

"Kinda late with the cinnamon rolls, aren't you?" Billy asked, looking at the limited display of donuts and breathing deeply the fried grease, knowing that the back of the shop had a fan heavy with oil-clotted dust.

"Oh, fryer broke down last night. Just got it fixed at six o'clock."

He watched her shove the tray into its slot in the glass-enclosed counter. He could smell melting sugar through the grease.

"I'll take three of those cinnamon rolls, Mrs. Nguyen," he said.

"Oh, got to bring Jesús his breakfast, eh?"

"Yeah, before I go to L.A."

"You gonna eat two grease balls, yourself?" she asked with a laugh.

"Uhmm," he responded, feeling anger at her tiny face and voice. "I'm only going to eat one; I'll put the other on the dash so I can look at it and concentrate on the image of la-la land."

"Maybe you like L.A., so many things to do, lot of pretty girls," she said, laughing again as she placed the three cinnamon rolls in a bag.

"All the pretty girls left L.A. ten years ago. They moved here," he said.

"Oh, you always funny, Wheelyam. You got pretty girl now?"

"I always have pretty girls, Mrs. Nguyen. Always."

She smiled, and then asked, "A cup of coffee?"

Billy thought for a second about the coffee. They used styrofoam, he hated the waste. "I'll take two, large."

She poured the coffee a few inches from the top of the cups and moved the milk carton where he could reach it easily. He filled the rest of the cups with milk and added two packets of sugar. She waited with the plastic lids, and when he was finished, she shoved them hard onto the styrofoam, making the edges crease.

"There you go," she said, punching the cash register. "Two, twenty-five for you, Wheelyam."

He pulled out a twenty and slid it over the counter top. He watched as her nimble fingers slid the bill off and placed it on a ledge of the register, where she could see it as she made change. She counted out the change, placing it on the counter even though he had his hand outstretched. He looked at the towel on the counter next to the money; it was damp and could easily be rolled up. The two ends could be easily gripped. They wouldn't slip. Billy stared at Mrs. Nguyen, feeling the styrofoam waste, grease, her laugh and his sudden anger.

"Your change, Wheelyam," she sang.

As he fingered the towel, two customers entered. He glanced at them, dropped the towel, picked up the bag of rolls and the coffee after scooping the money off the counter and into his pocket.

"You want to fry on Thursday, Wheelyam?" she asked as he touched the wooden screen door.

He stopped, the thin smile appearing again. "There's no future in donuts; fried dough is on its way out, Mrs. Nguyen."

He'd show everyone; he'd be flying jets soon. Later, Mrs. Nguyen, I'll be back, he thought. He got into Barbara's car, turned onto the highway, and pulled a cinnamon roll out of the white bag. It was gonna be a long day; there was a lot to plan, he told himself as he worked the roll into his mouth. He'd meet the artist today and later he'd see Calasan, but first, he'd go see Jesús and calm down. When he reached the road at the top of the bluff, he turned left. It was about two miles inland, then onto a dirt driveway behind a brilliant white fence dulled by the fog, the road lined with rocks and avocado trees, their trunks painted white about three feet high. He saw the small white bungalow and the large covered porch where Jesús and his family lived. There were dogs and they charged, barking, excited, one jumping against his window when he parked. He hated the dogs and bright white paint, grateful for the stagnant fog. The bungalow door opened and a woman's face peered out at him. He quickly waved as she turned away. Yolanda, the wife, she had always been cool to him; now he would have to wait until Jesús came out and called off the dogs. A long minute later the door opened again and he heard the familiar whistle, saw Jesús scratching his chin and waving him over.

"*Buenos días*, Billee," Jesús said warmly as he gestured at one of the chairs on the porch.

"*Buenos días, Señor* Jesús," Billy answered him with his biggest grin. "I brought you something." He dropped the bag on the table, opened it and placed one cinnamon roll on its waxed paper in front of Jesús's chair. He took a bite out of his before he slid a styrofoam cup of coffee next to the glistening, untouched roll.

"Ahh, you brought *café* and greaseballs," Jesús said with a smile.

Billy gulped at his coffee before he sat down. "Capitalist cinnamon rolls dripping with Vietnamese pussy juice."

Jesús chuckled politely, drummed a finger against the edge of the wax paper and said, "Your favorite donut shop."

"The only donut shop. Aren't you hungry?"

"No, but thank you. I just finished a huge breakfast. Yolanda spoils me, you know."

"You don't know how good you got it, living like a Don."

"Not too shabby," Jesús answered him with a wink. "And where have you been; we haven't seen you in over a week."

Billy leaned back in his chair, put his hands behind his head for a moment, and said, "I'm finally doing it, Jesús. All my connections are coming together." He slapped his hands together, took another sip of coffee. "I'm going to meet an artist, a woman in L.A."

"A *novia*?"

"No, this is business. I've got another new woman now with a nice apartment. That's her car." He pointed at the car and winced as he noticed the muddy paw prints on the driver's side window and door.

"You live a very full life, Billee."

"I have to make up for lost time. You know where I grew up?"

"Sure, you tell me many times. Fargo," Jesús said, folding his hands and placing them on his lap, the cinnamon roll and coffee waiting.

Billy spoke to the fog at the edge of the porch. "You know what we did in Fargo, North Dakota, for entertainment? We waited outside the local bar and watched the drunks slide on the ice. We would divvy up the change we found. This one kid would roll the drunks as he was helping them up. He smoked unfiltered Chesterfield's and had a switchblade knife."

"Fargo," Jesús enunciated.

"I ran into him again, when I was in high school, at a Byrds' concert in the San Fernando Valley. He pulled a knife on the bass player and got hauled away." Billy paused a moment, watching a seagull. "I don't think he would have cut anybody."

"No."

"Murray always hated tall guys and now I was taller than he was. He hadn't changed, but I was the one who felt like Fargo, North Dakota with a paisley shirt and blond hair, and he was still short, dressed in black with slicked-back hair." Billy sipped his coffee through the torn hole in the lid of his cup. "I was with my girlfriend, the girl I married while I was at Yale. She was scared to death. We drove Murray's woman home in the family Beetle. And my best friend was in the back with Murray's woman trying to put the make on her. We had to drive all the way out to Pacoima or some strange place." Billy began a chuckle that turned into a laugh.

"Childhood friends are the best friends; they never die," Jesús said, with a shrug.

Billy continued as if he hadn't listened to Jesús. "I never saw Murray again. But my high school friend, he was the first real Californian I ever met. That was Calasan Klor de Alva. He sat behind me in Latin and algebra class. That's how we got to be best friends. I lifted my arm during the tests."

"You miss him?"

"I miss my wife."

"Because she left you," Jesús said emphatically, but with reserve in his voice.

"We were in Italy," Billy mumbled, as if he were talking to himself. "I was teaching English at a college in Florence. She left one day, wouldn't answer any of my letters. I came back to the States to find her, but she wouldn't see me. She left me, and I was the one who changed her, opened her eyes."

"Uh-huh, and what about *El Californio?*"

"I'm going to see him in L.A.," Billy answered with renewed energy.

"So, it's been a long time?"

"Yeah, but we're still close." Billy turned away from the table and looked out over the orchard. The fog as it burned away had left a smooth clearing under the trees. Was this the potential of fog—to scrub clean? He thought of the first day of class at his new high school in California. Latin and algebra are what had made them friends—that, and alphabetical order. Johnson, Klor de Alva. Billy remembered the shirt his mother had let him pick out. A California shirt, yellow paisley covered with green parameciums, to show that he wasn't an outsider, and yet behind him sat Calasan, his bowling alley vision of palm trees and convertibles riding the hard molding of a student desk. Until that day, Murray was the only stranger he had ever known.

Billy wanted to take his "Californian" home and introduce him to his family. He thought that it would be good for them. He had. He remembered it too vividly: his mother, the housewife, and his father, the engineer, eating corn flakes at four o'clock in the afternoon.

He rubbed his face with both hands. "He's my dolphin brother, Jesús," Billy said with his thin smile.

Jesús touched the wax paper under the roll, stiff as a sugared trilobite on the table. "We can all use a brother."

Billy waited for a circling gull to land on an avocado tree. "And I'm going to L.A. today. It's the beginning of the Brotherhood. I'm doing it. Why don't you come down with me to the pyramids in Baja, you and Calasan? The dolphins will teach us."

"I can't leave, *amigo*. I've got work, *pues*, I got to go. Forgive me," Jesús said, standing up and pushing his chair in.

"Ah, come on, it's Baja," Billy whined. "I'll sneak you back across."

Jesús shrugged. "Not this trip, my friend, you will speak to the *delfines* for me. *Hasta luego.* I must go to work but bring your friend by. You know *aquí* you are *con familia*."

After Jesús left and entered the house, Billy remained at the table, hands folded on his lap. He was warm in the bare sun under a sweater Calasan had given him, the sweater he'd put on over his new clothes. He fingered it. It wasn't thick, but it was hairy and made of Argentinean wool. It was one of the few articles of clothing he hadn't lost or given away. His first Californian, the true Californian from the family of the *rancho*, the *vaqueros*, bull breeders, bear-baiters, baptisms and marriages at the San Gabriel Mission, and finally, the lost land. The myth of Califia. He tried to peer into the last of the fog that had escaped into the folds of trees. If he could only disappear into the fog, like light, the clever way it had of hiding white light.

Calasan would be the roots. He would respond to Califia. Calasan, the Californio, a Dolphin Brother. Billy had found him, and they'd go to the pyramids in Baja to swim with the dolphins. Jesús had told him to speak to the dolphins. He looked spitefully at the sun and wished now for the shroud of fog against a sun that would never approve of him. He was wasting time in that sun, wasting time with this old wetback.

Billy flung the stiff cinnamon roll to the dogs, settled into the fully gassed Honda and spun it around in a tight quick circle, narrowly missing one of the dogs by inches.

CHAPTER 12

The artist's apartment was in MacArthur Park, but since he had several hours before their meeting, Billy decided to stop at the Central Library. Once he had admired the library. Once he had come here gladly, with expectations, but what had that accomplished? It had been meticulous, the planning spirited, but unlike with Maggie, the execution had been dull. Yes, there were fire trucks, an institutional disaster and a female firefighter almost killed in the line of duty, but nobody knew, no one had really felt him or his ideas. What had the firefighter felt? Had she left the fire more aware of the library's cultural oppression?

He remembered her story, she was in Engine Company 12. It would be wonderful to meet her, find out how close they had been, united in the arms of a blaze. Now he stared through the chain-link fence thrown around the library, saw the statue of the goddess in the entryway, felt her calmness and power, but the longer he stared at her the more agitated he became. Too strong, imposing, the breasts jutting under the flimsy material. It was wrong, a carved image, made by the hands of a man who didn't understand women as he did. He left quickly in the Honda and, squealing away from the parking space, he knew something had to be done; sacrifices had to be made. He would find the firewoman and add a photograph to his art piece.

Billy made a right turn at First Street, and ended up near Tommy's Hamburgers. He was hungry now and would have liked a chili tamale, but he was in too much of a hurry to stop. Ten minutes later, after asking directions, he pulled up in front of an older apartment building in a MacArthur Park neighborhood. She answered his call on the second ring and told him she would be right down. Billy waited under the overhang, and looked at the paint peeling on the steel doors.

He had imagined an older woman, short and dark, with grey in her braided hair, big hoop earrings, and a loose tent of a dress splattered with oils. Instead, Lourdes María Monroy wasn't even thirty. She was close to six feet tall, model thin in tight black Levis and a black leotard top cut out at the shoulders, showing off arms that were as long as the fluorescent tubes in the Encinitas donut shop. She stood in the open door and stuffed one hand in a pocket pulled so tight, even a finger couldn't have fit there. She called him, "Bill." The hair stood up on his arms. He struggled with the smoky voice, but it was her face that kept him riveted. She must have bleached her hair, almost white, severe, cut as short as a man's, which made her high cheekbones and large, green eyes explode. The only makeup she had on was purple eye shadow and black mascara. He took three steps forward without knowing it, and she let the door close behind him.

"The elevator doesn't work," she explained as they stood in the foyer. She looked him over, and he could feel sweat run in the crack of his ass. "That is why I had to come down. How chic, if one wants to look at it that way. It could be Paris," she said, smiling with the fullest lips he had ever imagined. The smile melted into her eyes, which seemed to darken and grow and smolder all at the same time. He wanted to clean his glasses.

She led the way up the stairs, gliding, moving like an animal, body swaying, starting from her head and continuing as a question mark down to her feet as she walked. It wasn't just her hips; everything moved, like a marble sliding down a circular tube, the marble reappearing over and over as he followed her up the stairs. She didn't make any noise as she walked. Billy realized that she was barefoot.

The apartment was filled with art, framed art work, art in progress, a tarp and an easel, a canvas where the dining room should be. She asked him if he wanted a drink.

"Tea would be fine," Billy answered.

"To make tea I'd have to boil water. Wouldn't you rather just have a *copita*?"

The way she asked, he couldn't refuse.

"Is Scotch okay? On the rocks, or with a little water?" Her smile made him forget how to talk.

"Water would be fine," he said finally.

She went over to an antique, wooden liquor cabinet, poured him half a glass and added water from a glass decanter. She poured a Cointreau for herself.

"Now, tell me, you have a plan to expose the world to the art of the Third World?" She smiled, raised her glass and added, "*Salud*."

"*Salud*," Billy replied, taking a gulp that made his eyes water.

"I hear your ideas are revolutionary for a promoter, or should I say art dealer?"

Billy had to think. He felt a bomb go off in his stomach, the explosion stretching his ears. He took another gulp. What had the Sandinista told her? "Promoter," he said quickly, liking the word. "Corporate America and the Vatican have collaborated in structuring our culture, our minds, into continuing in lock-step formation along the road of feudalism." He felt better, warming to his favorite topic. "You see, the art that we have been told—forced to believe—is great art, is nothing more than propaganda. Da Vinci, Michelangelo, Matisse, even Picasso were working for imperialism. And now, by showing this art which they have funded, they can say that they are ennobling and giving culture to the people. But it is on their terms; the price is that we continue in the factory mode. Art should be Nature. They don't want us to see it; that's why indigenous art, which is as close to the Mother, the woman in all of us, is hidden." He took another drink.

"Here, let me top that off for you," she said, coming over and taking the glass from his hand with both hands, letting them linger on his for a moment, deliberately, he knew.

He watched her move to the counter and fill the glass. She added the water casually.

"But isn't Matisse a painter of Nature, and do you feel the same way about someone as defiant as, say, Van Gogh or Gauguin?" she asked with her back turned.

"Those are good examples of art that attempts to explain Nature. That was Matisse. The Impressionists were only an advertisement for the idyllic life of the bourgeois before the war. They were painting from Nature, but not of Nature." He enunciated the word "from," letting it hang in the air.

"But Van Gogh," she said, using the French syllables, "surely he worked from instinct, no?"

"Yes, but look how his art has been capitalized. It's as if, here was a genius, but look what they made him; he was a waste of a man. They use him as a message." He took the glass from her hands and watched as she slipped onto the couch, curling her legs beneath her. He pulled at the Scotch and continued. She refilled his glass twice.

"Isn't art, modern art, a reflection of the real world?" she asked.

"Hah! Modern art is an inside joke, a reaction to credit cards and television. I've seen enough modern art to know that it belongs on a black and white TV. It should be viewed with a Dr. Pepper."

"I see," she said, slowly. "But how would you propose to replace this art with that of Nature?"

"It will happen with the proper education. Everyone can feel the emptiness, but first I think a statement has to be made. The art of Nature must be shown so that people will be blown away."

"A statement?"

"Yes, I have a group of followers who believe as I do. In fact, next weekend we are heading to Baja to build a new pyramid and listen to the dolphins. You should come. I'm inviting you."

"Thank you," she answered. "I might like that." She waited a moment, scratching, he noticed, at her left breast. "So what is your statement?"

"Something to threaten the art community. Maybe, we'll hijack an important piece, something from the Getty."

"Too volatile," she said, laying her long arm along the top of the sofa.

Billy glanced around the room. There were many pieces hanging, some unframed. Most were vivid, color splashed. A few were very different, dark. He wondered which style she preferred. He would ask later, but for now she liked his ideas; he had her attention; she appreciated him.

"Are you here working for the Sandinistas?" he asked, twisting his head.

"I don't work for anyone." She leaned over, lowering her voice. "Are you an artist?" she asked.

"Yes. I use computer images and color them. I wanted to bring a sample, but there was no time." He tried to raise himself out of the chair, looked at his glass and saw that nothing remained but an amber spot.

"That's a shame," she answered. It seemed as if her face were one big smile. He tried to watch her lips move; he heard only noise. "You look tired," she said from somewhere behind his ear. He saw her smile. Then he was led by gentle hands and helped into the bedroom, where he was placed on a bed. "Rest," he heard her say. "We'll go out later and talk."

He could see her in the mirror as she left, surprised that he would agree to a nap, relieved because he couldn't keep his eyes open. He was sure he saw her hand reach in to close the door, a thin hand, and then he fell asleep.

Billy woke up wet. It was the Amazon again, and it wasn't right; he wasn't supposed to have the same dream over and over. His mind told him to get up, but he couldn't move, as if the sweat had glued him to the mattress. He wondered what time it was, heard a shower running. It was dark in the room, the shades closed tightly, the air close and humid. The water stopped. He moved enough to see light along the bottom of the bathroom door. When the door opened, he pretended to be asleep as she walked past the bed, wrapped in a towel.

Lourdes hummed, selecting clothes quickly. He listened to her return to the bathroom, then watched her reflection in the mirror as she did her face. He lay still, stiff from that dream, afraid to breathe, fearful that it would sound too labored. In the mirror, she had removed her towel, using it to dry her hair. He leaned forward, trembling on an elbow so that he could see past the doorway, the back of her knees, up her thighs, thin and long, past her ass, the tight waist, and up the long back that rippled as she rubbed her hair. Billy raised more of himself to see better, but then wished he hadn't, because now his neck was strained, and he couldn't see her in the mirror anymore. It was the mirror he wanted to see, to watch her in the mirror, combing her short hair with her fingers. He wanted to touch his own, just to pull it from the skull where it felt plastered. That dream. He lay back down to see her in the mirror and saw the brown hair of her vagina. She started to rub lotion on her legs, both hands climbing the insides of her thighs, up over the flat stomach and then across her breasts. They were larger than he had thought possible on such a thin woman and perfectly round without sag.

He wanted to concentrate as she started rubbing her breasts, the circular motion caressing, but then the dream hit him again: the Amazon, the rain forest of heightened light and shadows, a toucan on a branch, staring with head cocked, monkeys swinging in the trees. It was the part of the dream that he could live with; wandering in the jungle, picking fruit from trees, and watching monkeys. Why did it have to change after that happy moment, and why did it change when he looked at the toucan again? A panther began howling from far off and, as he looked next into the trees, the monkeys had disappeared, but not the toucan. The toucan was still there, watching him. It was always the same toucan. The panther howling, closer, and then he was running, branches whipping his face and arms, birds and animals he couldn't see screaming at him, a root that tripped him, the insects biting through his sweat. It should have been the end, with the insects in the dirt, the ground pounding from the panther closing in, but there was the toucan, twisting his head to catch him with one eye, the jerk of its tail and the real horror beginning: white, always blinding white shit splattering his face, covering his glasses.

He came back to the mirror with a start, upset with the memory of the dream. Lourdes was now in black panties and bra. How had she dressed? Had she sat on the toilet to slip into the panties, or done it standing up? Had she leaned over to drop her boobs into the cups? He fought back his anger. Now there was only the small black mini, tugged at, then zipped up the back, no nylons, a red top pulled over the head. She turned once in front of the mirror, found the earrings she wanted and put them on. He waited as she came into the bedroom, until she returned from the closet with a small shiny black coat; then he made his move, stretching, yawning, and rising up on the elbow all at the same time.

Lourdes stood at the end of the bed. "So. You're awake now," she said. Did she know that he had been watching? "I'm sorry," he answered, yawning. "I've been working hard, between my art project and last night with my friend."

"A *siesta* is good. Besides, we have a long night ahead of us." She put on her jacket which was cut high. "I hope I didn't disturb you," she added.

"I just woke up," he lied, believing that she had enjoyed it.

She adjusted her jacket. "Are you hungry?"

He visualized her still in the mirror, dressing in black panties and bra, the panther he never saw.

"Perhaps you need to wake up. A shower first," she said, startling him.

Billy sat up on the bed. She left the room and he could feel his shirt stuck to his back, but he needed more time before he actually moved. In the bathroom, he studied the man's razor, deodorant and aftershave, laid out on the vanity.

Lourdes was sitting on the same couch in the same lazy way, as if the couch were made more comfortable because she sat on it. She held a Campari in her left hand. The red of the Campari set off the red blouse under her black jacket. She stretched, obliging him, he thought, as she took off the jacket and he focused on her breasts. She patted the couch, at a spot next to her. He sat down and she handed him a Campari.

"It will wake you up, refresh you."

He raised his glass and looked into her green eyes. She started to talk, but he couldn't listen. Her nipples were erect, frightening. He had always picked thin, unassuming women, women without breasts, and now she was touching his arm, leaning into him with nipples fighting through two layers of cloth. They both drank again and he removed his glasses, lurched forward pinning his lips to hers.

Lourdes pushed him back. "You have awakened, ¿qué no? But I'm starving, Bill. Let's go eat. I know a wonderful little bistro."

He flashed her his brightest smile and then came at her again, groping, pawing clumsily. She frantically pushed him away and, just as suddenly, he stopped. Lourdes moved away from him and stood up, adjusting her top.

Before she could say anything, Billy blurted out, "I'm sorry. I don't know what got into me."

"Are you crazy?" she asked, her eyes wide, her voice thickly accented from the shock.

"It's your beauty. And you're an artist. I went a little nuts. Forgive me?"

"Is this how you act with a woman?" she asked, calmer now.

"Are they real?"

"What?"

"Your tits? They're plastic, aren't they?"

"I think you should leave now."

"I have to make a phone call."

"Get out!"

Billy left her standing, hands on hips. He closed her bedroom door behind him, sat on the bed and dialed Barbara's number. He thought of Nature and the improvements of science, but he didn't reflect on the white Honda Accord that ran perfectly and had been filled with gas when he left, the art hidden in the Vatican, the art planned for the new AT&T corporate headquarters, the art being created by indigenous hands, the broken down donut cooker at Encinitas Donuts, or tuna fishermen with dolphins in their nets. He didn't wonder why she had filled her chest with plastic. He had squeezed hard. Was that the bag of silicon? Is that what he had felt? Had they been injected with a huge syringe, like the one he had used on the jelly donuts, a glob of it leaking out the hole? He thought of Mrs. Nguyen. She had made him angry this morning. Styrofoam, he didn't like plastic. They were too firm.

Lourdes had been making fun of him, seducing him from the bathroom with her fake tits. He got an erection. It must be some kind of sport with her, a game, and he didn't like it when they played games. Women. Barbara wouldn't treat him this way.

When he got the message machine he was pleased, "No fog, just smog. Be home in a limo. I'll bring Chinese," he said into the phone. He replaced the phone and dug into his pockets, pulling out a baggie filled with sage, the leaf tied with a red string. He placed it in an ashtray on the night stand, found matches and lit it, breathing deeply. As he was sucking in the dark smoke, he saw the toe of a pair of nylons peeking out of the top drawer of her bureau.

"What are you doing?" she demanded as she came in the door.

"It's incense," Billy answered. "A blessing."

"Get out!" she coughed out as she went to the ashtray.

"It won't bother you for much longer," Billy said to the back of her head, and then yanked her against him as he tightened the black nylons around her beautiful, long neck. She was a better fight than Maggie, and she almost clawed him until he threw her face down into the pillows and rode her, the black nylons tight around her thin throat as he listened to the choking gasps that reminded him of the squeals of dolphins. After she had stopped struggling and he could let the nylon go, he turned her over, delicately removing her clothing as he breathed in the deep smoke of the sagebrush. His erection pounded and he ejaculated easily, needing only the slightest touch against her thighs, moaning as he jerked over her chest.

Billy left for Calasan's grandfather's house an hour later, slightly drunk and very pleased with himself. Lourdes hadn't really believed in him. It was a shame that she wouldn't be around to see it happen, but it didn't matter that Maggie or Lourdes wouldn't know; maybe his ex-wife would notice. It wasn't until he had reached the Echo Park Lake that he wondered if Barbara would understand. He was an artist, he decided; his revolution was moving forward and, more importantly, he was going to be powerful. He thought of the Central Library, books to placate the masses, and then, as he passed a Winchell's donut shop on Glendale Boulevard, he remembered that Mrs. Nguyen had told him he would like Los Angeles, that it was filled with beautiful women.

CHAPTER 13

That same day, in the late afternoon at Evergreen Division, Pete and Tony were working on the paperwork of the two gangbangers they'd grabbed that morning, 'bangers who had hit Elysian Park on a typical Sunday of large families, blankets and barbecues, lawn chairs, teenagers sneaking off into the bushes, popsicle vendors, and all those damn soccer games.

The gangsters hadn't missed; with an Uzi and a .38, how could they? But it was the wrong young guy, a *chavalo* bouncing a ball on his knee, and his little sister catching a bullet as well. They had been playing a game. *Fútbol*. The game the "nationals" played. Kick the ball to one end, then back to the other, trash cans for goalposts, a sweaty, red-faced *señor* as goaltender, and always run, run, run, and never enough points scored. Pete remembered when their Coachy had tried to get them interested in playing soccer, but they had wanted basketball, baseball, or American football. They had played another team once, but everything had had to be in Spanish with those *pendejos* and finally the game had been stopped because of fighting. Pete remembered the game, the *mexicanos* adept at defense and able to control the ball seemingly at will. Then, he saw the kid on the slab in the morgue and his sister in intensive care.

Had he and Tony been lucky on this one? They had the guns and the car, a ratty '53 Chevy lowered with skirts and in need of a paint job. It had been a good tip and they usually didn't get tips.

Tony shuffled the papers, stacking them and announcing, "Finished, Sleepy."

"Don't call me that around here, *ese*," Pete shot back. "I don't like it."

"Take it easy, dude. *Tranquilo*."

"Don't call me that here, ever again. You understand," Pete said.

"Hey, chill with your bad attitude," Tony said with heavy barrio inflection. "When're you gonna be done?" he asked a moment later.

Pete shuffled the papers, bouncing them on the desk until they were in a tight pack. "Finished," he said.

"About time. Christ, that was some luck, that squeal, huh?"

"Listen to me," Pete growled, leaning away from the desk and pointing his finger at Tony. "Don't be a dumb *chota*. We never got a tip. We don't know from a squeal; ¿*sabe*, dude?" He felt edgy about that tip, good information carried a heavy load. It needed protection.

Tony wasn't looking into Pete's face; he was staring at the finger.

"Don't point your goddamn finger at me. I ain't no fucking lame boy."

Pete's hand and finger became a pistol, the thumb cocked. "Don't talk corners, man. I don't wanna hear it."

"Jesus, what a hard-on you got. Up yours." They were both silent a moment and then Tony laughed, saying, "Let's blow this pop stand. I'll drop off this load with the lieutenant *chingón*. Comb your hair, and we'll go get something to eat.

I'm starving. How 'bout Tommy's? Man, I could go for a sloppy burger right now."

"I can't make it. I got to work on something else," Pete said, opening the desk drawer and pulling out the library fire file. His eye caught the phone number right off, the phone number he had penciled in, against division policy, on the file folder. It was for Sofía's house, Carmen.

"Lay it down, man. That don't have nothing to do with you anymore. You're gonna get in deep *mierda* on this one, Pete. Far as I know, that arson investigation got shifted to a special, and you ain't in that unit."

Pete brought his finger up again and cocked the mock trigger. "It ain't just any fire, *ese*."

Tony ducked and shielded his face with his hands, saying, "Sylvia Cruz, the barrio."

"Right, family. I don't need to tell you more, do I? You got it sussed, right?" Pete said, closing his hand into a fist.

"Yeah, fuck you twice," Tony said, laughing. "Still a humping homeboy."

Pete let it ride. He wanted to talk to Tony about Carmen, but decided against it.

"Come on; let's go get something to eat. We'll make it quick. Man, my *tripas* are twisting," Tony tried one more time.

"I'm not hungry, Tony. Do me a favor and go feed yourself."

"Knock yourself out," Tony said, picking up the Elysian Park file and leaving for Lieutenant Vasconcelos's office.

Pete watched him enter the glassed-in office before reaching for the phone. He dialed the first four numbers of Sofía's, then quickly stabbed the cradle and listened for the dial tone. He replaced the phone slowly. Not a phone call, he told himself; I'll drop by there in person. He opened the file. Tony was right; it was official, a special unit assigned to the arson investigation. Pete felt his weariness; he was hungry and needed to eat, but then he thought of the soccer game. He listlessly picked up the doctor's report on Sylvia: shock, pulmonary edema. He had already talked to the doctor, asked for a translation. "It's unusual for an inhalation victim to have a system breakdown hours after the initial emergency, but not impossible. Her lungs were partially filled with water, making her susceptible for trauma to take place."

Pete closed the file. He had almost lost an old friend. He stared at the phone, letting the ring startle him a second time before picking it up.

"Detective Escobedo?" a deep voice asked.

"Escobedo here," Pete answered, frowning as he placed the voice but not the face.

"Cornelius Bennett. The firefighter in Sylvia's company?"

Pete remembered Bennett at the fender with a pile of T-shirts. "Yes, I was just thinking about that fire."

"Uh-huh. It works that way sometimes. There's been another arson."

"The library again?"

"Not the library this time, an apartment; young woman died, but not from the fire."

"Murdered?" Pete shot back.

"I couldn't say."

Pete took a moment. "Is it connected to..."

"The Library," Cornelius answered for him. "I don't know, but this one's real strange."

"When and where?"

"We just got back to the station; you got a pen?"

Pete took down the address and asked, "What makes you think it might be related?"

"Art again. Artist's place was burned."

"And?"

"Something I overheard you might want to know about."

"What's that?"

"Deputy Inspector came as we were packing it up. First thing he finds is a bundle of burnt sage."

"That start the fire?"

"No way," he said. "I believe it's some kind of medicine man shit, you know, Indian blessing, incense; they sell it in all those new age stores."

"Never heard of it. How do you know about it?"

"I get around, detective."

He thanked Cornelius for calling and told him he'd stop by after checking it out. Coincidence? Pete wondered. He opened the file again and re-read the department's prelims. Nothing about sagebrush. Pete turned the page of his notebook to the interview with Cornelius, but there was nothing there to tell him that the brother had called because he had felt something in that apartment. Pete remembered Bennett at the fender with a pile of T-shirts, a new Sears power buffer in a box. Pete stood up and put on his coat. The last thing he saw before leaving was the penciled in phone number on the cover of the file, the phone number that had kept him at his desk. "Carmen" underlined twice, but he didn't make the call.

The address of the apartment was over by MacArthur Park. If it was the ratty section of MacArthur, the fire could be anything strange: drugs, angry pimp, coyotes wanting their money from the illegals they'd brought across the border. Pete parked in front of an older apartment building located outside the MacArthur Park war zone. There was debris on the front lawn, cushions still smoldering, and a blackened window on the second floor. It wasn't hard to find the right apartment: its door open, smell of smoke, two detectives and a fire department inspector. The two detectives looked up as he entered, one giving him a hard-ass stare, the other switching to a grin. Pete moved aside to let the fire marshall leave.

"Check it out. Didn't I tell you, Andy? Those Evergreen bulls got heart. Must have known we're understaffed and in need of top professional help," the Chicano detective said to his partner.

"That's what they say on the floor: help López out, he's easily confused. How's it going, Jack?" Pete said as he crossed the room to shake hands. Pete was introduced to Jack's partner; there was more small talk, and then he got the details. The call had come in immediately, so the fire hadn't spread far. The woman had been found on the bed. Nude. It looked like strangulation, black nylons found next to bed. Sexual contact unknown. They'd have to wait for the coroner's report on both.

A retired man in the next door apartment had called the fire department after he'd smelled the smoke. Yes, he had tried the door but there had been no answer. Lourdes María Monroy had had many visitors. An artist type. No, he hadn't seen anyone leave.

Pete walked into the bedroom, stopping just in the doorway to survey the room. Subdued, black lacquer, black bedspread, bathroom off to the left. Another regulation apartment bedroom. He walked to the bed, saw the dent of a head in a pillow, and a baggy containing a pair of black nylons. He searched through the rest of the evidence until he found what seemed to be a wrist- thick bundle of twigs tied together with red yarn and burned at one end.

Pete took the bag into the living room. "This sagebrush?" he asked López.

"Hell if I know. What's it smell like?"

Pete opened the bag. Dry and dusty. There was an aroma, but not like the incense he knew in the church, or on the dresser altars of old ladies.

"Get me the lab report on this?"

"Whatever you want, Pete, and seeing as how we're working together on this, what the fuck you got going on, anyway?"

"A possible repeat," he answered, thinking of what Cornelius had said.

"Likes to strangle the ladies?"

"Maybe. Likes fires. We'll keep in touch, Jack."

CHAPTER 14

Billy Johnson parked between a taco stand that was once an old gas station and a Quonset hut labeled simply, "Ray's Auto Body." He was meeting Sylvia Cruz here. It had been too easy. Yes, she was happy to grant him an interview this same afternoon, but since she was returning to the station for her first shift after her recovery, they would have to meet somewhere else instead of the station house. She had given him directions and that too had been easy. Ray's Auto Body was close to Calasan's grandfather's house in the hills of Silver Lake. He wanted a photo of her in her gear, but hadn't mentioned it. That would come later, after she knew him better. At the taco stand, he ordered a large Coke.

Waiting, he sipped the Coke. He watched as a young woman, a Latina, pulled up to the doors of the Quonset hut, jumped out and raced in. He heard an excited yell, "Ramón, *huevón*," over the sound of the traffic as a burrito, a white whale, flopped onto the formica counter. He slid off the stool and sauntered over to the auto body shop.

He entered Ray's, stopping at the doors, once he saw it: a Mercury painted deep purple. Billy smiled at Sylvia, then crossed the floor to stand close to the car.

"Can I help you?" a large Chicano with a goatee shouted from across the shop.

"Don't even breathe too close," Billy heard a young man say over his shoulder.

Billy stepped back a foot and announced, "The color on this car is a sunrise on the Gulf of Mexico. No, better, it's chiles drying in the sun. *Pasilla* chiles."

"Magenta, it's the twelve coats, man," Vinnie spoke up over his shoulder.

"Subliminal. That's art, what real art is meant to be. You are an artist."

"Talk to Ray, he's the man," Vinnie answered, shrugging as he walked off.

"What did he call you, Ramón? An arteest?" Sylvia laughed. "Watch yourself, that's my brother you're talking about."

"Are you Sylvia? I'm Bill Johnson."

Sylvia came over, her hand outstretched. "Ray, this is the guy who wants to interview me." They shook hands. Billy smiled.

"You from a newspaper?" Ray asked.

"No. I'm doing a book. You know, this car should be in a museum."

"Wait'll Paco hears that. Won't be able to whine about the bill!" Vinnie said, moving to the work bench.

"They rub it out after every coat. That's the work, hard work. I know," Sylvia said, smiling at Ray.

Billy turned to Sylvia. "You glow," he said. "You're a woman in a hard profession dominated by white males. I have to photograph you in your gear."

"Hear that Ray? I glow," Sylvia yelled.

"You do; you're the epitome of my work in progress, the courageous heart of women. The modern goddess evolved," Billy said excitedly.

Ray approached Billy. "What's going on?"

"Ramón, chill. It's just an interview," Sylvia said from Ray's side.

"I need a photo, too. How about at your station? You in your gear would be perfect." Billy smiled.

Sylvia, in spite of her independent attitude, waited for Ray's look and shrug. "Sure, the station house will be fine, but not tonight; it's my first shift back, like I told you. I'll give you the telephone number, the direct line."

"Fantastic. Thank you," Billy exclaimed. "Now, where can we talk?"

"Come on, we'll go into the office," Sylvia answered, giving Ray a wink as they passed him.

Billy sat in the chair, Sylvia on the cot. He unfolded a small notebook, took out a pencil and wrote a few words on the blank sheet. As Sylvia led him through the fire, they were the only notes he would take, but she didn't notice. He was sweating when she finished. He wanted to hug her, but he held himself back. The excitement he felt made his hands tremble. He was almost glad when she told him it was time for her to leave.

Before Sylvia left, she handed Billy a Company 12 card with the telephone number she had promised him. Billy slid the card into his pocket. Under the curved roof of the Quonset hut, Sylvia pulled Ray's goatee to give him a kiss. "See ya in twenty-four, big brother."

"Take it easy, girl," Ray answered with concern.

"Always do." She waved at Vinnie, got in her car and screeched out of the lot.

Billy remained in the open doors of the shop. Absorbed with the cars and the work, he didn't notice Calasan approaching until his friend was at his side.

"What made you pick this place to meet?" Calasan said.

"Look at this color, Calasan," Billy said coolly, ignoring the question. "You'll see that color over the bay, the dolphins leaping with joy."

"Yeah, still a dreamer," Calasan said, with a big smile as he slapped Billy on the back. Billy grinned and led him over to the table where Ray was working.

"How's it going?" Calasan said, shaking Ray's hand.

"You from around here?" Ray asked.

"Not really. My grandfather lives over off Allesandro."

"I seen you around."

"Like a small town here."

"Sometimes it is," Ray said. He turned to Billy. "Billy, right?"

"Bill Johnson. I'll catch you later."

Ray watched them leave and returned to the work bench.

CHAPTER 15

Pete left the apartment in MacArthur and drove to Ray's. He pulled up to the doors of the Quonset hut and got out quickly. He could hear a grinder going, but he couldn't see inside because of the late afternoon glare. He could smell paint, and the El Taco Loco in the old gas station next door. Two pumps with hand cranks on the side still stood in front, but someone had long ago busted out the glass over the gallon and price indicators. "Douglas Oil," it said in faded letters. For a split second, he wanted a Coke. He would have liked to shoot the breeze with Paco, the cook, take his Coke filled with ice to one of the tables and drink it slowly. He sniffed the air: *carnitas*, chile verde, hot oil. What did burning sagebrush smell like? Pete stood in the last of the sun for a moment longer and then walked into the auto body shop.

Ray was working at the bench along the back wall. Vinnie was grinding the left fender of a lowered Nissan pick-up. Pete stood a foot inside the doors of the shop, just out of the sunlight, and let his eyes recover fully. He listened for the sound of the ventilator, the whirly kind that played shadows. He heard it through the rap music that was playing, the new music that the high school kids were digging. The pick-up, which had looked dark grey when he had first entered, now took on the light grey of primer. The sparks off the fender stopped when Vinnie saw him standing there. Vinnie wagged his head. Pete raised his hand and walked between the truck and the classic Merc' over to the bench. Ray was in coveralls, and he wore a Dodgers cap. He was cleaning out the jet of a paint sprayer, on a workbench that was shiny as if it had recently been wiped, the tools laid out clean and orderly. Pete wasn't surprised; Ray had always said he wasn't a mechanic.

Ray shouted over his shoulder, "Wha's shakin', Vinnie? That fender ready to go?" He turned to look at Vinnie and saw Pete. "*Orale*, how you doing, *ese*?" he said.

"Just stopping by, homer," Pete answered.

"Vinnie, turn that shitty noise down," Ray shouted. "Fucking rap music, they don't know from R and B," he said to Pete. "I'll grab a couple of brews and we'll go into my office, detective."

Pete thought of the cold Coke he had wanted; churning, swirling Coke in a cup loaded with ice, as Ray went over to the antique chest of a cooler, the red paint faded and the Coca-Cola logo barely readable in white on the side. "So what's new?"

"Arson in MacArthur Park, young woman murdered, strangled with her own goddamn panty hose," Pete said, leaning against Ray's desk, the beer untouched at his side.

"War zone. MacArthur."

"I got the word from Bennett."

Ray sat hunched over on the edge of the bed in his office. His arms rested on his legs, the beer cradled in his hands. "Why's that?"

"The brother had a feeling."

"An apartment, in MacArthur? It was a dope deal!"

"No signs of heroin or other shit, fully stocked bar. Doesn't ring, homer."

"I don't know. Ratty fuckin' barrio."

"Sometimes it's more than that. How's Sylvia?"

"First shift back, you just missed her."

"How you dealing with it?"

"You think you could hold my sister back?"

Pete shook his head in agreement, then patted his jacket pockets.

"They're in that desk drawer," Ray said, pointing with his eyes. "I thought you stopped smoking?"

Pete shrugged, opened the desk drawer, found a pack of cigarettes, and saw the pistol. "Jesus, Ray, what the fuck you doing with your *cuete*?"

"Protection. Rough town, Angel."

"Don't shit me."

"I might have to guard my cousin."

The answer took Pete by surprise. He knew he must have looked surprised, and then he got it. Carmen. "Funny, homer, but you're not a comedian."

"You always say I need to lighten up."

"What you need to do is lock up this relic," Pete shot back, tearing open the pack of cigarettes.

Ray stared into Pete's eyes. Neither flinched. "Relax, I was cleaning it today," Ray said slowly. "I'll lock it up soon as I'm finished, but if it upsets you so much, take it."

"I don't want it, Ray. Damnit, you're too old for this shit," Pete said, tapping the cigarette rapidly on the edge of the desk.

"You haven't been gone that long," Ray replied, his eyes slowing to a half slit.

Pete reached for his beer and drank half of it down in one long swallow.

Ray looked past Pete, fixing on the calendar on the wall, the Snap-On Tool girl and then the *Virgen*. Two women and the Sacred Heart of Jesus. Sylvia calling him Ramón.

Pete heard a truck and felt the rumble as it passed the shop. Here he was dealing with family, his best friend, a loaded gun in a desk drawer, life in the barrio. What could police procedure tell him to do? The unwritten code made them strong, held them together, and kept them locked in. If you ran in the neighborhood, your neighborhood was family. It was that simple.

Vinnie knocked, Ray answered.

"There's a guy here. Looking for your sister," they heard Vinnie say clearly, and then his voice dropped, almost a whisper, "A black dude."

"Tell him I'll be right out," Ray shouted back.

Pete studied Ray, but then he dropped his stare into the open desk drawer. Ray stood up, clapped him on the shoulders, left the hand there a moment, steady and calm.

"It must be Bennett," Ray said with the same pressure of his hand.

"Came by to see Sylvia off to the station?"

"Yeah, they treat each other like a family," he shrugged. "I've got to get out there. You coming?"

"I need to make a call first."

"Help yourself," Ray said.

Pete tossed the cigarette he had pounded into a wedge after Ray had left the office. Then, he opened the folder and found the number he wanted. He tried to call Mrs. Delacorte at the Central Library, and was surprised when she answered. He looked at his watch: five-thirty. He identified himself and listened to details about books, the freezing of books, the efforts to allay the destructive powers of mold.

"In the Art Room," Pete interrupted.

"Why, that was where the fire was set. Not in the Art room, actually, but in a workroom next to it; it's called the art workroom..."

"Yes, I know. Cleaning up, did you find any incense or a bundle of sage tied with colored yarn?"

"Not that I know of," she answered sounding startled, "but I'll ask around."

Thank you," Pete said. "Would you let me know if you find anything like that?"

After he hung up, he remained seated at Ray's desk. He looked at the calendar from St. Teresa's on the wall above the desk, then smiled when he turned to the glossy Snap-on Tool calendar to its right. It wasn't like Ray, he thought. He opened the desk drawer again and pulled out the pistol. It was a .45 caliber, Army issue, heavy, recently oiled. Someone had filed a small section under the barrel. I.D. gone. The *cuete* was hot, but who would track it or care, a war pistol stolen in Vietnam. He had seen it before, shot it several times in the desert with Ray. It kicked. He held it for awhile, wondering whether he should take it. Why was he so edgy? Ray was just meticulous, cleaning it, and Ray had given his word; Pete couldn't change that now. He put the pistol back in the drawer, closed it, and got up from the desk. There was no sound of voices from the garage. Bennett had left. He wondered how much Ray knew about Bennett and Sylvia and how he felt about it. He tried to examine his own feelings. Why hadn't he gone into the garage to meet Bennett? Hadn't he trusted Cornelius enough to investigate the MacArthur Park murder? Pete thought back to the fight in the Salvadoran bar, the knife in his hand. Carmen had told him to stop enforcing borders, had reminded him that he was a police officer.

Stretching, he went over to the wash basin to wash his hands. He used hot water, hot enough to steam the mirror, scrubbing to get the smell of oil off his skin. He dried his hands with a paper towel and then used it on his face, soaking with sweat before he finally left the office. Vinnie was gone. It was quiet now, except for the hum of the coke machine and the ratcheting of the ventilator. The doors were closed. Ray was busy taping a section of the pick-up.

"Two-tone?" Pete asked.

"Yeah, cherry it out," Ray answered without looking up.

Pete watched Ray carefully attach one half of a side of the tape. He knew the other half would be for the paper. Ray made a cut with his razor knife, angled the tape in a zig-zag pattern, and then continued up to the inside rim of the bed.

"The Merc' is looking good, Ray," Pete said.

"You're the second guy today that's fallen in love."

"Chuy musta stopped by."

"Naw, it was some writer come to interview Syl. Said he wanted to put it in a museum."

"What kind of museum?"

"Art museum. Got all fired up over the color. Get this, said it was the color of chiles. *Pasilla chiles.* It was nature."

"A crazy *pendejo.*"

"Yeah, a funny white guy, almost an albino for chris'sakes. He was stroking me. All he really wanted was to take a picture of Sylvia."

"Why?"

"Put it in the book he's writing."

"Here?"

"No, at the station."

"Sylvia?"

"Yeah, with all her stuff on."

"You know this guy?"

"No, but I've seen his buddy around here. Guy named Calasan. Hey, I'll see you tomorrow at Sofía's," Ray said, leaning back into the truck.

"Thanks Ray."

"For what?"

"For letting me use your office."

"Get outta here," Ray said, not looking up from his work.

CHAPTER 16

The following morning, there was so much sun blaring through Pete's window at seven a.m., that Pete didn't hear the usual traffic. He washed down two aspirins in the shower. Still in his towel, he called the fire station. Cornelius came on after a three minute wait and told Pete to drop by, that any time was fine, unless, of course, he was out on an alarm. Pete dialed Sofía's, but he was relieved when he heard the busy tone. He didn't want Carmen to answer anyway. He picked out a double-breasted, the jacket edge hanging low, a dark shirt, red tie. He tried Carmen again, the line still busy. The kettle whistled and he rushed to turn off the gas. Poured a cup of hot water into a spoonful and a half of instant coffee. There was no milk. He remembered the couple of packets of creamer on the floor of his Trans-Am. Later, he wished he had a microwave as he drank coffee with lumps of greasy creamer. It wasn't until he had downed half the cup that he tasted the lack of sugar.

Before he left, he checked himself in the mirror, adjusting his tie, staring into his eyes the entire time. He should go by Evergreen first, but the fire station was closer. He called Evergreen and gave the sergeant a short line of b.s.

There was a crew working on the already hot asphalt at the corner of Glendale and the Aimee McPherson temple.

Echo Park Lake, off to his left, looked green in the sun. It was unusually quiet. The fountain in the middle wasn't on; the mothers hadn't arrived yet to put their kids on the swings, and the ducks weren't in their usual cruise near the lilies.

He parked on the street in front of Station Number 12 and went in to find Cornelius Bennett. He stopped at the pumper, noticing that the fender had been rubbed out and properly polished. Harrison was in his office, working. Pete walked past the office and headed up the stairs.

He found Cornelius in the dormitory. Cornelius put down the magazine he was reading.

"Caught me at my favorite chore," he said, wiping his hands on his pants before they shook.

"Can we talk here?" Pete asked.

"Have to. I can't leave until the bell goes off," Cornelius answered.

Pete didn't waste any time. "You thought of the library when you saw the murdered woman at the fire yesterday. Why?"

"Something clicked. I can't explain it, but you ever have a feeling about a place? It could be good, or it could be bad. The second I went into that room, I felt a presence, and it wasn't good."

Pete nodded his head. "Left his bundle." He waited, thinking for a moment and then asked, "Can you dig into the library fire, see if they found any sagebrush?"

"Already did. It wasn't in the report, and I spoke with the inspector, but that was one hot fire."

Pete nodded, thinking that he had been right in talking to Bennett. He asked Cornelius what he knew about arsonists. He heard jargon, a psychological profile. "You think we have a freak on our hands?" he asked.

"That's why I called you."

Pete got up to leave. The two men shook hands and Cornelius walked him to the stairs. "Thanks for your help. Let me know if you hear anything else, would you?"

"I'll keep in touch," Cornelius answered.

Pete took two steps, and then turned back. Cornelius was still standing at the top of the stairs. "Ray know about you and Sylvia?"

"What about it troubles you?" Cornelius replied.

Pete stared back. "It's none of my business. It was the wrong question."

"Still, you asked it. Now you tell me; what the hell does it matter, one way or the other?"

"It shouldn't," Pete answered, before continuing down the stairs.

Pete didn't see Harrison or Sylvia as he left the station. He got into his car and stepped on the gas, narrowly missing a pigeon, before he turned the corner and had to slam on his brakes. He was on Broadway, and Broadway was a mess. He honked his horn and edged into the column of people in the crosswalk. They walked around the nose of his Trans-Am, staring inside. A man in a black *Norteño* cowboy hat, the whole *ranchero* getup, passed by. Old women in *rebozos*, good-looking *chavalas* dressed in jeans or short skirts, women with babies and plastic shopping bags, sometimes with their men in baseball caps and long-sleeved shirts. A lot of kids; one wanted to wash his windows. Pete waved him away. An old man in a straw *sombrero* and *huaraches*, straight from the *campo*. A couple of drunks. Two tiny *Guatamaltecos*, dressed brightly in regional clothing and braided hair. Everywhere, there were shopping bags and dark hair, hats, and everyone looking, but not staring. A car with a loud-speaker pulled up alongside, the bored announcer talking and cajoling without seeming to breathe. No one noticed; the message was just part of the noise, the announcer selling, his voice of male authority. It had the proper tone, the cadence never stopping.

The light finally changed and Pete eased down Broadway, passing a *joyería*, *mariscos*, the Million Dollar Cinema playing India María and Roberto Guzmán, a *salón de belleza*, *tiendas*, more *tiendas*, and the May Company, Bank of America, the Central Market, smells of food and people and rot and gasoline. Los Angeles, he said to himself, using the Spanish pronunciation, but without *gabachos*. Why would he need to visit Mexico? A blonde passed with penciled mascara eyebrows, about forty-five, in pants too tight for her rump. María Madonna. He inched forward, and grabbed a cigarette. They were moving faster on foot than he was, hundreds, thousands, millions of them, weaving in and out, passing the yapping and waving of hawkers at each restaurant. One big sound and an overpowering smell. He puffed eagerly, angled over to the left turn lane at Seventh Street. The first block crammed with bars, *mariachi* and *Norteño* pumping out their doors, men sleeping against walls despite the constant .rush of the crowd. He found himself smiling. *"Madre,"* he muttered, throwing the finished cigarette out the window and lighting another. The hookers on the corners began and still the families, passing them by, eyes straight, always straight ahead. He neared the Greyhound Bus Depot, more people spilling out of its doors. Now he was in the territory of the homeless, box after box lined up on the street. He saw one bag lady with a shopping cart, and then another, but mostly he saw men, black men. Two patrol cars rolled by as he passed the bus depot and neared the train tracks, the area, all industrial space and art lofts now—complete with the color change to white homeless everywhere, a guy in Jesus robes speaking from the corner in front of a trendy restaurant. Everyone in their barrios, he thought. Los Angeles.

Once he'd crossed over the bridge and into East L.A., he felt more relaxed, but he didn't realize it until he switched on the radio. He could have come another way. A freeway would have been faster; a freeway would have cut over the cultural lines. In East Los, the freeways were everywhere, high off the ground yet spilling into every backyard, peering over every fence like a nosy stranger. He headed under the Interchange of the Santa Ana and Five Freeways over Seventh Street, reading walls as he drove by. "Chuy, Danny Boy, Sloopy got down here." "Flaco, Wiley, Big Ben, Droopy, Loverboy, Angel marched on Terrace 13." He saw the X's and the comebacks. "Seventh Street Underpass," appeared everywhere. Cruising the streets slowly, he spotted two kids on bikes. They stared at him defiantly. One, about ten years old, flicked his fingers off his teeth at him. *Chamacos*, just checking him out. He stopped his car in the street and got out, waving them over.

They circled on their bikes a safe distance from the car.

"You like baseball, the Dodgers?" He saw them look at one another.

"I got two tickets; you want them?" It was a game he'd been looking forward to, the Reds and the Dodgers.

They didn't stop circling.

"I got two tickets I can't use. You want to take them?"

The boy who had flicked his teeth slowed his bike and pedaled over, signalling his friend to keep his distance. "Whatta you want?"

"I don't want nothing from you bad dudes except for you to have fun at the game." He held out the tickets. "Take 'em. I can't make it that night. They're good seats."

The boy swung by and snatched the tickets out of Pete's hand. After he had circled away, he looked at them and nodded to his friend.

"I got a wrestling class. We work out at Evergreen," Pete said, getting into his car.

"You're a *chota*."

"Yes, I am."

"We don't like *perros*."

"No uniforms when we wrestle. What we need is some *bad* wrestlers, guys who can tough it out." Pete started up the car and waited. They weren't circling anymore, they had finally stopped.

"Wednesday night at six-thirty. I'll be looking for you. Ask for me, Pete Escobedo." He U-turned back to Seventh, heading once again for Evergreen Station, wondering what he'd just done. Those were two good seats, but what the hell did it matter, one way or the other.

CHAPTER 17

Tony Hernández looked tight. He came out of his chair as Pete threaded his way through the busy squad room. "Hey, what's going down, bro? The old man has had a rage-on all morning. Bulldog up his crinkly with your name on it," Tony said.

Pete moved Tony out of his way in order to get at the desk. "What's this noise?" he asked, not looking at Tony, but concentrating on the stack of files on the desk.

"More work, of course. It's been a busy morning. Now, you want to tell me what you stepped in, Pete?"

Pete didn't answer him.

"Mother humper, he's lighting the stogie."

"He's nervous, has an oral fixation," Pete said.

"He's gonna oral you, *pendejo*. You shouldn't have busted up that *Salvatrucha* bar. What's the matter with you?"

"A little fight was all it was," Pete answered, not wondering how Tony knew.

"It's more than that, isn't it? The *chingón* doesn't work himself into a rage over head-butting."

"Who the hell cares," Pete said, leaving Tony's worried face and walking towards the Captain's office. He hadn't walked more than ten feet before the Captain's splendid voice rang out through the squad room.

"Escohbeado, get your sorry ass in my office right now."

"On my way, Cap'," he answered, looking the *chingón* in the eye as he entered the office, headed for the closest chair, and sat in it. If he were ever going to sit in that office, it might as well be while he got a haircut, a righteous ass chewing.

"What the hell you doing over in Rampart?" the fat old boy started right in on him.

"Victim killed in an apartment. I think there might be a link with the library fire," Pete answered without hesitation. The question wasn't a surprise. He had known all along that he'd get called in for crossing the line into MacArthur Park.

"The library fire? For chris'sakes! Did I tell you, or didn't I tell you that case is nothing more to you than hand jive. There's a special unit assigned and your name isn't on it. Do you hear me? Am I getting through?"

Pete didn't answer because he knew it wasn't really a question.

"I'll ship you to Pacoima. You ever been to Pacoima, Escahbeado? Those bangers don't know you from Nancy Reagan in Pacoima. You realize that, airmahno? Am I getting through, Escahbeado?"

Pete sat in the chair, letting his fingertips rest lightly on the tops of his thighs. He stared straight ahead like he'd seen on Broadway, eyes so straight that the clock and the plaques on the wall in front of him were only shapes, nothing more. Carmen came to mind. Could he patch things up with her tonight?

"I take a project like you, work myself like a goddamn peon to help you out, and what do you do? You defy my goddamn orders. Look it here, look it."

Pete turned his eyes to the Captain. The cigar jerked like a cat's tail as the Captain pounded the top of his desk.

"These are goddamn applications from every coach and high school principal in your goddamn bare-ee-o. *Pachucos*, like you, that want to get in, and I just might have room for one of them. Am I getting through, Escohbeado?"

Pachuco. When are these old boys gonna get with it, he thought. The old boys were so far back they were about to be lapped, twice.

"I catch one more word that you're sniffing around Rampart, or the fire station, or anything to do with that goddamn library and you're outta here. Am I getting through?"

Pete nodded his head.

"That's good, Escohbeado; that's real good. I'd say you were never on arson detail. Do you hear me?" The Captain sat down and immediately began to push paper. He wasn't waiting for a reply.

Pete stood up, but he didn't move except to rest his fingertips on the desk. He waited. He was calm while he waited for the *chingón* to look up, but the Captain didn't look up, he just grunted out, "What's your problem?"

Pete wanted to tell him about the coincidence, a possible freak, but he let the moment pass, saying only, "Is that all, Cap?"

The *chingón* shot his head up and pulled his stogie from between his teeth for the first time. He used the cigar like one would use a finger in the chest. "Get outta here before I get upset," he said, staring at Pete with such slitted eyes that Pete could feel them on his back long after he'd said "Right, Cap," and closed the door.

In the squad room, it was as if he had entered a cavity, a cave, or had stepped onto the mat at a wrestling competition. The haunting silence, the sensation of his own beating heart, and then the realization that all attention was focused upon him. It only lasted a moment, but in that moment he could look into all their faces and remember, just as he'd entered into the eyes of his wrestling opponent. After that split second, the squad room returned to its normal level of activity, so that he was ignored on the way to his desk.

"Holy sweet Sister Angelina. Sit down. You need a cushion?" Tony asked under his breath, giving the squad room a hostile look.

Pete sat down.

"That was some kidney pounding. My old lady couldn't even come close. If you need to chill, I got a little baggy in my *carrucho* that I pinched off a banger. You're welcome to it, dude, rolling papers right here."

Tony's forehead wrinkled up and his chubby cheeks jiggled. Concern sprayed all over him.

"No thanks, I trimmed out on the *chingón*," Pete answered.

"Oh yeah, you gotta go into Buddha land, but don't tell me you wouldn't like to march on that fat fuck in some dark alley?"

Pete chuckled. Some of the bulls looked over at them, but then quickly turned away. Tony was too uptight to laugh, rearranging his glasses over and over as he muttered a few choice words under his breath.

"I need the desk, Tony."

"Yeah, sure," Tony answered, "I'll use Frank's."

"And take this load with you," Pete said, handing him the stack of new files.

After Tony had cleared out, Pete went into the top drawer for the library file. He called Betty in Records to punch up arsons referenced to murder by strangulation in the computer.

"How far back?" Betty replied with a dry snap.

"Last six months."

"How wide?"

He heard her inhale, smoking a cigarette. "County, Southern Cal, and State."

"You've got some nerve."

"I'll bring you a sweet roll."

"Thanks anyway, but I already got two on my hips. Call back in twenty, but I can't promise anything."

He hung up and called Jack López.

"What have you heard, Jackson?"

"I heard the surf's up. Six feet and clean. Grab your board and we'll catch a few."

"Can you even swim?"

"What I hear, you can't even tread water; your bunghole is far from watertight."

"Help me out, Jack."

"That's a fine whine you bottle at Evergreen."

"I owe you!" Pete heard a sigh.

"It's a confirmed strangulation. No penetration but the monkey shot two loads on her naked body and the sheets, about an hour apart, then he lit the place up."

"The prints?"

"The Captain didn't beat you up enough, did he? Let me tell you, there are a mountain of prints. A popular lady. We're running priors as we speak."

"Did they powder the bathroom?"

"What the fuck? Hold on a sec. Here we go, let me see. No. No prints taken in bathroom."

"Do the bathroom, this type likes to stay clean."

"What type?"

"Firebugs. They're orderly. Anal. It's in their profile."

"I'll get on it bro'," López said sarcastically. "I suppose you want to know what we dig up?"

"How far you want me to bend over?"

"You're far enough, *puto*."

"Thanks sweetie." Bun buddies, that's what Jack called him, and that's what they were. Pete owed him big time. He dialed up Betty.

"Thirty-two arsons in the last six months, two attempted murders. Father set his son afire with lighter fluid; the boy lived. Heroin addict beat near death with a shoe."

"That's it?"

"How about the guy who killed his goats in Topanga Canyon; then burned down the barn?"

"Did he strangle them?"

"No, he shot them. Look, I'm faxing you a copy of this report and the list of all strangulation victims in the last six months. Knock yourself out, Escobedo."

She hung up before he could thank her. He went to the fax machine and found a stack addressed to him. Six cases, not as long as he had expected, but she had included the files. He knocked the pages into order and began to read.

An hour later, Pete had narrowed it down to two cases. The first was in Malibu, a high school girl done on the beach at Zuma. Lifeguard found her under a guard tower at seven a.m. Popular student, under questioning a mile long, a fire in the sand. Still, he put it aside. The other was an older woman in Encinitas, another beach town. Found strangled with a garden hose. He wondered how anyone could be strangled with a hose, but what caught his eye was the barbecue—someone had burned papers and pieces of art.

"It's a sleepy town," the Encinitas Sergeant said.

"You had a choker recently."

"Yeah, a week ago."

"Nailed it down?"

"Nothing yet."

"Old woman?" Pete asked.

"Sweet old lady, political activist," the sergeant said dutifully. "Strangled with a garden hose."

"Tell me about the fire?"

"We found a few paintings charred in a barbecue pit, but the old broad was crazy as a loon."

"Any semen tracks?"

There was a long pause and then, "She was an old lady. I mean old. Tell you the truth, I don't think we looked."

Pete asked that the coroner's report be sent up and signed off. He read "sagebrush incense," and "Encinitas." New Age, Bennett had said. Arty. He could go around the shops and ask. Good luck, he thought. He pulled out a map of the state and located Encinitas, a beach community north of San Diego.

When Pete pulled up at El Patio over an hour later, he was surprised to see Tony's black Camaro. Pete had stopped at the Central Library after leaving the station. He hadn't known why he wanted to go there, maybe just to feel the place. Mrs. Delacorte, the head librarian, had shown him around.

"You can see the beauty. This building was an eccentric combination of styles, but where else would it be more appropriate than here, in our city? A grand repository of culture and literature almost destroyed," she had said.

Of course he had listened, but it was what he saw that affected him: mosaics, the charred and rotting smells, a pyramid in the center ceiling, the goddess at the entrance, books in crates. He had come to look for clues, an understanding of the man he was searching for, but saw only destruction, charring of culture.

Instead of answers, he had felt more confused. Seeing Tony's car made him focus on present time. He knew that he had to go to Encinitas. As he entered the familiar dark room he remembered dinner at Sofía's. Carmen. She was leaving in another day or two. What was he going to say?

He slid onto the stool next to Tony, in front of a ready, sweating bottle. Tony had the cocktail napkin spread out, hunching over the caricatures. Pete thought of Carmen again, her lovely neck and ears, the way she moved. Carmen at Stanford. Carmen coming to the neighborhood for visits twice a year. Carmen with some dentist or lawyer, naming their kids Luke, Trevor, Heather or Billy.

"Jesus, Sal, when are you going to change these sad napkins?" he heard Tony ask.

"When I run out. SOS, same old ca-ca, you know the procedure," Sal answered.

Tony laughed and nudged Pete in the elbow. "Sal thinks we're still in Mexico. Where they make these, Guadalajara?" he said, talking loudly.

"Hell, no. They print those in Monterey Park. Probably supply every bar in the Day Efe," Sal answered.

"East Los supplying Mexico City with Mexican humor," Tony said. "Too much."

Pete finished his bottle, thought of the library and ordered another round.

"Take 'er easy, *compa*," Tony said, "I hardly wet my whistle."

Pete cleaned the condensation off his bottle before getting into it. He told Tony about the apartment fire, throwing in what he'd just discovered in Encinitas, but he didn't mention stopping off at the Library. He waited while Tony analyzed the information, twirling his bottle on the bar top.

"So you want to cruise this town looking for sagebrush?" Tony asked. "It's rush hour."

"Not tonight, I'm having dinner with Ray at his *tía's* place."

"Oh! yeah. Hey, say hello for me. Tony from Frogtown."

"You haven't lived in Frogtown for years," Pete said with a grin. Frogtown is a strip of working class homes between Riverside Drive and the L.A. River, close enough to Echo Park to have caused an intense rivalry.

"So, what does that matter?" Tony asked.

"You know Ray doesn't care about that, anymore."

"Neither do I, but I knew Ray since he was one bad dude."

"Yeah, and now that's ancient history." Pete finished his beer and wrote down Carmen's telephone number in the corner of a bar napkin. "If you hear anything more, anyone has to reach me on that arson, call me at this number."

"It's your neck, *ese*. I'll cover you best I can," Tony answered, and they shook hands, barrio style.

Pete left El Patio and headed down Sunset, turning right on Echo Park Boulevard toward the Ravine. He parked in front of Sofía's and got out, straightening his tie and praying that he wasn't in for another hard time. There wasn't anyone in the front room, so instead of knocking, he went around to the backyard. She was there, in the garden, working in the tomatoes. Carmen in shorts and a halter top, white cotton gloves and no sun hat.

CHAPTER 18

Pete stood in the shade of the house built on a high foundation. Mud was splattered on the sides from heavy watering. It wasn't dark mud, but sandstone colored, the sandstone red of the neighborhood on the narrow clapboards, with paint thick and heavy, filling in the lapping edges like he'd seen on old-fashioned rowboats, the mud splatters like the splash of waves. He pushed at a green avocado with his foot. There were five of them in the driveway, resting in the cracks and valleys created by the bulging roots of the tree whose leaves reached the house and dwarfed the garage. The avocado rolled into a depression. It didn't start to wobble until it had gained speed, and then it twisted and made several revolutions before it stopped, the fat end pointing down into the crack of concrete. It was dark green, not yet purple, smooth and small and hard. He could tell when he bumped it with his toe. Sofía would save it, and place it in the basket covered with a clean white dishtowel on the shelf over the washing machine where it would sit with the others, like so many green eggs brooding over the Sears Kenmore.

Carmen was on her knees working at the ground with a hand spade. He could see her arms and shoulders glistening in the yellow light of Los Angeles. She worked hard, moving quickly, intent on the ground. He could smell the manure as she turned the soil, soil that was dark, that smelled sweet and rotting. She should wear a hat, he thought, as he watched her brush away hair that fell along her cheek and stuck there.

"Hey, Carmen," he called out, trying to sound cheerful as he left the shadow of the house.

She flicked her eyes up at him and then went back to work. "Here a little early, aren't you?"

"Am I?" he asked. She continued working in the tomato bed. "You should wear a sun hat," he said finally, after he had studied the fence behind her, overgrown with some creeping vine so that he could only see wood occasionally. It was still a fence that marked the property lines, although the way the fence leaned, the vine was probably holding it up. He imagined that the posts dug into the earth thirty or forty years ago had since loosened, becoming a home for worms and cinch bugs. He heard a child's voice, and then the mother from another yard. It startled him when Carmen spoke, slightly hidden because she'd moved to the next plant.

"The sun feels good, Pete. I don't mind it at all." She brushed at hair that had fallen against her lips.

He moved so that he could see her better. She looked good. "Yeah, but you know you could get cancer, sun cancer. There's a lot of strong rays from the sun. I read all about it in an article. It was in *The Times*." He wanted a cigarette while he talked to her, but he didn't want to light up in the sunlight. He didn't like to smoke in the sunlight.

"Skin cancer mainly affects fair-skinned people, Pete. Don't you think I'm dark enough? You don't think I'm too white, do you?"

"No, I don't think you're too white," he answered with a wide-handed gesture. "You could never be too white. It's just that the radiation affects everyone." He felt better now. They were talking.

"So you think I'm dark enough?" she asked.

"Yeah, I guess you're plenty dark. Maybe I shouldn't have been so worried."

"Plenty dark? *Negra?*"

"No, you're not *negra*. You're just dark enough. Like *café con leche*," he answered, wishing they were talking inside the house or in the shade because he was getting hot under the sun.

"Just dark enough, but you wouldn't want me to get a little burn, would you? You wouldn't want me to get any darker, would you?"

He didn't say a word for about a minute and Carmen didn't move. She was on her hands and knees, the garden trowel stuck in the dark soil. A few errant hairs had stuck to one side of her face, but she didn't move to brush them back, and she didn't take her eyes off him. Finally, he felt his mouth arrange itself. "I came by to tell you I can't make dinner tonight. I wanted..."

"Have something better going on," she said cutting him off. "A *güera*? A white girl from Silver Lake?"

He felt his feet planted firmly in place. He was aware that he couldn't tell them to move. It was like the time when he had shoved the fork into a electrical plug and couldn't let go. His *mamá* had screamed and knocked him away, then scooped him up, hugging and kissing him. A minute later she had spanked him. *Papá* had said that he didn't need any more beatings; he wouldn't do that again unless he was *menso*. He was still cautious around plugs. Finally, he stepped back a foot. "You know, I almost remember when I once liked you."

"You mean, when I was impressed with you? That was when I was a nice kid with skinny knees. Remember how I used to bang up my knees all the time? You said I was never going to find a boyfriend if I didn't stop banging up my knees."

She rubbed at the hair stuck on her cheek, pushing it back towards an ear pierced with one tiny pearl.

Pete looked at the vines on the lopsided fence, and then at her. "You fell down so much because you were clumsy and wanted attention."

"What?"

He grinned.

"I never wanted that kind of attention," she said angrily.

"You wanted me to play doctor, to touch your legs and make sure you were alright."

Carmen jumped to her feet and came at him. "*Cochino*, I was ten years old."

"I know. Just a kid, and a *mocosa*."

"Don't you ever call me a snot-nosed brat," Carmen said while swinging at him with the garden spade. He started to laugh. It was the first time he had really laughed all day. When she kicked him in the shins, he turned away. Doubled over to protect himself, he thought he might get sick, his sides hurt so much from his belly-laughing. She punched him on the back and called him a macho pig, and a *viejo raboverde*, an epithet which was usually reserved for old men who chased young girls. He turned to her, protecting his head, and grabbed her around the waist, swinging her as she hit him.

"Let go of me, *pendejo*," she screamed in his ear, trying to push his head out of her chest where it was firmly placed. She hit him hard with her fist in the kidney, causing him to grunt and twist so that he felt his balance give way, and even though she tried to shove away, he held on firmly and they landed in a tangled heap on the lawn.

"I hate you," she yelled at him. "I hate you."

He rolled over on top of her in the hot prickly grass, close enough to smell the tomato plants and the soil of the garden. Carmen tried to hump him off, but he was quick. He hadn't wrestled under Coachy's direction for nothing. He moved up quickly and sat on her stomach, pinning her arms above her head. She was sputtering, but she continued to hump her groin in an attempt to throw him. He took one hand away, holding down her wrists with his right and found a twig. He stuck it in his mouth, and replaced his left hand on her wrists.

"Pete," she screamed, "let me up."

He bent his head over until he could gently touch the twig against her neck. Then he started to tickle her with the twig. She slashed at it with her head and he went for her exposed right armpit.

"Stop it right now," she screamed, wiggling as hard as she could. He saw that her eyes were dark and hot and wide, and he almost dropped the twig because he wanted to laugh. He tickled her other side and she started to giggle.

"Damn you, stop that," she shouted, but he was getting good now, remembering all the moves, the twig torture. If she wiggled too hard when the twig was under her arm he would get her neck, or sometimes her ears, but she was laughing now, between screams, and he was ready to drop the twig and kiss her neck, her ears, and her lips; what he'd wanted to do all along, since he had seen her bent over the tomatoes when he was still hidden in the shadow of the avocado tree. He dropped the twig and bent down. Her giggling didn't stop, but her lips opened as he dropped slowly, getting closer. Suddenly, she twisted, throwing him off as they heard the shout, "Carmen? Angel?"

Sofía stood on the porch, staring at them with a mouth open wide enough to accept one of her green avocados. Pete tried to speak, but Carmen, standing behind him, was pulling back on his ears with such force that his eyes watered and only a grunt came out.

"*Mamá*, you let this two-timer sneak past your window and attack me."

"I'll file a complaint with the *chotas*, *m'ija*," Sofía responded. "What do you say in your defense, blondie boy?" Carmen said, forcing his head back even farther.

"Gah, gah, gah."

"You're worthless, what about her?" she asked, giving him a kick as she released him. Sofía roared with laughter, and when Pete finally heard the screen door slam, he tried to reach out and grab Carmen's leg, but she was too nimble, leaping from his lunge. He tried again and again until, resting on his knees, breathing hard, she came to him.

"I don't know if it will make any difference, but I stopped seeing her because of you."

Holding his head in her fine fingers, she leaned over as if to let him drag his thirsty lips over hers, but instead, she only whispered, "You stink like a frog pond. You need a shower." And then, when he thought he hadn't a chance, she surprised him, bending down to greedily suck his heart onto the tip of his tongue.

She dragged him by the hand, and he followed her, stumbling into the house, through the kitchen, past Sofía cleaning a chicken in the sink. He heard Carmen say, "*Mamá*, this man needs a shower."

"Leave him outside and I'll hit him with the hose," she shouted back.

Pete stumbled in the hallway, like after he'd just finished a reckless ride on his bicycle down a hill no one had ever attempted before. He stopped abruptly, causing Carmen to pull up, wanting to look at her, but she yanked on his arm and pushed him into her room.

It was a bright room, covered with posters and art work and lacy stuff on the windows. Carmen closed the door, smiled, and pulled her halter top off with both hands. It was a room decorated by a seventeen-year-old girl and then forgotten. She came towards him, and he could see bits of grass stuck to her chest and belly. Grass that had worked itself up onto her brown breasts, and the dark nipples that contrasted with the lace over the windows. He would have liked to let his eyes feast, but then she was on him, rolling him onto the narrow bed covered with a frilly white spread, pushing at his coat and then his shirt, kicking at his pants as she slid out of her shorts, while he tried with his lips and his tongue to clean the grass that stuck to her.

"What about your *mamá*?" he stuttered.

She pulled his head up until their eyes met and she kissed him, sucking on his lower lip as he entered her so he couldn't speak, and then she went at his neck and his chest, using his skin to absorb her own desire as she pulled him in deeper and felt him grow tight and smooth until it was he who had to clamp a hand over her mouth.

After they had both showered, he listened to her as she spoke of her studies. She was going to be a doctor. He would come up and visit at least once a month and she would come down once a month. "The city is wonderful," she assured him. He wagged his head. He still had the towel wrapped around his waist, while she was carelessly naked, lying against him with wet hair that she wrung out once on his shoulder.

"Are you sure you can fly down here once a month? Can you leave your studies that often?" he asked her, watching the shadows begin in her room.

"Of course I can. For research. Humping *cholos*," she laughed, slugging him in the arm.

He smiled and kissed her belly, tonguing her belly button. "Did I say that?"

"You bellowed like an old rooster." She punched him in the stomach this time.

She was as strong-minded as her *mamá*, which pleased him and worried him at the same time. The worries came along with his hard-on. A strong woman, educated, and he knew her family too well, but still the towel rose.

"You'd better get the time off," she said seriously.

"Anything for you," he said, bending over to suck one of her nipples, pulling it into his mouth, wondering if they should chance it again in her room, with Sofía in the kitchen banging pots.

"Don't sugar me. I'm not some little *mamacita*. Uhmm, tell me why couldn't you come up at least once a month?"

He let go of her nipple with a pop. "I didn't say I couldn't come."

"I'll say," she said, laughing as she went under the towels with her hand and shrieked, "Look what I have here. My own pet iguana."

He turned to her and then there was the knock at the door and Sofía calling out, "My God, it's dinnertime, you two. I hope there hasn't been a scandal in my own house. *Madre mía*, what would the *abuelito* say?"

Pete was in his shorts and grabbing his pants before they could hear her heels clacking on back to the kitchen, a loud laugh and her voice calling out to someone at the front door.

Pete came out first, saw that the kitchen was empty, and entered the living room, hoping that he wouldn't find Uncle Pete. He relaxed when he saw that Carmen's father wasn't at home, but then tensed up when he found Ray and Cecilia sitting on the couch. Sofía wagged her finger at him and tried to act serious. "Her *papá*'s buying a shotgun from Alfredo, right this instant." Pete touched his tie and brushed his moustache. At least, Ray was serious, and then, Cecilia started to laugh.

"What's goin' on?" Ray asked.

"Nothing, *m'ijo*," Sofía answered, looking over at Cecilia which made her grin.

"How's it, homer?" Pete asked, shrugging his head.

"Not bad. Wha's shaking with you?" Ray answered.

"*Tranquilo, ese, tranquilo*," Pete said before turning as Carmen came out in a colorful dress with flowers and open shoulders. Ray stood up and turned to say hello.

Carmen gave Ray a hug and a kiss. "Glad you could make it." She motioned to Sofía and Cecilia with her hands, finally helping Sofía off the couch. "*Mamá*, Ceci, would you help me in the kitchen, right this minute." Carmen guided them from behind, between the men. They heard her as she went through the swinging door into the kitchen, "*Mamá*, you're a monster," and then watched the door swing shut on laughter.

Ray hadn't moved. He was still standing next to the couch and the coffee table. He leaned over, retrieved a sweating bottle of beer, took a long pull and asked Pete, "What the hell's goin' on, Angel?"

"Search me," Pete answered, shrugging his shoulders.

"They're like school girls, and my *tía's* the worst."

"They act crazy sometimes."

"I don't know what sets them off," Ray said, motioning toward the kitchen door. "That's why I go to work every day. Can you imagine dealing with this kind of *locura*? And they see each other all the time. Sometimes I like to work on Saturdays just to get away from it."

"What a burden, you and that sander. I can see it must really bother you, itching to get it on," Pete ribbed him.

Ray shot him a look, took a pull on his beer, and said, "Oh yeah, you say it now. Wait until you have to put up with it. Listen to my wife; she's gonna split her dress. What kind of example is that?"

A pot clattered on the kitchen floor.

"Should we offer them help?"

"Why, you starved?" Ray asked slyly.

"Yeah, I could chew through the chrome on your Chevy about now."

"Now I know what they're laughing about."

"You don't know a damn thing about women," Pete said.

"They're laughing at you, *vato.*"

"At me?" Pete's voice rose as he turned and looked at the door.

"Yeah, at you. Who else would they find more comical? Not me, I'm only funny when I screw up," Ray answered, smiling and tipping his can at Pete.

"You? Screw up?"

"You better believe it and be happy about it, because it's when they stop laughing at you is when you got problems, man." Ray smiled at him and shook his head.

"That's what it is? They like it when you make a fool of yourself?"

"That's what it is."

They sat there quietly for a few minutes until Cecilia came out with two more beers, a smile for Pete, and a kiss for Ray. "Dinner's in five minutes," she told them, kissing Ray once more.

Ray winked at Pete.

Pete watched Ceci leave. "You ever hear of some place called Encinitas, near San Diego?" he asked Ray.

"Yeah, they do a lot of flowers down there. I was stationed next door in Oceanside. Nice town. Why?"

"I've got a murder in Encinitas to check on."

"When are you leaving?"

"Soon as I get some free time. Captain threw me off the case."

"Why's that?"

"I crossed some lines when I went into MacArthur. The library is officially an arson and I'm wasting time."

"What does Harrison say?"

"He hasn't. Most likely, he'll play it by the rules. I'm out of his picture."

"And Encinitas?" Ray paused. "If you're running on the sly, you'll need all the help you can get."

"Could be," Pete answered, thinking it was as much of a commendation as Ray would give. But Pete had already thought about it, knew he and Harrison might have to work together. Still he'd wait; even though he trusted him, it would have to be the right time or else he wouldn't like it.

"How's Sylvia?" Pete asked.

"Busy. She called, said it was like old times except for her photo session."

"The guy who came in your shop?"

"He's gonna shoot her after her shift is over. He's an artist, works only on women, but loves cars," Ray said with a grin.

The dinner began seriously enough, the women were quiet, subdued, but it didn't last long. It was Sofía who blasted the calmness from the table. "So tell us, Pete," she said, dishing out *arroz con pollo*, "this cure for sun cancer, did you really read about it in *The Times*?"

"Yeah, it was in the paper, a couple of weeks ago," Pete answered, looking at Carmen who whispered, "*Mamá*," as she smiled at him. Then Ray innocently asked, "What's the cure, Angel?"

Cecilia had to drink a half glass of water while Sofía pounded at her back to stop her from choking. Carmen called it the grass cure, and when Pete looked at Ray and smiled weakly, Ray started to laugh. Pete could only shake his head at the women who made this family so damn crazy.

After dinner, Pete followed Carmen into the back yard. He watched her move the garden hose across the tomato plants. Neither said anything, Carmen working her way gently between the rows. It was enough to see her in the yellow light from the porch, at times dwarfed by the full plants.

"I have to leave the day after tomorrow." Carmen told him as she was shutting off the faucet.

Pete didn't want to think of her leaving when she came to his arms. He wanted to stay with her as long as possible.

"I'll take you to the airport."

"I always go with Sylvia. But, maybe this time, I can make a change.

"It's too soon, baby," he said, kissing her.

She held him tight. He heard a phone in the house ringing, a shout, and they both turned as Ceci banged open the back door screen.

"There's been another fire at the library. Let's go. Sylvia's there."

CHAPTER 19

Harrison was on the squawk box as the team came out of the library, Sylvia leading the way.

"Is this the way you treat my return?" Sylvia yelled at the guys filing in as she dropped her pack and began to pull hose.

"Drop that hose and let's go to a bar. I'll celebrate your return."

"There's the Biltmore. You wouldn't be worn out and cheap, too?" Sylvia answered Red with a grin.

"They don't have Miller Lite. Red wouldn't know what to do with his 'self," Bennett said.

"Don't be talking trash around our girl, scrub. She won't be covering your ass next time we have to come back here."

"I don't ever want to see this library again," Sylvia said.

"Damn shame and a waste of our time."

"You reliving past glory?" Red asked Cornelius.

"There wasn't much left to burn, the books gone," Cornelius said somberly.

"A freak making a statement," Sylvia shot back.

"You're not sensitive enough, Cruz. He came from a home with no love; daddy was strict, mommy was working; they expected good grades. He's angry at society," Red said tiredly.

"Yeah, and let's roll up and get outta here," Sylvia demanded. Coming back to the station had been better than wonderful, she thought. Just touching familiar wood and metal, the sound her locker made as it shut, the feel of her turn-out boots and jacket had given her a buzz all day. She'd had to catch herself several times, almost choking up with the fullness of it, like when the guys, working overtime to keep their usual sarcastic edge, had laid out a cake they'd baked at dinner. It had taken her more than a moment to make the speech they demanded, pounding the table with their fists, clinking glasses with spoons and knives. She had fought it back, the clutching sob right there, pounding so hard behind her eyes she had to step on her left foot to grind it away. Then, she had given them a mouthful before cutting up the cake. But this, coming back to the library, wasn't supposed to be in the cards, not on her first day back. Again, she found herself breathing hard, but the earlier delirium had been replaced. It was anger she was fighting, and worse, hatred.

"Let's party," Red shouted as Sylvia threw herself into the job of laying hose in the bed of the pumper.

Harrison walked over as they were finishing up. "How you feeling?" he asked Sylvia.

"Fine physically, but returning here makes me sick."

Harrison shrugged. "It's ugly. The good news is that there are no injuries."

"Arson?" Harrison heard over his shoulder. He turned and recognized Pete. Ray, Cecilia and Carmen, rushed by him to talk with Sylvia.

"Detective Escobedo. You knew that first fire was an arson without me telling you. I might've called you on this one but your Captain got to me first. You shouldn't be here."

Pete brushed Harrison's comment aside. "You know about the MacArthur Park fire. I'd like to know if there's similarities."

"Apartment fire in MacArthur, woman strangled. That's a reach, Detective. Profile says this one wants a big show; you know, get all the trucks out here, the media," Harrison answered.

"Excuse me, don't mean to butt in." Pete and Harrison turned to stare at Bennett, Sylvia next to him. "The fires aren't related in complexity, but I believe there may be a connection. Location is close; there is a profile that shows an arsonist that looks for human damage as well as property; and this may sound like I'm reaching, but I believe the man has a cultural itch. First fire here was started in the Art section; the woman murdered was an artist; this fire was started in the Early California History section."

"What's that have to do with Art?" Harrison asked.

Pete jumped in, "There wasn't anything left to burn anyway, but if I remember correctly, there was a mural..."

"It circled the room," Sylvia spoke up. "Our cultural history with loads of landscape, chaparral and sagebrush."

"You mind if I take a look inside?" Pete asked.

"I can't give you permission to do that," Harrison snapped back. "Bennett, I've got to wander over to headquarters. I counted an axe missing. Do what you can to find it. Find me in an hour; you can ride back with me." He didn't wait to receive an answer, and he didn't look at Pete or Sylvia. He just turned and walked away, crossing the street to the Biltmore Hotel.

Pete watched him for a moment, and then turned to Sylvia. "What about you?"

"Looks like he made it perfectly clear I'm not part of your show."

"Two men searching for an axe might be too much," Cornelius said.

"I see one man, who's the other?" Sylvia snorted.

"Are you calling me a boy, 'cause I be fetching for the man?"

Pete cleared his throat.

"Take'er easy, Pete," Sylvia said. Clutching Cornelius by the arm, she pulled him aside, whispering, "I'll be the one fetching. I want the real welcome back."

"Tonight?"

"I'll wait for you at the station." They both knew the search might continue past their shift.

"Sounds too good to be true."

"Yeah, well you better produce."

"*Señorita* Cruz!"

"The library, Romeo. Concentrate on what's at hand."

"I am."

"Yeah, me too." She took his hand and rubbed it hard for a moment. "I'll see you in a couple of hours."

"I'm looking forward to it already."

Cornelius waved to Ray and Cecilia as Sylvia went over to them. He watched Sylvia take her place in the pumper. He waved once more, and then he rejoined Pete.

"We need to bring an axe with us?" Pete asked.

"Don't see why we should. It would make Red nervous. He's already put them away."

They entered the Early California History Section, the only area lit up with high powered lamps on tripods. There were departmental types with notebooks; one looked their way and then returned just as quickly to his notes.

"This is it; we only have an hour," Cornelius muttered.

They started together, but split up gradually as they focused on their own areas. Pete was looking for the bundle of sagebrush, a stem, seeds. It was like searching for marijuana, only everything was charred and this wasn't a one bedroom apartment. Time was running out; he was ready to pack it in when he heard a low whistle and his name called softly.

"Over here." Cornelius pointed his light above the door they had entered in. There, in the thick doorjamb, lay what looked like a small bundle of twigs tied together with red yarn.

"Odd place to put it," Pete said.

"Like he wanted us to find it on our way out," Cornelius answered.

They alerted the investigation team, stood aside as it was bagged for evidence purposes.

"That start the fire?"

"No way. Man used barbecue starter or something with a low flash point. Get that broom and we'll sweep this cleaner."

Pete saw nothing but hardwood floor.

"You have to see this from an angle. I caught it out of the corner of my eye when I found the sage bundle."

Pete looked and saw the scratches made from dragged furniture, footprints, scuff marks, the grain of the oak.

"Here, follow my broom handle."

Pete followed the tracing handle, saw a faint stain.

"It burned here. He set the fire in the middle, where you see the desks and chairs in a pile, but he tried to light it over here."

Pete looked at the mess in the middle of the room, saw the trail coming back to them. "Like a kid pissing his name in the snow."

"That's it. Can you read it?"

"I got some of it. The Bro. What do you see?"

"The Brotherhood of Dolphins," Cornelius said, tracing the line so that Pete could read it.

"What's that mean to you?"

"Literary reference? A terrorist group?"

"No, he believes he's an artist. A loner. He murdered the woman in MacArthur Park by himself. He set it up, framed it," Pete said as if he were building up his case mentally. Then, he told Cornelius about the Encinitas murder and fire.

"Did they find sagebrush?" Bennett asked.

"Didn't look for it. But I'll find it. I have a feeling," Pete said.

"I know how that works. And you believe this is the same torch who set the first one?"

"What do you believe?"

"I hear you say artist but I wonder why an artist would come back to a empty performance?"

Pete shrugged. "Why didn't it burn where he began writing?"

"That's why I think it was barbecue starter, doesn't flare up, needs help to get going."

"So when his signature didn't fire up, he got anxious and went to the big pile."

"Should have used spray paint," Cornelius answered, "if he's an artist."

Tomorrow was Pete's day off. He was going to drive down to Encinitas just to look around, see what he could dig up. He gave Cornelius his beeper number. It wasn't until he had parked in the Evergreen lot that he remembered tomorrow was the day that Carmen left. He thought of Carmen, told himself he could make it back, and headed for the computer room.

Cornelius rode back with Harrison. Both were silent until they turned the corner onto the street of Engine Company 12.

"You find that axe?"

"It was there, tied with red yarn."

"What'd he use to start the fire?"

"Low flare fluid, barbecue starter, I believe. He left us a message. The Brotherhood of Dolphins."

"That mean anything to anybody?" Harrison asked.

"Not yet, but it may help."

"Barbecue starter, huh? You've been working overtime, studying. Stick around, you might make it yet," Harrison said as he pulled into the station.

"Thanks for everything, Tom," Cornelius said before he got out of the battalion GMC.

"Don't thank me. You owe me a steak dinner, barbecued steak dinner, if that report says different."

"I'll take you up on that bet."

"Damon's in Glendale, best damn steaks in town. Barbecue starter!"

Bennett went upstairs and stripped down. Red came out of the shower.

"Candy-ass fireman," he shouted, toweling off. "You gonna wax the Chief's car 'fore you leave?"

"With your mustache, bro'."

"Don't bro' me, sucker," Red said, stretching out sucker and swatting at Cornelius with his towel before heading off to his locker.

Cornelius sat down on a bed in his shorts, scratched his chest, stood up, went to his locker and found his shower kit. "Where's Cruz, ain't she here?"

"What you wanta know for?" Red shouted back as he pulled on his pants.

Cornelius stopped at the entry to the shower room. It was tiled white, but had yellowed over the years to look like any gym shower. "How was she doing?"

"She was doing fine. Had to run and meet the arteest."

"Yeah?" Cornelius asked with a very surprised tone.

"Took her gear for her photo shoot. I hope he's from *Playboy*," Red said, tucking away his shirt. "Ain't I cute?"

Cornelius had his comeback on the tip of his tongue, but nothing came out as he stared at Red.

Red gave him a big smile and said, "You're not my type Bennett."

"The photographer?" Cornelius asked as he stared into a blank space, the investigation in the library filling his thoughts. Pete had said the freak thought of himself as an artist, liked to frame his work.

"Called as soon as we stepped foot inside, like he knew we were home," Red continued.

"That same guy that stopped by to see Sylvia about an hour before the library alarm went off?"

"Yeah, the dipshit with the ponytail. Don't know why..."

"Red, what did Sylvia tell you? Where was she going?"

"What's it to ya?" Red answered back.

Cornelius came across the room in three long strides that Red could never make. Red backed up. "Damnit, I'm not fucking around. I think he's the arsonist, Red. Now where'd she go?"

"Christ, we were talking. She didn't say."

"Think!" Cornelius screamed.

Red had a line of sweat working his clean-washed face; he pulled at his upper lip. "Said she had to clean up her crib."

"Her place!"

"What do you want me to do?" he shouted as Cornelius leaped to his locker and began throwing on clothes.

Bennett ran his hands through his uniform pockets until he found Pete's card. He tossed it on the bed nearest him, yelling, "Call this number, tell the man what's going down. Call 911."

"What's her address?"

"Harrison has it! Move," he shouted and sprinted down the stairs to his car.

Red caught Harrison closing his files up. He only half explained the situation before the Chief burst into action. Red held down the phones after Harrison had left with roof lights blazing. Thirty seconds later, he got the call from Pete Escobedo and relayed the information. The phone rang again and it was a TV station wanting to know if they could come by for an interview. After he slammed the phone down and wiped his face, he wondered if he would ever remember what he'd said to make the reporter shut up so fast.

Pete was halfway out the door when he thought of calling Ray. Time was short, but it would take him ten minutes at least to make the drive and Ray lived two houses down from Sylvia. He ran back, dialed Ray, and got Carmen.

"Hi hon, how you doing?"

"Is Ray there? I have to talk to Ray. NOW." He heard her mutter a curse and then Ray was on the line. All it took after that was ten seconds and he was out the door. He fishtailed into the freeway on-ramp and broke every traffic law. Still, he was too late. He knew it before he saw all the lights on, Harrison's car lit up, the engine still running, two squad cars following him, and Ray hugging his mother on the front porch, Sylvia's *mamá*, holding her so she couldn't enter.

"Can you take her back home?" he asked Ray, looking into his best friend's eyes, seeing nothing but pain in return. He squeezed Ray's shoulder and passed into the living room.

CHAPTER 20

As Pete entered the living room, he knew that of all the crime scenes he had witnessed, and all those he had yet to see, this one would never leave him, etched sharper, more clearly than his name on the stairways. It wasn't the light, not bright enough for an investigation, but bright enough. What he would never forget was Carmen on the floor cradling Sylvia in her arms and lap, Cornelius at her side. He couldn't remember the last time he had cried, but if Ceci and Sylvia's father hadn't bumped him on their way out, he knew he would have broken down.

"Take him home, Ceci. Please. I'll be over as soon as I can." He had touched the old man on the arm, but he couldn't speak to him. He hoped Ceci would take him home, or at least out on the porch with Ray and Sylvia's mama. As he passed through the circle he acknowledged Harrison, but he didn't speak to him. He grabbed the nearest uniform and told him to close off the scene and get outside—now! Then, he went to Carmen and Cornelius. She looked up at him, but couldn't say anything, and Cornelius wouldn't acknowledge him as he continued to caress and comb back Sylvia's hair, once long, now very short. Carmen turned back to Sylvia when he touched her, holding Sylvia even tighter as he squatted down to speak to her.

"Carmen, we have to take care of this. Come on, baby."

"Leave me alone."

"I can't do that. You have to understand; we have work to do."

"She was my *prima* and best friend. Do you understand that?" Carmen cried out.

"Yes, I do. I love her too. Cornelius will take you back; you need to be with the family now," Pete said, grasping Cornelius on the neck, squeezing until he got the recognition he had hoped for. Pete backed off as Carmen kissed Sylvia's brow, her eyes and lips, sobbing as she finally laid Sylvia's head down. Supporting, but not pressuring her, Cornelius helped Carmen up and guided her out of the house, and finally, the room clear of all but one cop, he breathed deeply and began his investigation. A chair and a lamp had been knocked over. There were bloodstains on the tiled floor and on Sylvia's uniform shirt. He looked at her fingers and found skin and blood under the nails, but no cuts on her that he could find. She had put up a good fight. He rocked her head from side to side, saw the marks of lividity, blood swelled to the area of tension, pressure and fingermarks on her neck. As he stood up, the room filled with medical examiners, lab techs, and Joe Wilson, the detective he'd pounded in the squad room a week ago. Pete didn't waste any time, and he didn't care if there was bad blood between them.

He offered his hand and Wilson took it. "We have a repeat offender, a choker, only women so far. There was a similar case at MacArthur a few days ago."

"Latina?"

Pete glanced at the detective. A week ago, Wilson might have said something cute; a week ago, they had been different cops. They weren't perfect, and none of them was without bias, including himself, but he knew they could work together.

"The victims are latinas; the suspect is a male caucasian. He's used panty hose, and maybe a garden hose," Pete said, including the Encinitas murder because he felt certain of it. "This one struggled, blood and skin under her fingernails. Make sure they test for semen."

"Vaginal?"

"No, he's a jack-off artist." Pete left him and continued his search of the room, but he couldn't find the murder weapon. No belts, panty hose, garden hose, nothing. Pete knew he had done it with his hands. It was that more brutal now. Pete began looking for the bundle, the calling card. He hadn't smelled anything when he entered, but then there had been a dozen people, and he hadn't been thinking of odors. He found nothing in the living room and went into the bathroom, the bedrooms. It wasn't until he entered the kitchen and turned on the light, first searching the counter and then the sink, that he found it. A sodden heap half way down the garbage disposal. He yelled for assistance and watched as they bagged it. Had Sylvia objected to the smell, the burning, the smoke, and tossed it? He left and walked the two doors down to the family home.

There was a crowd in the living room. He hugged Sofía and nodded at the group. With a head gesture, he beckoned Ray into the parents' bedroom.

"It was that blonde photographer mutherfucker."

"I think so," Pete acknowledged, his rage turned inward, remembering that afternoon in the garage, wishing he had just concentrated on the matters at hand, the man, there in the afternoon. Another afternoon he couldn't bring back, an empty cage, the baboon gone.

"What was his name?" Pete asked, focusing, his fury stored away in deepening shadows.

"Billy Johnson. He was white like a light bulb, blonde hair thinning on top, but pulled back into a ponytail, at least six feet tall."

"I know that. And, you remember his friend's name?"

"Calasan Klor de Alva."

"That's it. He stays with his grandfather. Do you know where the *abuelo* lives?"

"Off Allesandro, in the hills, that's what he said," Ray answered. Then, closing his fists he beat at his chest, raised his head and choked out, "I let her go with him. Sylvia."

Pete went to Ray and held him. He didn't have to say a word. There wasn't anything he could say that would help.

"Ask *la Tiá*," Ray said, pushing himself away and collecting himself, "She'll know, she knows everyone around here."

Pete left the room and found Sofía. "He lives on the hill," she said, "that curvy street with the view and a Frank Lloyd Wright Jr., next to the Mendoza's. Those old ones are cautious, call themselves Spanish because they don't want anyone to think they have any Mexican blood."

"I want to go with you," Cornelius said, appearing suddenly at his side, the dark face grey as if he had sprung out of ashes.

"No, you need to stay here, take care of the family." He didn't tell Bennett he wanted to handle it by himself.

He parked on a winding street in front of a narrow old Spanish house built into the hillside next to a Wright Jr. modern. A black iron gate and two stories of painted red stairs led to the front door. He tried the gate at the street. There was no lock; the latch had long been broken, and the gate swung open easily. He went up slowly, on his toes. Since it was late, he didn't expect a quick answer. He didn't know what to expect. A young woman, a girl, from El Salvador or Guatemala, answered his ring after two minutes, her hair in a black braid.

She wasn't wearing nylons and hadn't ever shaved, gold appeared in her front teeth when she spoke. This *guanaca* is pure country, he thought to himself. He asked for Señor Klor de Alva. She stared at him, rattled away in the quickest Spanish he'd heard in a long time, and then she held the door open, finally saying one word he could understand, "*Pasale.*"

He went into a living room that could have been the movie set for a forties picture starring Ramón Navarro. The furniture was dark. Red velvet drapes that must have been fashionable at one time hung from iron rods that resembled spears. There was a large rug in the center of the wood floor, but it was dark like the furniture. A shield with two swords on a wall caught his eye, but he didn't bother to stare at the coat of arms lacquered on the shield as he followed the girl up a half flight of stairs, through a sitting room, and out the open french doors onto a flagstone patio carved into the hillside. The patio was loaded with flowering plants, a pond among sandstone boulders filled with fat goldfish under chicken wire. There were Japanese lanterns in the grape arbor above the pond connected to a extension cord he couldn't see. Smoke from the one lit Tiki torch fluttered over the water before passing through the high trellis heavy with green grapes. Pete thought of the ventilator in Ray's shop as he watched a fat ugly fish, white with black and orange splotches, open its mouth to burp and suck, a hole opening and closing in the thick dark water line. He touched the gun in his holster just to know it was there.

"I have to keep the cats away. That's why there's wire. A shame."

Pete turned toward the voice and saw the Californio smoking in a wooden lounge chair laced underneath with ropes to hold up the bloated vinyl cushion. The old man had a shawl draped over his shoulders, even though it wasn't that cold. He was thin, dressed in nice slacks and good shoes over thin socks. He smoked slowly, touching his perfectly trimmed moustache after he exhaled.

"Fish like that would be an easy target for one of the cats around here," Pete said.

"Would be. Disease gets 'em, anyway. Not enough filtration. Need a pump."

"Uh-huh," Pete said, turning to look at the hole in the pond again. "*Señor* Klor de Alva," he said after two more openings had broken the surface.

"Mister," the old man answered sharply. "This is America, son, and you don't look like any of the worthless wetbacks I have to hire."

"Mister Klor de Alva," Pete said sharply, staring at him. "Pete Escobedo, LAPD. I'm here to ask you a few questions." He didn't move closer to show the old man his badge.

"What can I do for you, Detective?" the old man asked, stubbing out his cigarette and lighting another.

Pete was cut off as the girl came through the doors and said something to the old man while wiping at her apron. "Gin," he coughed, "*con limón, rápido.*"

"I want to talk to your grandson, Calasan," Pete said, after the girl had left.

The old man hacked into a handkerchief and stuffed it between his legs. "Why?" the old man asked.

Pete looked up into the grapes growing from the arbor and answered, "I have to ask him a few questions."

"María!" Klor de Alva shouted. Pete jerked, surprised at the ferocity in the old man's voice.

The girl came rushing out with a tall glass. There was a lot of ice and a slice of lime floating on top. He could smell the gin as she passed him. The old man's hands shook as he took the glass from her. He spilled some down his chin as he sucked at it.

"So, what are you, the new boy in the department?" He sucked away at the gin as the glass shook between two hands.

"Where's your grandson?" Pete asked.

The old man's eyes rolled. "Get out of here," he hissed. "Goddamn East L.A. greasers. Chicano," the old man swore, starting to cough. "You call that a culture. Now leave before I call your boss." Pete took the ten steps to the old man's chair quickly, leaning over with his hands firmly set on the armrest, close enough to smell old sweat and cologne mixed with gin.

"Where are they?"

"María," the old man tried to yell, but Pete clapped his jaw shut.

"We're gonna get some answers here, *viejo*," Pete whispered as he moved to the back of the lounge chair, tilted it up on its wooden wheels, and rolled the old man to the edge of the pond. He dropped the front end, came around, and tore at the wiring over the goldfish.

"What're you doing?" the old man wailed.

Pete picked up a pot, heavy with an ambitious geranium. He held it over a mouth on the surface, looked at Klor de Alva, and then let it drop. The water exploded, an immense bloom from the center of the geranium that spread over the pond as well as over his pant legs and those of the old man. When the surface had subsided, there was the flower pot, the edges leaking scum onto the belly of a goldfish, like his own feet in thin shoes.

"I'll get your badge; you'll be looking for work at a car wash," the old man wheezed.

Pete hefted another pot, raised it high.

"He scared the girl."

"Who?" Pete asked, fondling the pot.

The old man's eyes followed the pot. "I don't know."

Pete let the pot fall. The bloom wasn't as pretty this time. His wet pant legs stuck to his skin. He turned his eyes on Klor de Alva and said, "You're lying," as he reached for another pot and placed it on the wet stones at his feet.

"Billy Johnson," the old man groaned, starting to hack. "Please, no more, my babies."

Pete saw a movement through the doors. His hand went into his coat pocket. He saw the girl in the shadows, wiping her hands nervously on her apron. He removed his hand. "*Lárgate!*" he yelled at her, and she disappeared around a corner.

"When did they leave?"

"An hour, two hours ago."

Pete waited as the old man had another coughing attack. He waited longer as the old man lit a cigarette and sucked it in.

"Who is Billy Johnson, and where did your grandson go with him?"

The old man sucked on the butt, staring cross-eyed at the burning end until Pete began to tap the flower pot noisily. It got his attention, Klor de Alva's eyes now glued to Pete's foot.

"They were going south."

"How far south?"

"San Diego."

Pete lifted the pot, but he didn't wait for a goldfish. The only holes in the water now were caused by geraniums. He let the pot fall and it had the same effect as before. The old man jumped. The same two fish continued to float belly-up on the surface.

"You're lying to me again, *Señor*," Pete spat out.

"Encinitas, a town near San Diego. I wasn't lying. Please," he whined.

Pete went for another pot and placed it at his right foot. "He left with his friend, a white man with blonde hair in a ponytail? An old friend from high school, correct?" Pete tapped the flower pot twice.

"Yes, I told you already. It was Bill, Billy Johnson."

"The address?" "Huh?" he shouted this time, pushing the flower pot with his foot until it tottered on the edge.

"The address I don't know, my grandson didn't tell me, but I have something that will help you. Believe me, please, no more." His eyes jiggled with the flower pot. "María!" he yelled.

Pete watched as the girl came to the shadows behind the french doors.

"*Dame el papel que le dejó* Calasan. ¡*Pisale!*" the old man shouted. The girl hurried away, apparently knowing what paper the old man wanted.

Pete relaxed his foot and watched the old man stare into the pond at the three flower pots sitting in a foot of water.

The girl returned with a scrap of paper. The grandfather snatched it from her, and without looking at it, waved the paper at Pete. "The telephone number. Here's what you want. Now take it and leave me alone."

"Was the caucasian tall?" Pete asked, not yet ready to leave.

"He was a little above average. Thin, no fat to speak of, and he wore glasses that were slightly tinted. He dresses miserably, never had a manicure," the old man enunciated, ticking off points on the tips of his fingers while staring at a spot above and to the left of Pete's head. "His ears are overly large. By his accent, I would say he is from the Midwest. No moustache or beard. I doubt if he could grow much of one. He's about thirty-six, looks younger than his years. There is a small scar on his left eyelid, the suture work extremely unprofessional, probably done by a country doctor. It made his left eye droop slightly. His hair is almost white and not cut in any modern style that I'm familiar with, balding on the top, and tied in a pony tail," he continued, ending with a sigh. "María!" he yelled, and then, "I suppose I should offer you a drink, detective."

"Now, why don't we start at the beginning, *Señor* Klor de Alva, and maybe I can find your grandson for you."

Pete didn't leave until an hour and two gins had passed. *Señor* Klor de Alva went on a roll before the first drink was dry, but his eyes never lost their shine. The ponytailed friend of his grandson, a "conniver," really worried him. The grandson had left for Encinitas in a Japanese car. He couldn't tell what make or style; he was only good with people. The blondie talked a lot of intellectual crap that his grandson ate up.

The old man gave him a picture of his grandson that was about ten years old. He had long brown hair and a moustache, and that open face that good kids from college had.

Pete offered to clean up the mess in the goldfish pond before he left, but Klor de Alva waved him off. "María will do it. She doesn't have anything else to do." Pete told him he'd call as soon as he'd found his grandson and that he'd send over some live fish. The old man shook his hand, and said, "Forget the goldfish; just find my Calasan."

CHAPTER 21

Pete pulled off the freeway and into a gas station on Encinitas Boulevard. He remained in the seat for a moment, not because he felt stiff from the drive, seat half in recline, head back, and pushing the fast lane. He liked a long drive; it was just that he had expected more than a couple of gas stations and a Denny's on a boulevard named after the city.

There was a cashier in the station, and a sign over the door, "Pay First—Then Pump."

Pete slipped a twenty under the window. "On number 4. Hey, where's Vista Del Mar Street?"

"*No sé*," the *mexicano* said under the window, rubbing his eyes.

Pete looked at his watch. This *huevón* was almost asleep, but it was almost one in the morning. He'd made good time. Pete was pumping the gas when a beat-up junker pulled in. Three teenagers jumped out, one shouting something. Pete changed hands on the pump, putting his right hand into his jacket just to touch the pistol under his arm as he jerked his head around, checking the area. There wasn't a lot of light in this station, a Denny's across the road, one car getting off the freeway and racing by. Nobody else on the streets except this one carload of wired kids. The teenagers ignored him and went in through the station's wide-open doors. Teenagers, he told himself, as he glanced at the read-out on the pump. Edgy; no, not edgy, just watchful, the way he was.

Pete finished up and walked into the station, over to the twelve-pack of Millers on the counter, a twenty dollar bill laying next to it. He eyed the kids in ripped Levis, flannel shirts, long hair, and clean, high-school faces. He exchanged a knowing look with the guy in the booth. "Now, where is fucking Vista del Mar?" he asked in Spanish.

It was three blocks down, an apartment building, as ugly as any he'd seen in L.A. Like the Denny's at the off-ramp, L.A. didn't have the lock on trashy architecture, just more of it. He parked on the street and walked though the carports until he found the stairs. A thin, slouchy young woman in a baggy dress answered while he was knocking, his hand still raised at the door. Pete introduced himself and held out his badge. She looked as if she were going to cry, her skin transparent, the glasses too large for her face, but instead she asked him if he wanted a cup of coffee.

"When did you last see Bill Johnson?" he asked, after he had drunk half the cup. She was standing in the kitchen under the fluorescent lights. He placed his cup on the formica counter.

"He went to L.A. almost a week ago. I haven't seen or heard from him since. What happened?" she asked in a voice that was stronger than he had imagined.

"He may have gotten into some trouble."

"Oh no, Billy!"

Pete waited a moment, thinking she would begin to cry, that she had expected a cop to show up eventually. "Do you know what day he left?"

"Yes, it was Monday." She didn't have to check a calendar.

"He took your car?"

"Yes," she answered, shivering a little.

He looked at her and took another sip of coffee. "Where is he?"

She started to shake. "I really don't know," she answered, looking directly into his face for the first time since he had come to the door.

"Has he ever done this to you before?"

"I haven't known him that long." Then she breathed deeply, but it didn't stop the tears. He waited, noticed the hum of the refrigerator and the glow from the lights overhead. His eyes followed the shaking of her shoulders, feeling the stiffness in his own.

She took off her glasses to wipe at her eyes. Then Pete said, "There was a woman in Los Angeles."

"Yes," she answered, breathing deeply again, and he was concerned that she would break down again, but this deep breath was the one to cleanse her. Her glasses went on as she turned to the refrigerator, opened it, took out a bottle of white wine, and asked him if he wanted any.

"No thanks."

She poured a large glass. Pete watched her take a long drink, and then another. It was almost two in the morning.

"Did you know her?"

"Yes. No. Not really." She finished the glass. "I know her name is Lourdes," Barbara said, after pouring another full glass of wine. "She's an artist or something from Nicaragua."

"You know for sure he was with her?"

"He went to see her and Calasan. Billy talked a lot. Too much. But, I mean, we were just friends." She blinked when she said "friends," and Pete looked down to give her space in case she wanted to cry some more, but she gathered herself up with another slug of wine and continued. "Billy really does live in another world. I just wish he would have called by now. He said he was an artist, but I'm not so sure."

She hesitated. Pete waited, knowing it was going to happen. The words came out between sobs. "I'm worried about him."

Pete waited a moment. "You expected him to return?"

"Yes," Barbara said emphatically. "Billy said that he was going to become wealthy and powerful, and we would have babies and a big ranch in Mexico." She paused. "I just don't know. I didn't really believe him, but..."

He let the silence expand for a good minute. "Why did he go to see the artist in Los Angeles?" he asked as soothingly as possible.

She was staring into the glass of wine. For a moment he thought he had lost her, but then she spoke. "He said he was working on an art commission. He was going to change the way the world views art. He was always talking about it, how we had to get rid of established art and bring back Nature." She said it as if she were reciting from a seed catalog.

Pete asked her, "Did he call you while he was in Los Angeles?"

"Once is all. He left a message on my machine. He said that they were planning an art escape; that's what he called it. And that he was going to be famous."

"Who? Did he mention any names?"

"No."

"How about Maggie Stevenson? Did he ever mention her?"

"Maggie? She was a good friend. A supporter of the arts and migrants. She was murdered a week ago."

"Billy knew her?"

"Oh, they were great friends. Such a shame. Are you sure you won't have a glass of wine?" she asked.

"No thanks. Does he have any sagebrush here?"

"No, he took it all with him. I hated the stuff."

She didn't ask him how he knew about the sagebrush. Relief for Barbara swept over him. Billy had obviously burned the sage here and she was still alive. "Did he leave anything here?"

"He scribbled things down on a laptop. You want to look at it?"

"Yes, please." He followed her into the living room and watched as she unfolded the laptop. She logged on, and the screen filled with green. She worked with him until she was assured that he knew what he was doing, and then she excused herself.

An hour later, he was finished. He accepted a glass of wine from the new bottle she had opened. He watched her, readying himself to help her out, thinking she should be half-looped as she sat down on the floor opposite him, but she didn't spill a drop of wine.

"I waded through those disks. Most of it is letters, some of them very angry," Pete said over the top of his wine glass.

"He was angry," she answered.

"Did he like women?"

"Oh, he loved women, yes. He said we were superior beings." She smiled as if it were a small joke.

"How about Chicanas?"

"Excuse me?"

"Mexicans, Latinas, women from East L.A.?"

"He loved the Third World," she said, smiling.

Pete coughed. She was serious. He imagined what Carmen would say when he told her she was from the Third World. He had to cough again to keep himself from smiling. He looked at Barbara, thought of Maggie Stevenson, an activist strangled with a garden hose, and wondered if it was more than a cultural thing with Bill Johnson. "Did you ever cross him, do anything to anger him?"

"I didn't know him that long. You mentioned Maggie and asked me about his opinion of women. What happened? What are you investigating?"

Pete stared into the still lit computer screen. "Why weren't you surprised that I came here?"

"Oh, I don't know," she said, rubbing her face. "I even knew when you knocked. Does intuition sound stupid?"

"No," he answered, and he meant it. It seemed like everyone had a feeling before he did. As he told her about the murders of Sylvia and Lourdes, her eyes never left his face.

"Did he strangle the firefighter too?"

"I think he used his hands." Pete let it sink in. It was a theory on his part, Billy becoming more brutal and close. He reached over and switched off the computer. The screen continued to glow as he stood up.

"You're not leaving."

"Yes, I'm going back to L.A. He's not here," Pete answered. He started to move toward the door.

"But he's not in L.A."

"Thank you for your help," he said, reaching out with his hand.

She didn't take it.

He rubbed his hands together. "Okay, where is he, Barbara?"

"Baja. He's in Baja."

"You mean the place with the dolphins and the pyramids? Boca del Mar, that place he mentions all the time in the computer?"

"He always felt safe down there. That's where he would go. You'll just be wasting your time in L.A."

Pete looked at her, thinking this freak's not gonna go hide out in the desert. He's got big things planned, more women. Intuition again? He looked at his watch. It was 3:30.

"Go visit Jesús tomorrow. Maybe he'll know," Barbara said.

"Jesús?"

"One of Billy's best friends. Billy would hang out with him and his family a couple of times a week. Real nice people. You'll like them, except that I don't know where they live."

Pete grinned. Like them? Why, because they were Mexicans? He reached for the doorknob. "I've really got to go, but I appreciate your help. I know it was tough." He held out his hand.

"Yes, it was," she answered, but still she didn't take his hand. "You're not returning to L.A. You have to talk to Jesús. He went directly to the pyramids. I know that's why he didn't come here to see me, because something has gone wrong."

This was definitely not the same woman who opened the door, Pete thought.

"One more day might be all you need. If you drive back to L.A. and don't find him there, which you won't, you will have lost valuable time. Give it a shot, detective. Here, I'll make up a bed for you on this couch."

She smiled when he brought up regulations, asking him if he weren't out of his jurisdiction anyway, as she made up the couch. After bringing him a pillow, she wrote down directions to places in town where he might find someone who knew Jesús's house. She wrote down her phone number at work and told him to come in for lunch.

He lay down, but how could he sleep? The Captain, *El Chingón*, would love it. Not only was it the case he was supposed to drop, but he was sleeping over in the apartment of the suspect's girlfriend. He turned on his side, telling himself not to worry about it. He was already in such deep shit, why worry anymore? But his eyes wouldn't shut. Carmen. He couldn't take his eyes off the phone. It was within reach of his right hand, a lit phone on a glass table.

A moment later, he heard Carmen's sleepy voice say, "Hello, Pete."

"Hello, baby," Pete murmured.

"Where are you?"

"Encinitas. At his girlfriend's."

"So what's she like?" Non-threatening, but very worried about him. How are you holding up?"

"It's been hell. I had to get away for a few minutes. Everyone's still next door. I'm glad you called."

"I miss you madly."

"I've been thinking about that. It happens with disaster, doesn't it." Carmen breathed hard and then stopped.

"You OK?"

"I canceled my flight."

"You shouldn't do that. I know they need you, but..."

"I wish I could come down *en la mañana*, just to see you."

"Johnson's not here. I'll be back in the evening," Pete said. Then, he told her what he had found out, and Carmen surprised him. She agreed with Barbara, told him she thought it was smart to stay and talk with Jesús.

"I'll bet he headed down to Baja, Pete. It makes sense. He's running; he's going to hide out."

"No, I don't think so," he disagreed. "Woman's intuition isn't going to cut it this time."

"You are a very sweet man, Pete, and I'm crazy about you, but I don't think you're going to make it back tomorrow."

"I will. Besides, if he is in Baja, I can't arrest him or go after him. The only thing I can do is alert the authorities and start proceedings."

"I'm coming down. I want to see you. I need to see you."

"No, Carmen. I don't know where I'll be."

"I could take the train. You could meet me in Del Mar; they have a station there."

"I'll be back, believe me," he told her.

It was almost light when they hung up, and although Pete was tired, he still couldn't sleep. He lay on the couch thinking about Bill Johnson, trying to get into his head. He couldn't figure out why someone would live or act the way this guy did. It didn't make sense that a guy would get so worked up over art. Didn't he have anything to do with his life? He was thirty-six, and from what Pete had discovered, he had it all going for him. Educated, intelligent, middle class, and white. What was the problem? He thought about his own life. Was he satisfied? He realized that he hadn't really thought about it much in those terms. He was a detective; he was making it. He had a beautiful, sharp girlfriend. A *chavala* at Stanford. It sounded fine to him. He hit the pillow once, wondered if he would be able to sleep and woke up at eight-thirty to the smell of coffee.

He said hello to Barbara and headed for the shower after his first cup. Barbara was gone by the time he had finished his shower. After he had dressed, he poured himself another cup of coffee and made some notes from last night. He debated running through the computer again, but passed on it, knowing he wouldn't find what he was looking for. What *was* he looking for? The library, Sylvia, Lourdes, Maggie Stevenson? The evidence wasn't in the computer. All he had was intuition. He reconstructed the events: Johnson had killed Maggie Stevenson a week ago, set a fire in the barbecue pit and burned a few paintings. Three days later he was in Los Angeles. If Johnson had called from Lourdes's apartment there would be a phone record and a time of call. He had met

Sylvia at the body shop, and the following day he had set fire to the library and had met Sylvia at her house. Had Johnson been in L.A. earlier to set the first fire at the library? Barbara wouldn't know because she hadn't been living with him then. But it didn't really matter much to him; what he wanted now was hard evidence, fingerprints, a witness. Calasan, his high school friend. Had he gone with Johnson to Sylvia's house? But Calasan was most likely still with Bill Johnson. Pete called Evergreen and luckily got ahold of Joe Wilson. He didn't tell him that he was in Encinitas. Wilson told him that finger-prints matched at Sylvia's house and Lourdes's apartment. There were a lot of William Johnsons. It would take more time. Try Encinitas, he told him, the Maggie Stevenson case. Wilson paused, but didn't ask the question. He had to spell Encinitas twice. He called Tony, caught him at home. A dog yapped in the background. He'd be back this evening. Yes, he knew he was in deep. No, he didn't want Tony to drive down. What he needed was Bill Johnson. When he hung up, he knew that was all he really wanted. Find him and drag him in. What if he was in Mexico? Barbara and Carmen thought so. They were going on feelings but what more did he have? If Bill was down in Baja and Pete found him, he could only bring him back with Johnson's consent. Or? He tried to let it pass, but couldn't stop thinking of taking Johnson out himself. Nobody would ever have to know that he had been down there.

He left the apartment, and after starting his car, looked over his notes. He debated stopping at the police station and decided against it. They wouldn't throw in with a L.A. cop, free-wheeling a hunch and out of jurisdiction. He had time. Why not use it on background? He found Maggie Stevenson's home using Barbara's directions. The street was quiet, upper middle class to wealthy, except for the one ramshackle house he wanted. The house was locked up, but he didn't need to go inside. He found the barbecue pit and bits of ash. There were no paintings, no sagebrush, no garden hose. He'd find those in plastic bags at the station. He stopped at the edge of the patio and took in the view. A campground on the beach, the highway busy, the cool, calm ocean. He wandered through the gardens with no purpose, found the room at the bottom of the house and, pushing aside the warped plywood door, went in. He went to the bulb in the center and pulled the cord. He looked around and, when about to yank the light off and leave, he noticed the bare patch on the wall. He went to it and figured it had once been a picture, the tack still in place. He left the room, got in his car and headed north on the Coast Highway. He drove slowly, checking the terrain. There were a lot of bicyclists. He was concerned about them, not too many bicyclists in L.A., so he drove slowly when he came up behind them. A car honked. Surf shops and Mexican restaurants. They must be the leading economy, he thought. He pulled into Gene's, "Regular breakfast-type food, and friends of Billy's," the note said.

Gene's was noisy. He sat at the counter with the *L.A. Times*, read the sports section, and half-listened to the dialogue. Construction types and working people. The hefty young Chicano taking orders acted as if he owned the place. He got his coffee and some small talk thrown his way. Sal was popular, but he wasn't the owner. The skinny red-neck at the griddle was Gene. Pete wasn't sure he wanted to eat after watching the cook in action. He ordered eggs over hard and bacon. Make it easy for him. He ate, intent upon Steve Sax's errors at second base and Fernando's pitching problems. By the time he finished, he had convinced himself that Lasorda was using up Valenzuela's arm. That's why they're in fourth place, he told himself.

"Hey, you a Dodger fan, bro'?" Sal asked, pouring him another cup of coffee.

Pete nodded, looking Sal square in the eyes.

"You from up there, homes?"

"Yeah," Pete answered again.

"East Los, right? I know a lot of bad dudes from up there. We party down. Hey, you know Hueso or Yogi from Terrace?"

Pete knew the Terrace.

"Where do you hang, man?"

"Echo Park," Pete answered. He wanted to smile, listening to this rap. Wait'll this *vato* heard that he was LAPD.

"Echo *Parque!* Yeah bro', that's a cool barrio, dude. The *locos*, eh?" Sal spoke in perfect *cholo* rhythm, more emphatic than when he talked to the regulars at the counter sitting on either side of Pete.

"Right, the *locos*, homeboy," Pete said, mimicking Sal. "Who do you run with?"

"*Puros pendejos.* There's nothing going on down here. This place is dead. Waves, fish, flowers, and cruising with my *vieja*. That's it. I'm gonna pack out of here first chance I get."

Pete smiled. "Yogi's cutting brush in Tujunga at a work camp by day, and letting some *veterano* shove ink into his skin at night. You ever get tattooed with a sewing needle and a ball point pen?" Pete shoved his right hand forward towards the cup to show Sal the cross between his thumb and first finger and the serpent bracelet on his wrist.

Sal flicked his eyes at Pete's wrist. His voice got tougher. "No man, I ain't been to camp. What the..."

"You're making it fine here, *ese*," Pete said, cutting him off. "We don't need no more bad dudes in East Los, homer."

"Oh yeah," Sal said pulling himself up. "You don't look so bad. Wait here, don't go nowhere, I'll be right back, the meatheads want me. Hey you," he shouted with mock hostility.

"What you want, more coffee? Sheet, I already poured you a dollar fifty worth."

Pete waited until Sal had made the rounds. When Sal returned, Pete spoke low, cutting Sal off before he could get started again. "I'm looking for a paddy. You know Bill Johnson?"

"Billy Johnson?" Sal asked too loudly, leaning back. "What'ya want with Billy? The dude's bent. You know, earth to Billy."

"That's what I heard," Pete answered. "Where can I find him?"

"What is this, a stakeout? Man, you sound like a bad cop show," Sal answered, snickering.

"What'ya know, homeboy," Pete answered, watching the surprise on Sal's face as he flipped his badge open.

"*Orale*. Hey man, I didn't mean to give you the wrong impression. I was just working some shit, having fun. I'm clean, a very clean, upstanding dude."

"Don't sweat it," Pete said quickly. "I know where you're at." He put his badge away. "I need to find Johnson before he gets himself into trouble, know what I mean?"

"That's the *güero*," Sal answered, making a face. "Don't know where the next train is coming from, but he has big ideas, money-making schemes. Last time he was in here, he was talking about doing in the rice-eaters because they were fishing out the ocean."

"He ever talk about art?"

"Oh, yeah! Man, I was gonna get my own Picasso, hang it up in my ride or something. Shit, he wants to take all those ancient Figaro dudes downtown."

"You know Jesús?"

"I know a lot of Jesse's."

"This Chuy is a national."

"Then you're referring to his good buddy. Yeah, I know him. A *viejo*, still a *campesino*, but you couldn't be thinking of this Jesús. I tell you right now, Jesús walks the line, man; he's too wet for any crazy shit."

"It's not about Jesús. I want to talk to Billy and I heard he hangs at the *viejo's* crib. You know where it is?" He gave Sal his full attention while the directions were scribbled on a napkin. Sal told him he'd probably have to wait until the afternoon since the old man worked for a construction company. Pete thanked him and got up to pay his bill.

"It's on me," Sal said, waving his hands.

Pete left a ten dollar bill on the counter anyway, and walked out into the fog. He stood on the sidewalk for several moments as if to catch his bearings, but actually he was mesmerized by the sensation of light and swirling fog, and the lack of noise. There hadn't been any fog when he had entered the cafe, and now it was so quiet and peaceful and strange that he sat in his car for another several minutes and lit up a cigarette. He stubbed it out after three puffs and threw the butt out the window. As he drove off, the discarded butt bothered him. "Small towns," he said out loud.

He drove on the Coast Highway, conscious of how much faster he was driving than the others. It was as if he had been transported back to East L.A. on a Friday night when every lowrider in his short was cruising. *Tranquilo, ese,* that was the mood in a lowrider. Take it easy, *cabrón,* slow and easy. The Chicano twist on Detroit. Take a V-eight and hold it down to twenty-five miles an hour. Make it clean, bad, and beautiful. "A work of art," he heard himself muttering. But these cars in North San Diego county weren't lowriders; they were mini-trucks and imports. Nothing elaborate. Utilitarian. He saw nothing exciting here, so why was everyone driving so slowly. Checking Barbara's notes, he turned into the parking lot at Beacons, found a spot to park, and got out. He stood at the wood railing and looked over the edge of the bluff. The ocean in bright sun sparkled, greenish rather than blue. In the lot, what looked like boys, got out of cars and put on rubber suits. Only one man looked different, homeless, sitting on a bench with a blanket wrapped around his short squat frame, tangled hair, oblivious to the others as he listened to a new transistor radio.

Pete leaned over the railing on the cliff's edge and noticed the surfers in the water. He thought that the object would be to see who could ride the wave in the farthest, but they weren't doing that. They were falling off before the end of the ride. It looked like a friendly scene from where he stood, a bunch of kids hanging in the waves. He listened to two young blonde kids, his ears prickling on the squeaky voices, slang he couldn't understand.

"I slid into a gnarly tube when this valley snaked me, but I put an awesome ding in his new Fletcher, dude."

"Righteous, dude. Check that kook on the log, I thrashed him on one wave."

Watching the kid paddle out into the waves took Pete back to the gym and wrestling. Images blanked out the ocean: the circle on the mat, the heat of the gym, a referee checking his headgear, his opponent staring into a point behind his eyes. The referee had dropped his hand, and he and his opponent met. Pete had been thrown, the wind blasting out of his body, Coachy standing at the edge of the circle shouting, "You'll get him. You'll get him. Dig in, now. He's all yours, Pete." He remembered that he had thought it wouldn't happen this way. He had been sure that he would go in and throw the other boy, win the next point, and then it would be over. But now he was already behind, as if being one strike down was all he had needed to lose in front of the others. It had become quiet as they went to the mat on all fours, and then, as quickly as it had happened before, he was down again, but not pinned. He had struggled, using every muscle until it hurt, but he couldn't gain an advantage. "The frog, use the frog," he heard Coachy shouting. It was a difficult maneuver, the timing had to be perfect, or else he could end up backwards and defenseless. He had pushed backwards, had felt the strain from his opponent to keep him straight, and then he had lunged. He had been as surprised as anyone to see the boy tumble over his shoulders, the pin easy. He had fought the urge to look over at Coachy to feel the approval, his face tingling with pride. The next point would do it, would decide the match. He had thought about how proud Coachy would be when he won a trophy, here, at his first city match. In his mind, he could hear Coachy's voice as if he were next to him at the railing, looking out at the ocean, and telling him again, "You weren't all there, Sleepy. You were someplace else." Pete stared out at the ocean, but he didn't see the surfers, just as he hadn't seen anyone after that loss.

Angry, he had said that he would never wrestle again, and had walked away from the van. When Coachy came by his house a week later, he had hidden in his room until his mother had made him come out. He had looked Coachy in the eyes and told him that he wasn't interested in that silly shit anymore.

"Pete," Coachy had said, "I can't tell you that it won't matter if you don't come back, because I want you there. You're a great kid, and I don't think you're a quitter; I think you're a fighter, but are you gonna run out, or are you proud enough to take this guy next time you meet? What's it gonna be? Whose man are you? You afraid of that guy, or afraid of yourself? Be proud. You're Stairways, aren't you?"

He had stared back, saying, "I'm Stairways, but we don't have to wrestle. We're tougher than that."

"We'll see about that at the practice tonight."

Pete had watched Coachy get into the beat-up Dodge van that was his trademark and a constant source of their ridicule. The boys had liked to tease their Coachy about his ride. Once, after they had all piled in, on cue, they had pulled their watchcaps over their faces and had ridden that way for a mile until they couldn't take it anymore, and broke up laughing. Coachy was square but he had the scene down for a paddy, even if he was still in college doing social work.

Pete had spent that day in the house only going out once to feed the chickens in the backyard. When his *papá* had come home from work it would be another hour until dinner. He could hear his sisters in the kitchen, but he hadn't been hungry and left the house. He had ridden his bike down to the lake and had thrown a few rocks at the ducks until, bored with the ducks and the lake, he had left for the gym. He could have stopped at the newsstand to check out the nudies or gone to the Burrito King for a Coke, but instead he had cruised to the gym, hoping that he was late, and then had circled the playground twice until he heard enough noise inside. He had told himself that he was only stopping to check out the action, to see how dumb they looked, working out.

Pete's hands tightened on the wood railing at the edge of the ocean as he remembered standing for a good ten minutes at the door of the tiny, windowless gym, just large enough for one basketball court, one bench along the sidelines. The mat had been set in the middle of the gym where Coachy shouted out instructions, in his sweats, high-top sneakers, silver whistle, and Dallas Cowboys' hat. Either they were ignoring him, or they hadn't seen him. The homeys and Ray doing mat work, Ray looking good, but Chuy was dogging it. He had noticed, and so had Coachy who yelled, "You wrestling with your sister? Copping a feel, or what?" Coachy had turned to Pete, "What're you looking at? Get over here. Chuy needs a workout."

Pete had shrugged. He didn't need this, he had told himself. He was only gonna do it to help out his friend, Chuy.

He listened to the waves, the memories as sharp as the salt spray. What had happened to Coachy? Pete had gone on to win his division two years running, and it was Coachy who had taken him to the Police Academy, introduced him around, and had gotten him started. A few months after he had finished his training, Coachy had been offered a job in Texas. Pete never saw him again.

Pete didn't look at his watch until the wind came up, the breeze off the cliffs in the afternoon. It was time to go. He followed the instructions that Sal had given him, surprised at how rural Encinitas became after he had crossed the train tracks and gone inland a mile. He tried to remember how many times he had crossed these train tracks, this town like a strip center alongside the tracks, not like L.A. where the tracks were an intrusion, a place for the down and out. He pulled into an avocado orchard and followed the dirt road, past the main house into the back, where he saw the neat, white wood shack, geraniums along the sides in old tires and coffee cans, a lime tree at one corner. The house was small, almost dwarfed by the porch which held a table and three chairs. As he drove up he didn't see any life, but as he turned off the engine the dogs appeared, baying, with two little girls chasing after them. An older woman came out on the porch, rubbing her hands on a towel, and a man appeared from a shed behind the house. The man wore boots, khaki pants, a flannel shirt buttoned almost to the top, and a sweat-stained Norteño straw hat. He was short and heavy, but he moved

easily, rolling over the ground. The man called off the dogs as
Pete got out of his car, assuring him they were harmless, and
then he waited with his arms folded and his grey moustache
set, drooping around the corners of his mouth.

"*Señor* Jesús Pérez?" Pete asked.

"Yes," the man answered, not moving.

"I'm here to ask you a few questions." Pete saw the fear in
the older man. It was a slight movement in the head, and a
quick look back to his wife on the porch. She called out to the
little girls, "María, Lucy, *vengan por acá*."

"You have nothing to fear," Pete said quickly to Jesús,
hoping to minimize his presence. Perhaps they thought he
was from the INS. "I am not *la migra*; I'm from the Los
Angeles Police Department. You're not under investigation."
He spoke calmly, deliberately not using the strident bureau-
cratic voice that he was trained to use, and he didn't mention
Billy. He would wait for that. Wait for a sign from the older
man.

Jesús came forward. There was a thin line of sweat on his
brow. He held out his hand. "Jesús Pérez, *a sus órdenes*."

They shook hands and Pete responded, "*Soy* Detective
Angel Escobedo."

"Come, let's sit on the porch," the old man said in
Spanish. Pete had hoped he could conduct the interview in
English, but decided to follow the old man's lead.

"Café, Inspector?" Jesús asked, as he pointed the way
with his left hand to the table.

"*Gracias,*" Pete answered, reflecting on the use of the
word "inspector."

"*Mamá, dos cafecitos,*" Jesús shouted through the screen
and, turning back to Pete, spoke somberly in English, "Now,
what is it that you came to see me about?"

"Bill Johnson. I hear you know him well, *Señor*," Pete answered respectfully, grateful that Jesús had switched languages.

"Well, and not so well, but he comes by here often. We talk here like this, sometimes late into the night. He is a good boy."

"That's what I hear. I'll get right to the point."

"Why not. We have to get there sometime," Jesús said.

Pete told the old man about the fire, the murders, the connections with art and then listened as Jesús talked.

"I don' think he set that fire. Not to burn the books. Why would he do that on purpose? No, *señor*! I know him too well, and books are what he loves. Nooo, that Billee, he talks all the time, *siempre*, 'bout everything he reads, all the time. He learns everything from those books. Things I never hear of, and then things I know a little about, like plants and the stars and the *pirámides*. Oh, he's *loco*, that one, over those *pirámides* and the *indios*. Always the *indios*.

"He wants me to take a trip with him. To this place he says is sacred in Baja, California. He builds a *pirámide*, see, at this sacred place on the Sea of Cortez, and the dolphins come from all over, from everywhere to watch. Tha's what he says, the *delfines* come right up near the shore and watch because they are in tune. I'd like to see that, the dolphins in a big bunch watching this *gringo* build a *pirámide*. But I can't get away, you know; *mi vieja*, she just don' think much of this talk.

"So, maybe it's true we not in tune with the cosmos like those big fish. I wish I had the time to see all those *delfines*, but we have to eat. He talks about the cosmos all the time, but he likes to eat, too. He likes to eat *mi vieja's* cooking.

"The perfect diet, he says: *frijol*, *tortillas de maíz*, and *chile*. Tha's why we are so advanced. The Maya ate that food and come up with the dolphin who is a god of the cosmos. The spiritual foundation of the *pirámide*, he says. I don' know; tell you the truth, I like a little meat with my *comida*, and I don' know much about those people in the Yucatán. I never been there, but I seen the pictures, and I think a lot of work went into building those *pirámides*. Those short people must have had some free time and a little meat, eh?

"You ask me, if I think he done these things? And I tell you that it is possible, but I don' think so. Not the books. *¿Me entiende?*

"All the things he talks about, and he gets excited when he talks, like he is a little angry, because what it is, you see, he says we have to save the world. It's not the books; it's this other thing he speaks of, all of the time, that we are deprived of, Nature. I know what he means, but I don' know. It's like the burning of Tenochtitlán by the *conquistadores*, he says. Billee, he knows a lot of *español* for a *gringo*; he even calls them *gachupines*. The rape of my culture, he says. Hell, I ain't no Azteca like I ain't no Maya. He knows more about those *indios* than I ever did. I don' know nothing from them. I come from a *rancho* outside of Mexico City, the day effe, but I ain't no *chilango* either.

"No way could I stay. You know, that damn government won' help us with a *pozo*, a well. Not the *campesino*. *Madre*, you can' do nothin' without water where I come from. Tha's why I'm here sixteen years, because of those *pinche ladrones* in Mexico. Four kids and I just got a raise to eight dollars an hour. Tha's not much, but is better than a *rancho* with no water, eh?

"Billee don' know from problems, land with no water, *niños*, because he all the time in his own head. It's all in his head, but he's a good boy, a good boy. Talk to him, then you'll see."

Coffee came, and then more coffee. Pete had talked more than he normally felt comfortable with a stranger and yet he was at ease, relaxed on the porch with Jesús and his family. They had talked through dinner and a smoke outside, Pete opening up the life that he had always smoothed over, comforted by the closeness of family. When he realized that it was nine o'clock, long past the time he should have left, it was difficult for him to leave. It had been so easy with the *mexicano* and his *familia* as if he were at home again. He wanted to blame Los Angeles, a sharp salesman, deftly flirting the success of the elite, but that would be too easy. He thanked Jesús finally and began to leave, but the old man made him wait until he could place a letter in his hand.

"This will introduce you to my family. I wish that I could go back, but like I told you, I can't. It would make me very happy to know that you will visit my village. Take your woman. Together, you will understand."

Pete looked at the letter, read the carefully written words, "Nepantla, Morelos." The old man hadn't written, "Mexico," but then he didn't need to. When they shook hands, Jesús pulled Pete to him and gave him an *abrazo*, each clapping the other on the back.

Jesús had told him to go to the Gulf, had given him directions to the Boca del Mar, the pyramids at a small bay where dolphins gathered, and he had asked him to be kind. Billy was a good boy, led astray. A good boy. But how could Pete forgive him if he had murdered Sylvia? How could he be kind if Billy had killed the others too? It was up to him to bring the man in, to get to him first before he killed again. A man must be responsible for his actions, and yet Jesús had asked him to be kind. Jesús, a man who couldn't return to Mexico because of a death he had caused in self-defense many years ago in a pueblo near his home town of Nepantla. Fear of *la migra*, the longing to return home. Now Pete couldn't imagine never returning to his neighborhood. As he drove out through the orchard of avocados, the trunks painted white, he felt the loneliness of being cast out, of having to run, of looking in at the gym and staying in the shadows as Coachy yelled at the boys. He had felt it in a small way then, and now he realized that he had made the right decision back then, to return to the mat, to enter the light.

He drove aimlessly for half an hour in the direction of Los Angeles, but he didn't get on the freeway. Instead, he stayed on the Coast Highway where he could drive slowly. The streets were empty, the gas stations closed, the lights turning green for him. He crossed lagoons filled with the white shapes of birds he imagined were sleeping, some at rest under the train trestles always there on his right. He wanted to turn the car around, to cross the border at Mexicali and go on past San Felipe and stand at the pyramids and wait for the dolphins to come into the bay. But he knew that he couldn't. He would have to go through channels. Proper police work. He thought of Carmen to take his mind off it, knowing that he wanted to hear her voice. He stopped at a pay phone in Oceanside and called the house. It only had to ring once before Sofía answered.

"*M'ija?*"

"*Tiá*, it's Pete," he answered.

"Angel. Are you calling from Rosarito?"

"No, I'm in Oceanside. Where's Carmen?"

"Carmen's not with you? I told her not to leave. You're not in Rosarito Beach with her?"

The phone booth tightened. Pete saw the scratched-in messages on metal, torn pages from the phone book that littered the floor, the coin slot hanging open.

"Angel, are you there?" He barely heard the question. He was thinking of Jesús and his family in the orchard, Nepantla at the foot of the volcano Popo. Finally, he answered, "Sofía, I'm here. *Calmate.* Now tell me what's going on? Rosarito Beach?"

"She's gone crazy. She wanted to be with you. I told her no, but what can you tell her? She went to cross the border, to go to the Rosarito Beach Hotel, where she's supposed to meet you. Don't you know what I'm talking about?" Sofía's voice rose, higher than Pete had ever heard.

"No," Pete answered sharply, "Tell me what happened."

"She said your friend called. She's so impulsive. She wanted to be with you. I told her you have work to do..."

"Which friend, Sofía?" Pete asked loudly, cutting her off.

"I don't know," she wailed. "A man from the fire station. She said he worked with Cornelius, but she didn't tell me his name, and I didn't think to ask her. She left so fast. Oh sweet Mother, find her, Angel, please. Find *mi hija, por favor.*"

"Of course, Sofía, of course. I'll leave right now, and I'll find her. Everything's going to be fine, you understand?" Pete said soothingly, even as his blood pounded.

She gave him the name of the hotel in Rosarito again.

"I'll call as soon as I get there." He paused, noticing his reflection in the glass. "Did you tell Ray?"

"What could I do? I was so worried."

"Call him and tell him not to leave. Tell him I'll call as soon as I can. Got it?"

"Yes. *Vaya con Dios*, Angel."

He slammed down the phone and left the booth at a run, firing up the Trans-Am and pulling away with tires screeching. It was Bill Johnson. But how had he known to call Carmen? He wouldn't need to keep Ray away from him; he'd kill the bastard with his own hands. Goddamn crazy woman.

At the border, he asked directions to Rosarito Beach. The guard gave him a bored look and told him to follow the signs. As soon as he left Tijuana, the road to Rosarito became better than he had expected. It didn't feel like he was in Mexico until he saw a massive bullring, smelled the animals, and until he noticed the shacks, the crosses on the sides of the road painted white. He made it to Rosarito in under an hour. His watch read eleven-thirty. He wondered if he would have to change the time. Were they in a different time zone down here? He exited the Mexican highway into Rosarito and found the Rosarito Beach Hotel. It was pink and white, surrounded by a wall whose top was covered with broken bottles. The driveway into the hotel was bumpy with cobblestones, but he didn't slow down. He parked in front of the office and ran inside.

"Number 114," he said to the clerk who was rubbing his eyes. "Has Carmen Sánchez checked in yet?"

"*Un momento, señor,*" the clerk said sleepily, moving slowly to the register. He turned the page, then looked up at the room key slot. Pete followed his eyes and saw the note. The man moved slowly, fumbled for the note, read the outside, and asked, "Are you *Señor* Escobedo?"

"Yes, I am. Is that for me? Let me have it."

"May I see some identification, *por favor?*" the clerk answered.

Pete touched his revolver as he fumbled for his wallet. He had to stop himself from giving in to the urge to whip it out and wake this *pendejo*, but he found his wallet and flipped it open to the badge and his I.D. The clerk worried over the identification with his finger. "You are a detective?" he asked.

"Yes," Pete shouted, jerking his wallet away. "Give me the note." The clerk handed him the stationery folded in half. Pete turned his back to the clerk and opened Carmen's letter.

"Detective," he read. "I know you'll be furious with me when you read this, but I just had to find a way to introduce you to the beauty of Nature. Your heart is not calm. Come swim with the dolphins at the Boca del Mar; they will teach you the meaning of bliss. I want so much for us to be friends. Come with an open heart and we will build an understanding. You will see what I have envisioned, but do not bring anyone else. You see, I'm with friends. Carmen is very beautiful and intelligent, a paragon of womanhood, proud, just like her cousin, Sylvia, don't you agree?" It was signed, "The Brotherhood of Dolphins," and at the bottom of the page, "I love you, Carmen," in Carmen's handwriting.

Pete didn't have to read the note a second time, but he did, trying to absorb as much of Johnson as he could. After he had finished the second reading, fury took control of his hands, and he crumpled the note violently. Finally, he stopped himself, folded it up carefully, and started for the door. After he had gone outside he turned back and returned, slapping his hands together loudly.

"*Oye,*" he said to the startled clerk who was on his way back to sleep. "Did you see the two men who came for the young lady?"

"*Sí, inspector.*"

"*¿Gabachos?*"

"*Un chicano y un gringo,*" the clerk responded after thinking a moment.

"*¿Un gringo alto con pelo blanco?*"

"*Rubio,*" the clerk answered. Blonde, Pete reminded himself, the word was "*rubio.*"

"*Gracias. ¿El teléfono?*"

"*¿Pa' dónde?*"

"Los Angeles."

"*Para la policía, sí hay,*" the clerk said, smiling as he hauled a phone up on the counter.

Pete dialed Tony's number. It rang three times before it was knocked to the ground and a sleepy voice grumbled into the receiver, "What?"

"Tony, it's Pete. Wake up."

"Sleepy?" Tony growled.

"Billy Johnson has Carmen down here in Mexico."

"What the..."

"The freak has Carmen." From the guttural response he heard, he could tell that Tony was fully awake now.

"You sure, Pete?"

"Damn right, I'm sure. He must have called Carmen, but what I can't figure out is how he got a hold of Carmen's phone number."

There was silence on the other end of the line.

"I'd like to shoot myself," Tony finally answered and then told him about the call he had received, from a man who said he had evidence, but who would only talk to Pete. So Tony had given him Sofía's phone number, thinking that Pete would arrive at any moment.

Pete stared at the phone in his hands. He wanted to scream.

"I'm coming to meet you down there, Pete. Pete?"

"No. Go to headquarters; spill the situation."

"Fuck headquarters," Tony answered. "What're they gonna do? I really screwed up. I'm coming down. You need back-up."

"I'll go in on my own."

"No way, I'm coming down. I'll never be able to live with myself. You hear me?"

Pete tried to think. "Alright," he said finally, and gave him directions to the Boca del Mar.

"Bring your firepower," Pete told him. Tony had an arsenal that included a sawed-off shotgun and an Uzi that he had kept after a crack raid.

"What about Ray?" Tony asked.

"We can't bring Ray in on this."

"We have to, homeboy. Carmen's his cousin, two of you down there."

Pete squeezed the phone. "Ok, Ray knows anyway. For all I know, he's half way here already. Bring him, but on one condition, and if he doesn't agree, then he doesn't go."

"What?"

"He doesn't touch the freak. I want him."

"I hear you. I'll fill in El Ray, but don't go in alone. Wait for us."

"I'll wait," Pete lied, and hung up the phone without saying good-bye. He thanked the clerk who saluted him, and then he took off running. He came back again, shaking his head, to ask directions. After ten minutes of going over the map, he thanked the clerk again and this time he didn't return.

The clerk had pointed out two ways to go. One route involved going back to Tijuana, then over to Mexicali and down the coast. The other would take him on a road through the mountains just south of Rosarito. The road was "*sinuoso*," the clerk had said more than once, but quicker if he was able to drive fast, and best of all, "*no chotas*," no *pinche* police. Pete chose the mountain road. As he left, he checked the time. It was now almost three o'clock in the morning. He figured it would take him about four hours to reach San Felipe if there were no problems, and another hour or so to reach the bay. As he drove through the mountains he swore at Carmen for coming down, but it didn't help relieve the fear that caused him to drive faster through the mountain passes, alone on the black road except for one donkey, which he narrowly missed, the tires screeching. The *burro* didn't slow him down, but the near miss, his car sliding towards the edge of a cliff, suddenly came to him after he'd eaten up another ten miles, his back jerking against the seat, his foot backing off the gas until he focused his concentration on Billy Johnson. The freak was smart, abducting Carmen to keep him out of L.A., watching his moves, maybe even knowing where he was at all times. Billy Johnson would be waiting for him at the Boca del Mar, waiting with Carmen. As Pete came to another tight mountain turn, he strained to see around the corner, not letting up, but readying himself for another *burro*, knowing he'd better be quick but careful.

He pulled out of the last pass, dropping into a wide plain, as an edge of the sun broke free like some kind of fierce red moustache. The countryside at daybreak was not what he had imagined. Farms and *ranchos*, land planted, windmills, adobe houses, and cactus. It wasn't until he neared the Gulf that the scene changed, or was it the sun finally fully released that transformed it, as he saw the Mexico of his imagination, a Mexico of desert.

CHAPTER 22

He tasted the Gulf long before he saw it, but it wasn't until an hour later that he stopped in San Felipe for gas. He could have used a cup of coffee, but he instead took off immediately, a can of Pepsi between his legs, the condensation soaking into his crotch.

Jesús had told him that the road he wanted was on his right, that Billy had told him to look for a red house on the edge of an *arroyo*, about forty miles from San Felipe. He would have missed it, if a scrawny, ears-back and tail-between-the-legs missile hadn't run out and caused him to brake. Three tiny children paused at the side of the highway, one with an arm cocked for another throw at the dog, which was now cowering on the other side of the road. Pete gestured "stop" with both hands, and then ducked as a rock sailed past the window. He swore loudly, but when he looked up for the children, they had disappeared, running towards a red house. Pete crossed the *arroyo* and made a right onto a dirt road. He stopped after he had gone ten feet, and got out into the dust cloud that had engulfed the car. Could this be the right road, he asked himself? The road was just two tire ruts. He backed out and drove up past the *arroyo* a mile, but couldn't find another road. Returning, he drove slower this time, past the spot in the dirt road where he had first stopped, got out again to look carefully down at the dirt. There were tire marks, lots of tire marks, but they didn't tell him a thing. Who was he kidding? he thought. What did he know about tire marks? He got in and drove.

Jesús had told him that the road would be rough, but that it wasn't far to the Gulf, and then only another twenty minutes or so past the fishing village to the pyramids. "Not far" took thirty minutes and should have taken over an hour, but Pete wouldn't slow down. He could only clench his teeth as he hit one ditch or serious rut after another, hearing the shudder of fiberglass. A good piece of the spoiler that had once hung low under the front bumper tore off, enough to snag on to something on the underside of the car, enough to scrape across any notion of a high spot. His car, that noise, his teeth clenching with every dragging impact, reminded him of the time the gears had slipped on his bike and he had dropped a bare foot off the pedal to drag a toenail across asphalt. He had pedaled home at a crawl, his toenail flapping, only to have his mother rip it off and show him the tiny piece of flesh the toenail had clung to so valiantly. It would be painful but not at a crawl, as he gunned it through a deep ditch, felt the excruciating rip, a clunk and then a crazy, pleasurable silence. He checked the rear-view mirror and with relief saw his fiberglass spoiler, and then the road before him flattened out and a fishing village appeared, bare of trees, but bright from the paint on the houses and shacks.

It wasn't until he had passed though the fishing village that he actually saw it, as if it were a Polaroid developing on the dash in front of his eyes. At first, he recognized only four colors, none of them white. The houses took shape mainly in pink and blue, the doors in turquoise, unless the order had been reversed. He saw an occasional green house, the green of frogs and their ponds, and fishing boats piled on the beach. A

mountain of abalone shells took shape and dwarfed the cemetery behind the only picket fence in town. But it was only the
cemetery that used the white paint of seagulls like the border
of a photo.

Jesús had told him to look for the road that followed the
beach, that there would be many roads, but to find the one
that headed for the dunes. He found the road, the dunes in the
distance, and was relieved that it was sandy, that his bottom
didn't scrape. For another fifteen minutes, the car flew over
hard-packed sand, the Gulf off to his right and the dunes
ahead. Pete spent the time slapping at his leg, trying to
relieve the anger that wouldn't allow him to think or plan.
Pete knew he had to use the anger like he had on the mat,
wrestling. Stay cool, Coachy had always said; don't let your
opponent know you're afraid. But Coachy hadn't known
Carmen. Pete twisted the wheel hard to keep the car on the
road. "Stay cool," he shouted, slapping his thigh harder this
time.

Pete braked to a stop when he entered the dunes, getting
out of the car to look for pyramids. Nothing. Should he drive
in like an old friend, or scout it out first? He thought of Sylvia,
the old lady in Encinitas, and Lourdes, then got back into the
car and pulled up next to a Saguaro cactus, aware but unconcerned that the shade it created formed a cross on the roof. He
felt for the *filero* under the seat, and stuck it in a familiar
place—his sock, and touched the revolver under his arm
before dropping two boxes of shells into a pocket. He didn't
lock the door, noticed that the sun was high, but didn't think
that this would be any advantage, nor did he bother to wait
for Tony and Ray as he set off down the road at a trot before
heading off through the dunes.

It was hot, the sun beating down and reflecting off the
white of the sand. As he trotted, he could feel the heat of the

road through the soles of his thin shoes. Had he known, planned better, he would have brought water since he was already thirsty. Two hundred yards later, he dropped to his knees. A boat. He went to his belly and crawled across the hot sand until he could see over the edge of the dunes. He was above the beach, a small cove surrounded by dunes, the water clear and aquamarine, a color of water that he had never seen, blue-green and glowing. An expensive-looking fishing boat sat out in the cove, a rubber dinghy leaving its side, a lone male rowing towards the beach. Water rippled from the dinghy, extending in a wedge, a triangle, pyramids. Where were they? He looked across the cove, expecting pyramids like those of the Aztecas, the Mayas, but not these puny, plywood tents sitting on a low dune.

A man came out of one of the pyramids. He was half as tall as the tallest structure, a *güero* with a blond ponytail, shading his eyes. Billy Johnson. Billy must have been waiting for the rubber boat as he jogged down to the beach, arriving there just as the dinghy beached. He watched Billy wade out into calf-high water as the other man climbed out, and together they pulled the dinghy clear of the water. The rower reached into the dinghy and came up with a rifle. Was that Calasan? The rifle looked high-powered; Pete could see the scope even from this distance. Pete thought of the old *Californio*. His grandson with a rifle?

They climbed the dune and Billy went into the larger of the two pyramids, while Calasan remained outside and searched the area with binoculars. Pete dug in lower. Carmen must be in that pyramid. As Pete lay in the hot sun, watching Calasan with the rifle on the platform, he felt his shirt deteriorate and melt into skin. He made up plans of attack, but could come up with nothing other than to wait until dark and sneak around the back of the pyramids. He knew it wouldn't do any good to give himself up; the freak would never let Carmen go, and he had to get her away safely.

The day passed slower than any school day ever had. Sweat poured out of his scalp, leaving rivulets of salt down his cheeks. He felt more thirsty than any of those days he had dehydrated himself in order to make weight for an upcoming wrestling match. He dreamed of water, a glass of water, and then beer, cold beer in a frosted glass at El Patio. He tried to envision the cartoons on the napkins at El Patio, but could only remember them soaked with glass rings. He kept an ear open for the sound of Tony's car, and played with a huge red ant that had crawled near his chin. He formed sand traps, waiting for the right moment to crank over a wave of sand that would tumble the ant down to the bottom of the pit after it had worked so hard to make the top.

Suddenly, Billy came out of the larger pyramid dragging Carmen by a rope tied at the wrists. He pulled her down the dune and onto the beach. Pete started to jump up, but stopped himself. He had always thought this scene in the movies was unreal, the men acting crazy with love, screaming out, "I'm gonna kill you." Yet, he was so upset at the sight of her that he wanted to charge across the dunes towards her, to cause action, anything. Pete calmed down, knowing that he couldn't play his hand. Instead, he shaded his eyes and focused.

At the water's edge, Billy jerked on the line tied to Carmen's wrists. She pulled back, shouting at him.

"Stay cool, baby," Pete whispered. "Don't get stubborn on him; don't make him mad."

Billy was yelling and waving his free hand, but it wasn't at Carmen. Calasan shouldered his rifle, ducked into a pyramid, and came out carrying two red plastic containers, the kind used for gas.

As he watched the two men climb into the rubber boat with the gas cans and shove off, pulling Carmen into the water behind them, he felt an irritating itch on his cheek which he tried to ignore until, scratching at his cheek, he found the red ant. He held the ant in his fingers, the pumping action of the stinger giving voice to his dry tongue. "You can do it baby, up, up. You can do it, up, come up." The pulsing in his thumb was a relief as his eyes followed Carmen, fighting to break her head out of the water enough to take a breath before she would go under, again and again, until at last, reaching the fishing boat, she lay limply on her back, face up in the sea. They pulled her up the side like a fish and dumped her on the deck. Calasan helped Carmen sit up and pounded her back until she coughed, while Billy watched. Pete flicked away the dust of the red ant he had pulverized between his fingers. Not more than a couple of minutes passed before Billy disappeared below with Carmen. Pete started to wiggle backwards, but stopped when the cabin door opened, and Billy came out wearing a hat, a baseball hat, and then Pete continued to back up after checking that the gas cans were still visible on the deck. When he felt that he was hidden from their view, he stood up and ran back to the car. The sun would set in another couple of hours, and still there was no sign of Ray and Tony. He left a note under a wiper blade explaining the pyramids and the boat with Carmen in it. Pete had already decided that he couldn't wait any longer for nightfall, reckoning that the setting sun in their eyes would give him an edge.

He slunk off to his left, following a gully down and through the ravine, his pistol in his right hand. He took it fast in the shade of the ravine, until it started to level out, the ravine he had planned to use for cover flushing out into flat desert. From behind a boulder he studied the pyramids above him and to his right, silhouetted against the orange of the falling sun. Was Billy on his way back from the boat? Could Pete wait another hour for darkness? Deciding that he couldn't, he twisted out of his drenched white shirt, and in the humid heat ran like a fullback up the bank to the back of the larger pyramid. He had imagined that the pyramid would be enclosed; instead he found a short wall of adobe bricks, about ankle-high. Two-by-fours pierced the wall. Two-by-fours in the shape of triangles. It reminded him of a playground. He'd climbed on these before. The triangles, haphazardly covered with plywood, allowed him to see into the pyramid. Pete saw the two men before he climbed in. They were tied up.

"Shhh," he hissed as he slithered through an opening.

One turned a puffy face towards him. The other didn't move.

"Please don't hurt me."

Pete slid up next to him, then looked down into the bay. He remembered that sunset over Silver Lake and the full orange above the cages. He had never found out where the baboon had gone. "I'm not going to hurt you. I'm going to get you out of here," he said, trying to calm the fear in the man's eyes. "What happened to him?"

"He doesn't breathe anymore. He stopped, he stopped..." the man mumbled.

"Okay, okay, I understand!" Pete growled, an inch from the incoherent face. The man blinked and shut up. Pete scrabbled over to the one who wasn't breathing and felt his wrist anyway. The skin was cold, the hand heavy, eyes and mouth wide open, a rope still tight cutting into the neck. It wasn't just women anymore. Billy loved his work. The profile on throat specialists talked about the rage, the angry childhood, a rage to be close, an embrace so intense that material was usually found imbedded in the skin of the throat.

"When did he do this?"

"This morning, when we came in off the boat," the man coughed out the dry words. "He stopped his breathing. Stopped his. A sign for the L.A. detective," he chanted, hypnotically.

"I'm the detective."

"They got your girl," the man continued, his chin on his chest. "He said she will swim with the dolphins. Dolphins. All about dolphins. Loving animals..."

"Yes. The dolphins. Can you tell me about Billy? He strangled your partner. What else is he planning?" Pete spoke softly. He could tell the man was in shock and he didn't want to lose him.

"We weren't going to harm them. I wanted to show Jim the dolphins, we came ashore... pyramids on the beach. He didn't have to get so angry; we weren't going to hurt the dolphins."

Pete pictured the scene, two rich Americans fishing in the Gulf. Probably would've invited Billy aboard for a cold one, but Billy had gone berserk over dolphins or over their intrusion. They had come at the wrong time.

"I told him we would never hurt a dolphin. I told him."

"Yeah. You're gonna be all right, but you have to trust me. Hold on a little longer." Pete put his knife back in his sock. He'd have to leave this one tied up. "How many rifles did you have on your boat?"

"Please let me go. I have a lot of money."

"How many rifles were on your boat?" Pete asked, shaking him roughly.

"One," the man croaked.

Just one with a scope. For what? Plinking beer cans? Pete headed out the side of the pyramid into twilight. There was already a moon and he could easily see the boat and the dinghy still tied to it. The moon would be a problem, as light as it was, but if he circled behind the pyramids, they would shield him from the boat. It seemed to take forever, this southern route, but finally, as he gained the outer arm of the little bay, Pete felt elated when he saw the back of the fishing boat. He took off his shoes and socks, worried about his gun getting wet, and then slid into the water. It was incredibly warm. Must be eighty degrees, he thought, and salty, not at all like the Pacific that he had watched yesterday. He tried to keep his pistol out of the water, but he wasn't having much success.

The boat hadn't looked that far off the beach, but somehow the swim took longer than he had expected, and the longer he was in the water, the more he worried about dolphins swimming under him in the dark water, dolphins ready to protect their territory, or friendly dolphins wanting to play, pulling him under. Why hadn't he learned to swim better or shed his pants, less for the dolphins to grab hold of, and then as he neared the boat, treading water alongside, he bumped the pistol against the hull. The sound was as loud as a knock at a door. Trying to float and quiet his breathing, he headed for the back of the boat where there was a platform over the water, a transom. He slid up, and caught his breath again thinking about what he would do once he had Carmen. Swim for the shore? He looked down into the water. Not another swim; they'd take the rubber boat. One rifle. He'd take Ćalasan by surprise, put his pistol up behind his ear, let him feel wet steel, and then deal with Billy. Where was Billy? Still down below with Carmen? He felt anxious, the boat rocked and, losing his balance, he grabbed at the wood slats, only to watch his pistol pop out of his hand and slide off the end of the transom, hitting the sea with a plunk. He watched the gun disappear. He cursed himself, looking up with knife ready, waiting to spring at Billy Johnson. Then over his wet toes, out past the edge of the boat and into the sand dunes, he saw them, car lights, near where his car was parked, and then only moonlight. Tony and Ray?

"Bill, he's here. I just saw the lights."

Pete felt the boat move again. Billy walking across the deck?

"Good," the voice, low and droning, answered. "Took him long enough. Give me the rifle; I'm going ashore."

It was Billy Johnson, going after him.

"Why, Bill? Let him go; we've got the boat. Let's throw the girl overboard and get out of here, go south to Cabo."

"You're not thinking clearly; you're a Dolphin Brother now. Remember that, and remember our plan. We're going to achieve a balance with Nature. There have to be sacrifices."

"You're not going to do that thing again. Please, don't do it, I'm begging you. It was horrible."

"You're such a pussy, Calasan. Think of how interesting it will be. He'll put up a good fight, better than that dipshit fat *gringo*. It'll look like the detective did it. Murdered those two nice fishermen and then got caught in a terrible boat accident with his girlfriend. I'm going to take care of this. Trust me; we'll be swimming with the dolphins and there won't be any witnesses."

"I don't like it, Bill. Let's just get out of here."

"Relax," his voice barked harshly.

The boat lurched and Pete heard the splash of oars.

"If I don't come back, use the flare pistol on those gas cans and remember to jump."

It would have been easy to jump up and shoot Billy in the water, but then... He swore instead. He waited until he couldn't hear the splash of oars, waited, then peered over the transom. Calasan was at the rail watching the beach, the moon on his face as Pete slid on to the deck and pressed the

filero against the throat, jamming his left hand over the
Dolphin Brother's mouth and feeling the sharp intake, the jaw
jarring open, body rigid.

"Don't move," Pete said harshly into the ear as he
wrenched the flare gun from Calasan's grasp.

Calasan grunted, and Pete shoved him face-down on the
deck.

"I don't want to hurt you, but I will if you cause me any
problems. You got that?"

He heard a muffled "Yes."

"I'm the detective, in case you haven't figured it out yet.
Now you're gonna be in deep shit if you don't cooperate, but
listening to you and that freak you call a friend, I'm sure
you're going to be very helpful. Am I right?"

He grunted "Yes."

"Good. Man, your grandpapa was right to be worried
about you."

"You talked to my grandfather?"

"I sure did. Now we're going down below to get my girl.
You'll be a good boy, won't you?"

"He strangled that man. A rope, he used rope. Please help
me, I'm scared. I didn't do anything. I didn't want to hurt that
man."

Pete pulled him back hard, lifting his feet off the deck.
"What happened at Sylvia's house? Were you there?"

"I didn't see it."

"You were there."

"He made me wait in the car."

"Let's go." Pete shoved him forward.

Lazy water slapped against the hull, the boat rocking in
the dark of the cabin like a woozy silk cloth across his face. He
tightened his grip on Calasan's arm, twisting it sharply

behind his back. They crossed the cabin towards a sliver of light under a door.

"Pete!" Carmen cried happily, after he had pulled the tape off her mouth very slowly and carefully.

"It's okay, baby," he said, kissing her neck and face. He tasted her chapped lips, his own stinging from the salt.

They both turned and saw Calasan in the corner, attempting a shy smile.

Pete wanted to belt him.

"He's scared too," she said. "He was good to me; he kept the other one away from me." She went hard. "That bastard."

Pete held her, rubbed her head and kissed her face.

"I have to warn Tony and Ray," he said after a minute had passed.

"You told Ramón?" she asked accusingly. "Now mother will know."

Pete could only shake his head and raise his hands. "I hope that's the worst of our problems." He took Carmen's hand and led her to the cabin door. "What about him?" Carmen asked.

"He's on his own now."

"We can't just leave him with that monster."

Pete looked at Calasan. "He's not my problem."

Carmen grabbed Pete by the shirt, tightening her grip.

"Okay, he goes with us," Pete said finally, staring at her.

Carmen beckoned to Calasan.

On deck, Pete climbed a ladder onto the bridge above the main cabin. What was he looking for? He pushed buttons, flipped a switch, and the engines roared to life.

Pete gunned the engines. The boat didn't move. Gears, it wasn't in gear. He felt around for a lever and instead came up with the flare gun. Leaning away from the pistol pointed into the air and toward the beach, he pulled the trigger. Nothing happened. With the safety released, it went off with a whoosh. The flare exploded in the night, over the beach, just like in the war movies. There was rapid fire; it sounded like automatics. Ray and Tony he thought, standing on the open bridge, under the piercing light of the flare, like a *menso* angel on a Christmas tree, until the windows in the bridge blew out.

"Get down!" he yelled at Carmen, as he protected his head from splintered wood and flying glass. "Those idiots," he muttered, thinking it was Ray and Tony.

It was quiet for a long moment before the next clap of a rifle split the moon over the pyramids, a slug ripped into the deck, then another, closing in on the gas cans, and Pete realized who was shooting, his mind struggling as he braced himself under the wheel on the bridge and yelled down at Carmen to stay low. When the shot zeroed in, spraying the taut red gas can like a duck landing in Echo Park Lake, Pete reacted, anything to get them away. He went to work on the boat controls, pushing and pulling them. The fishing boat lurched backwards, then forward, straining and kicking up water over the stern. "Cut the anchor line!" he yelled at Calasan.

Standing in front of one of his pyramids, Billy Johnson could see that the boat had broken one anchor and was dragging the remaining anchor in the direction of the pyramids, away from the dunes that held Pete's reinforcements. Billy grinned. He only wanted that one good shot, but it wouldn't be for Pete. No, he would save Pete for later. The detective would be interesting; he was a work in progress. He waited until the back of the boat turned in his direction, sighted in on Carmen and pulled the trigger. He had seen movement, a body, but then the boat had turned away from him.

"Pete!" Carmen screamed.

Pete jumped from the bridge onto the deck, twisting his ankle on impact.

She was holding Calasan. Pete saw the blood splattered on her neck, cheeks, chest and arms. He pulled Calasan away from her.

"He must have come over to get me out of the way," she said.

"Come on, we have to get off this boat," he said, towing her away. Pete saw the pyramids loom up under the moon. He saw they were heading into the beach and screamed, "Carmen, Carmen!" The impact threw him into the open cabin. The engines roared, spitting sand as well as water.

Billy howled. "I'll give him five minutes to get off that boat alive," he told the fisherman under his foot. "You'd like that, wouldn't you," he said with a nudge of his toe. "Your new buddy wants to swim with the dolphins, but first we will communicate."

Pete crabbed back on to the deck, shoving Carmen towards the rail. She mumbled something as he bumped her head against the side. He could see that they had grounded on a sand spit, so close they could walk out through shallow water to dry land. The noise was incredible, engines straining, smoke, the boat shuddering as it tried to crawl further onto the spit but his main concern was the gas. It was all over the deck, on his hands and knees, the smell overpowering.

With Carmen in his arms, Pete's thoughts turned to Jesús, how he had mentioned the turtles coming ashore, the men ready with knives. They dropped into six inches of water, the pyramids on the dunes above them. They were out in the open, exposed. They had to reach the dunes. Where were Tony and Ray? He would have to go after Billy later.

As if in response to his thoughts, gunshots fired up the night, and he heard a clip go off as they ran across the beach. They had just made it off the beach when the boat went off, the explosion hurling them against the dune where he covered Carmen with his body.

Silhouetted against the pyramids in the flames from the boat, unconcerned with the gunfire, Billy looked down on Pete and Carmen. It would have been an easy shot for a hunter, two for one, but he was in no hurry. He thought of those days with his father hunting deer or duck in North Dakota. How he had hated the woods and the gutting, his father silent and hostile if he came in empty-handed, the time he was slapped down in front of the others.

Pete pulled Carmen up and ran into the night. He only turned to look back once at the boat and the young man on it engulfed in flames. They stumbled behind the shadow of the dune, the boat hidden now, the blaze silhouetting the pyramids. He stopped. Carmen rested on one knee in the sand as Pete stared at Billy in the pyramid.

"You stay here, baby; I'll be right back."

"Pete," she whispered, "don't leave me."

"I have to get him. Wait for me here." He touched her face, but kept his eyes on the pyramid.

She held on to him tighter. "What are you doing, Pete? Let's just get out of here."

"He's waiting for me, Carmen. Look at him."

She didn't look up at the pyramid. "Damn you, no."

He squeezed Carmen tightly and tried to kiss her, but she wouldn't let him. Instead, she grabbed on to him, screaming his name as he pulled away. He quickly climbed the embankment, found the pyramid he wanted, and circled the back of it, wary, the knife in his hand. There was a dense glow from the fire, the plywood-covered triangles reflecting the flames, but no Billy Johnson. He waited for a long minute and then slipped into the pyramid and cut the ropes that held the fisherman.

"Get up; we're leaving."

"I don't think I can walk."

"You can't stay here," Pete answered. It was taking too much time. Billy was out there. "Get up," he shouted as a shadow filled the doorway.

"Nice work, Angel," the voice said, a voice that clawed at him with the Spanish "Angel." "You weren't worried about this miserable dolphin killer, were you? What a nice guy, leaving a pretty girl alone in the night," the voice in the doorway said, the tone mocking.

Pete shielded his eyes from the glare of the burning boat, trying to draw in the features of the dark shape. But all that he could make out in the doorway was a skull on top of shoulders, a skull with little or no hair.

He slipped his knife into his palm.

"Throw it down, homeboy, unless you want to hurt your *chavala*."

Pete saw them both now, as Billy turned sideways, letting the light flicker over his grin, his hand clamped tightly on a rope around Carmen's neck, his rifle prodding the air in front of Pete.

Pete did what he was told.

"That's a good boy, Angel."

Pete stared at him forcing himself to talk. "You don't have to do this. Think of how good you'll feel if you let her go. You can do it. You're the one with the power. You can let her go, and I'll let you walk out of here. I won't stop you. Look at what a beautiful person she is."

"Of course she's beautiful. She's a woman. They're more intelligent, aware, and one with the universe than we are. I want to spare her from the pain of living with men, and then I'll deal with you."

Pete could feel the sweat rolling out of him, carrying with it the sharp, goaty smell of fear. "What about Barbara? Barbara loves you."

"Barbara has never hurt me, never made fun of me." He pulled the rope at Carmen's neck, making her gasp.

Pete flinched, jerking forward. Billy stepped back, yanking Carmen. She cried out and Pete stopped, held out his hands, the tip of the rifle two feet from his chest. He watched Carmen claw at the rope, her breathing becoming difficult. He felt his own breath pumping so hard it wouldn't remain in his chest, his lungs working for air as if there were chicken wire pressing, closing him in like the *viejo*, the baboon in his cage.

"Barbara would want you to let Carmen go. Barbara wouldn't want to see you hurt Carmen. Billy, think of Barbara."

"We've never been this close, but then she might like it. The struggle is so pleasing, like sex. We're almost one. Look at us. United. As close as you'll ever be to another being. You might like it too, Angel."

Pete saw Billy's hand work the cord tighter, his grin widening, Carmen beginning to choke in tiny gasps, as the boat, which had now burned for long enough on the sand spit, slid into the water and fizzled out like an old sparkler. In that instant, believing it was his only chance, Pete lunged at the rifle shoving it aside, the pyramid filling again with light, a flash from the muzzle.

Billy screamed. Carmen had bit into the skin of his wrist.

"Move it," Pete yelled to Carmen, as Billy clubbed the side of his face with his now free hand. Pete buried his face in Billy's chest to protect himself, but he wouldn't let go of the rifle.

"No, Tony, no. It's Pete," he heard Carmen scream. A flashlight illuminated them wrestling over the rifle.

"Drop it," he heard Tony yell.

Billy swung the butt end of the rifle deep into Pete's ribs, and, releasing his hold on the rifle, took two strides and leaped headfirst through one of the open triangles in the back of the pyramid.

Tony ran out to the side, and they heard the grunt of a double-barrelled sawed-off. "I think I got him," Tony yelled.

Carmen wrapped herself around Pete, which didn't help his breathing. He felt broken ribs, but it didn't stop him from holding her. Tony searched the slopes of the embankment.

"Ray," they heard him shout, "over here, I found them."

When Pete finally looked up, there was Ray. They started to shake hands, but then Pete pulled him in, against himself and Carmen.

"*Madre*," was all Ray could say, squeezing them both tight.

Tony broke it up, running in, yelling and waving his light. "Hey, I know I hit him. *Vámonos*."

They followed Tony, and with the help of two lights, walked the area behind the pyramids. If Tony had hit him, and they did find a short trail of blood, it hadn't been enough to stop him.

"What are we going to do?" Carmen asked, after they had searched another half-hour.

"Wait until light," Pete answered, pointing the barrel of Billy's rifle toward the east.

"Let's call it," Tony answered. "I want to get him as bad as you do, but look, he's taken off. We're not going to find him out there and he's not coming in. I have a *primo* in Tijuana, a detective on their force. He owes me a few favors."

Ray agreed. "We're not giving up, Angel."

"What if he makes it back to L.A.?" Pete asked tiredly.

"Then we'll take him out at home," Ray answered.

They walked back to the cars under the full moon, Ray helping the fisherman along.

"*He* was the one. With Sylvia," Ray said, breaking the silence, as they neared the cars.

"Yeah, he was," Pete sighed.

"He's got to show up sometime, and if it's in our barrio..."

"You won't be that lucky, homer. I'll get to him first," Pete answered.

By the cars, under the moon, Pete could make out the faces of his best friends and Carmen. He hugged her to him. "He won't get away. I promise you."

She buried her head against his chest, and then backed away so that he could see her. "Take me home, now."

"What's the matter, baby?"

"I can't change you, Pete. I love you, but is this the way it's going to be? Are you going to leave me out there, out there in the dark and the sand?" She hit him lightly in the chest with her fists. "Don't answer me now, because it's too soon. But when you've thought about us together, tell me what you see out there."

Ray and Tony waited. They might never have moved, if Carmen didn't speak up finally. "Can we get out of here now?"

They all agreed by shaking their heads.

"Follow us to San Felipe," Tony said, as he, Ray, and the fisherman piled into his car.

"Be right behind you," Pete answered, but he was grateful for the moment alone as he held her, without a care for his ribs. After five minutes, it was Pete who said, "We'd better get going."

"Pete," Carmen said quietly, holding his face and looking into his chest.

He kissed her cheeks, hoping that he was reassuring her, wondering if it wasn't he who needed the reassurance as he looked out into the desert.

They got into his car. He let it warm up for a minute, and then put it into drive.

They were on their way. He breathed easier. Off through the dunes he could see Tony's car. It had stopped as if waiting for them. Pete flicked his lights to let them know they were coming. They saw a pod of dolphins under the bright moon and he slowed so they could look at them. He thought of Billy, alone with his dolphins now. He looked away from the dolphins, over at Carmen. For a split second, he thought he saw a movement behind him. Then his head bounced as the rope jerked him back. He felt the clenched fists and the face of Billy. Carmen screamed. The car hit a rut and knocked them forward, but his head was instantly jerked straight back. The only thing saving him now were the two fingers that he had slipped under the rope when the car had bounced in the rut. Billy pulled harder. Pete thought his neck would break. He heard laughing and lost sensation in his fingers, felt the car bounce off the tracks, across sand and into brush, Carmen grunting now as she beat furiously at Billy.

Billy's fist drove into his ear, almost knocking him out, but it was nothing like the intense pressure on his neck. Another fist, and a backhand to shut Carmen up. Billy held the rope in one hand, twisting it around the metal bars of the headguard while he beat at Pete's head. Pete felt the darkness arriving like sleep. He could nod off and never know that he had dreamed. He tried to reach for the knife in his sock, but his foot was too far away from his left hand, the fingers of his right still fighting the rope around his neck. Another fist. Pete needed to free his right hand, and suddenly, from far off he could hear Coachy yelling at him. "The frog, use the frog."

Pete slammed on the accelerator, and in that brief moment when he felt the rope tighten, Billy thrown backwards, he hit the brakes. The rope loosened. He shook his hand free and went for his knife. His fingers had just reached the butt end, the *filero* in his grasp, and he was just stretching for a better grip when Billy yanked on the rope with both hands, slamming Pete's head back again, the knife clattering to the floor. Without his fingers under the cord, the blackness came quickly. He felt the boat rocking just as it had when he had gone below for Carmen, like a veil covering his eyes or the moon splintering the windshield. He saw Nepantla in the morning, clouds over Popo, smelled coffee and *atole*. He thought about his woman, Carmen; he would never be able to bring her there, and then the streak of light—the door below decks with Carmen behind it, or was it her smile?

That's what he thought he had seen when he came to. Her smile. Of course, she hadn't been smiling. She had seen Pete going for the knife, she told him later, and when it had dropped on the floor, she had found it. Maybe the streak of light he had seen, she tried to explain more than once, was the blade slicing through the air. That's all she could remember. But Pete knew. After she had revived him, he was the one who had pulled the knife out of Billy's throat, shoved in with such force that the tip had wedged into the spinal cord.